The Weird Fate of Amanda Wyrd

Siobhan grew up in north London and for part of her childhood she was lucky enough to share her back garden with sixty-four animals. Some of the animals would accompany her and her mother on their regular visits to walk on Hampstead Heath. She has fond memories of sharing the back seat of her mother's clapped-out Volkswagen beetle with two dogs and a double-jointed duck called Phoebe. The front seat was reserved for Horace, the sheep. Boudicca the goose, on the other hand, preferred to stay at home, patrolling the garden and keeping out any unwanted visitors – including many members of the household!

Due to undiagnosed dyslexia, Siobhan had an acute horror of putting pen to paper and came to writing late in life. She still finds the process somewhat terrifying but is enjoying it more and more. She now lives in south west London and is down to one cat called Lola.

The Weird Fate of Miranda Wyrd

by

Siobhan T. Campbell

© Siobhan T. Campbell, 2015

All rights reserved. No part of this publication may be reproduced, stored in a retrieval system, or transmitted in any form or by any means, electronic, mechanical, photocopy, recording or otherwise, without prior written permission of the copyright owner. Nor can it be circulated in any form of binding or cover other than that in which it is published and without similar condition including this condition being imposed on a subsequent purchaser.

Illustrations by: Siobhan T. Campbell
Cover design by hayesdesign.co.uk
Typeset by: Fenn Typesetting, Cardiff, Wales

Contents

Prologue		1
Chapter 1	No. 3, Stillwater Lane	4
Chapter 2	Hallowe'en	12
Chapter 3	The *Wilderness*	25
Chapter 4	Stavros sticks his beak in it!	54
Chapter 5	The Truth is finally revealed	67
Chapter 6	Red's Island	90
Chapter 7	Secret Passages	122
Chapter 8	Circus Maximus	148
Chapter 9	An Embarrassing Moment	187
Chapter 10	Forgiving is so hard to do	202
Chapter 11	Hangman's Noose	213
Chapter 12	The Tower	227
Chapter 13	Maze on Fire!	242
Chapter 14	Mer Island	259
Chapter 15	The Lost City	272
Chapter 16	The People of the Crystals	280
Chapter 17	Was it all just a Dream?	297
Glossary		304

Acknowledgements

There are many people without whom this book would never have been written. My thanks go to you all. In particular, my good friend Patrice Monroe for her complete belief in this book. Without you Pat, I doubt I would have completed it and the journey wouldn't have been nearly so enjoyable. You're a star. I would also like to thank another great friend, Victoria Templeton, for putting me through writers' boot camp. You really helped me raise my game and I cannot thank you enough for that. You're a wonderful, though long-distance, friend! Thank you Penny McKay, for all your help; Zahara Lemon, my first young reader and number one fan and, of course, my great niece Aurora, my number two fan, who read the book from start to finish in one go and loved it. Thanks for the encouragement, it was much needed at the time. Thanks are also due to Clifford Hayes for bringing the book cover alive and to the amazing Eira Fenn Gaunt for her wonderful typesetting skills and for doing a cracking job of editing and proofreading my manuscript; she has become a close friend. Last, but certainly not least, my thanks to Madison Alexander, Kathryn Cullen, Leslie Clyne, Lisa Lintott, Aliki Rousseau and Fiona Robson for your generosity, wonderful friendship and encouragement.

To my daughter Olivia and grandson Phoenix

Prologue

Have you ever experienced that feeling of falling through your bed, just as you're about to fall into a deep sleep, when the shock jerks you wide awake? Well, that had been happening a lot to Miranda Wyrd recently, and each time she seemed to fall a little further down. It was as if her bed was some sort of invisible trapdoor which opened into a transparent tunnel but as soon as she reached a certain point she always awoke with a start, only to find herself safely tucked up in her bed.

    These experiences always left Miranda feeling very strange but also rather curious for, in the distance, she would always see the same magnificent old-fashioned sea galleon, its white sails billowing in the wind, rising and falling on the great ocean waves. Leaping gracefully in and out of the water around the galleon were two beautiful dolphins that seemed to be laughing and beckoning her to join them.

    The dreams would stop suddenly, only to be replaced by awful nightmares where she was stuck in a damp, dark, cold cave she couldn't find the way out of. The stench of stale tobacco, rum and the sea invaded the cave, followed by a STEP… TAP… STEP… TAP that echoed loudly off the cave walls. A huge, menacing, filthy, ugly old pirate with a peg leg would appear, limping towards her and clutching a giant pair of scissors.

Every time she had this nightmare, just as the pirate was about to cut off all her hair, she would wake up with her heart thumping. Then she'd go straight back to sleep to dream muddled and confused scenes, where a giant rat would offer her some cake and a Native American Indian would give her wise and knowing looks.

To top it all, the dreams that she'd been having on and off since she was a young child had returned. They were about two girls, who were identical in appearance to her – they looked like scruffy urchins – and who were locked in a cell. Miranda had been born one of triplets but her sisters, Scarlet and Wilde, had died at birth. She wondered if they might be the girls who were haunting her dreams. Not only had she lost her sisters but also her father, Gideon, had disappeared in strange circumstances when she was just a baby. Whenever Miranda tried to broach the subject of her missing father, her mother either changed the subject or told her that she believed he would return one day.

These weren't the only strange occurrences that were happening at No. 3, Stillwater Lane. For the past two weeks Miranda would find herself at her bedroom window in the middle of the night – completely unaware of how she had got there – and looking out, she'd see a silhouette of a flying carpet with an exceedingly large man sitting on top of it. From what she could perceive, since it was very dark, he seemed to wear a different type of hat every night. Sometimes he had a young boy with him, at other times it was a very small man wearing a top hat. Like clockwork, they arrived each night, and she had the strange sensation that they were there to protect her. *Protect me from what?*, she wondered and then, realising that she was having a conversation with herself about flying carpets and strange men, she'd shake her head thinking she must be losing her mind, especially as her hair had started whispering at night, telling her to find the two lost girls.

Miranda had no idea what to make of all this and wondered whether she should tell her mother, but she decided against it since Karmela, as her mother insisted on being called, would probably send her to bed with some foul-smelling poultice on her head.

1

Number 3, Stillwater Lane

Miranda could hear the alarm clock jangling in her ears and, opening one eye, she reached out and turned it off. Trying to remember what day it was, she realised that it was Hallowe'en. Her heart leapt for joy, and then the activities of the night before came rushing back like a speeding train. She'd had another nightmare about the pirate with the scissors and she could have sworn that she'd seen a flying carpet with the mysterious man sitting on top.

Boudicca the goose suddenly began hissing and honking in the back garden. Boudicca had several different honks, and this one was her battle cry. Miranda immediately leapt out of bed and ran to the window, where she spotted Nerdy-Nigel, her next-door neighbour, throwing conkers at the goose over the garden fence. Opening the window she shouted out: 'Oi, YOU! Did you know that our bees sting on command and if you don't get lost, I'll get them to attack you?'

'Yeah, as if!' the boy sneered, looking around nervously. His mother had informed him that their neighbours were all witches and had forbidden him to have anything to do with them.

'I'm not scared of a silly old bee,' he shouted, with more bravado than he felt. Nerdy-Nigel wasn't nearly as bold when he was without his gang of geeky, spiteful friends.

'Yeah!' she sneered. 'Well, watch this then,' and shouted out: 'BEES ATTACK!'

Suddenly, a swarm of bees was flying straight towards him at an extremely rapid rate. For a second, he stood gawping at the fast-approaching buzzing cloud, but then his adrenalin kicked in and he turned and ran back into his house as fast as he could. Miranda stood at the window, having a lovely time watching him racing up the garden path, with the bees gaining on him by the second.

'Should've listened to me!' she shouted, and burst out laughing.

* * *

Miranda and the Nerd, as she liked to call him, had been bitter enemies for as long as she could remember. She had long forgotten why they hated each other, but stubbornness on both sides prevented them from becoming friends. As far as she was concerned, he was a very large thorn in her side who made her life pretty miserable at school with his spiteful comments. Thankfully, at home, things were a bit different: she had the upper hand because her animals generally terrified him.

Flying through the kitchen door, Miranda tripped over Sharbe, her Afghan hound, and landed head first in a laundry basket. She instantly knew it was going to be one of *those* days. She got up and lurched towards the table, spotting her grandmother Mimi eating breakfast, dressed in biker leathers. *Oh no!* she groaned inwardly. *What is she up to NOW?*

'Why the outfit, Granny?' asked Miranda, dreading the answer.

'I've decided to exchange my sports car for a motorbike and thought it a good idea to get into the swing of things,' replied Mimi, looking as pleased as punch.

'A MOTOR BIKE!' exclaimed Miranda, absolutely appalled, though not in the least surprised. 'But they're dangerous!'

'Not if it's got a sidecar,' snapped Mimi. The rest of the family had reacted in an equally appalled manner, and she was fed up with their lack of enthusiasm.

'A s-sidecar,' Miranda stammered. Flashing through her mind were images of herself and Mimi hurtling along at 120 miles per hour, with Miranda gripping onto the edge of the sidecar for dear life, terrified that when going around a corner Mimi would go one way and she the other.

'What colour is it?' she asked, already knowing it would be loud and garish.

'Bright orange, of course,' replied Mimi, pointing to her sleeves, which had two vivid orange stripes going down the sides.

Miranda's heart sank. *And I thought things just couldn't get any worse*, she thought despairingly.

Miranda stared at Mimi and wondered if she was ever going to grow up. She made Peter Pan look like a grumpy old man. Miranda was very fond of her grandmother but she was definitely different from other grandmothers she'd met. In fact, when she thought about it her entire family seemed to be very different from other families. Her friends' parents had 'sensible' jobs in offices but her mother, Karmela, was a spinner and weaver. And as if that wasn't unusual enough, her mother Karmela looked like a genie from a magic lamp. She liked to wear long, flowing kaftans and bejewelled turbans and would sit at her spinning wheel, spinning wool and twisting strands of the family's hair in order to weave it on her special loom.

Miranda grabbed her hairbrush from the sideboard, and tried to unravel her mane of hair. Like the rest of her family, she had the most extraordinary head of hair. It was a riot of different colours and textures. It was also very long, very wild and totally untameable. Some of it was curly, other strands were dead straight, whilst others were wavy. As for the colours, there were streaks of copper, auburn, raven-black, chestnut-brown, white blonde and dark blonde. In fact, her hair contained all the colours that natural hair can possibly have, plus the odd strands of violet and gold. She couldn't stand it and longed to cut it all off. However, her mother wouldn't hear of it and wouldn't even allow her to have it trimmed. Every time Miranda moaned about it, Karmela would tell her that her hair was a gift from the universe. Miranda, who didn't really get what she was talking about, just thought her mother was being neurotic.

She pulled a chair from under the table to find Rigor – one of their lazy, fat cats – sleeping on it. Pulling out the chair next to it, she found Mortis, the other lazy fat cat, curled up with Ratsputin – the pet rat – fast asleep under Mortis's great paw. Getting increasingly annoyed and frustrated with the general chaos in the kitchen, she pulled out another chair to find a pile of newspapers ready for the recycling bin with a bag of knitting on top. 'One day, a miracle will happen, and I will wake up to find it tidy!' she grumbled under her breath. Miranda shoved Rigor off the chair, and the cat promptly buried his claws in Sharbe who was innocently meandering past.

There was a tap at the back door and Fortuna and Destina popped their heads in. They were Miranda's aunties and lived three doors down at No. 6, Stillwater Lane. They, like their sister Karmela, were also spinners and weavers and came every day to work together. The three of them were very different in temperament, although they were all eccentric in the way that they dressed and behaved, and were at least a foot taller than everyone else. Karmela was the spiritual one, always muttering on about karma and saying things like 'What you sow is what you reap!'

Destina, on the other hand, was rather severe and definitely a lot more sensible than the others. She, too, liked to wear long, flowing robes but they tended to be less flamboyant than Karmela's and in earthier colours such as browns, greens and black. Destina wore her hair in two long, thick plaits which reached past the back of her knees. Around her waist she wore a heavy silver chain with three sets of house keys hanging off it, as Mimi, Karmela and Fortuna were constantly losing theirs.

Fortuna was the most fun of the three sisters and was always getting up to tricks and playing practical jokes on the others. Her sense of dress was also outrageous, but her choice of clothes was far more modern, preferring miniskirts and thigh-length boots with very high heels which made her at least two and a half metres tall. She even had a tattoo on her shoulder which said *The Goddess* and she wore her hair in two long plaits which she coiled into two giant cones sticking out at 45-degree angles from the top of her head, with several diamante hat pins poking out from them.

'It's Hallowe'en!' exclaimed Fortuna, with child-like enthusiasm. She sat down and asked, 'Have you got your costume ready?'

Miranda just shrugged her shoulders.

'What's the matter?' enquired Destina, joining them at the table. 'I thought it was one of your most favourite times of the year.'

'I'm just tired', she answered, 'and I've been having this awful nightmare about a pirate.'

There was an awkward silence around the table. Mimi, Fortuna and Destina gave each other furtive, worried glances and quickly changed the subject, leaving Miranda feeling even more bewildered.

Karmela arrived then, stinking of heavy patchouli oil and draped in yards of brightly coloured psychedelic fabric.

'Have you had breakfast yet? I'm just about to hitch Bert to the trap and I'll drop you off,' she said brightly.

Miranda picked up a hard, burnt piece of toast and let out a deep, loud, grumpy sigh. That was another annoyance: not one member of her family could stick a piece of bread under the grill without completely cremating it. Karmela didn't believe in modern appliances, so a toaster was out of the question.

Miranda's shoulders drooped; she was hoping Mimi would take her to school. Even Mimi's death-defying driving was better than being dropped off by pony and two-wheeled buggy. She was fed up with being teased and called horrible names by her fellow classmates. At least in Mimi's red open-top sports car she had been able to show off a little.

It's absolutely totally and utterly SO. NOT. FAIR, she groaned inwardly. *Why do I have to have weird, freaky hair? Boy-oh-boy! We make the Addams Family look sane and normal.*

Miranda grabbed her coat in the hallway, pleading with Karmela to drop her around the corner from school so she could sneak in unnoticed.

'You're not embarrassed by me, are you?' asked her mother, trying desperately not to smile.

'No, of course not,' she lied.

The truth of the matter was that Miranda found all of her family members a huge embarrassment. Her home was nothing like those of her friends. The rooms were always shrouded in a cloud of incense. Instead of net curtains, brightly coloured saris hung at the windows, along with crystals and wind chimes which were constantly tinkling in the breeze. African masks adorned the hallway and a giant Buddha took pride of place in the sitting room. Karmela's display cabinet even had a crystal skull in it, which lit up whenever she walked past. Miranda tried to introduce her mother to Ikea by casually leaving their catalogue around where Karmela was bound to notice, or by sitting with her grandmother Mimi on the sofa umming and ahh-ing over it, but her mother wasn't having any of it.

Miranda slowly made her way out to the front and climbed up next to her mother. Karmela handed Miranda her packed lunch. It weighed a ton, which meant her mother had put in a couple of her homemade rock-cakes.

As they clip-clopped their way through the village, several people shouted out: 'Weirdos!' Miranda's hair fizzled with electricity, sending out multi-coloured sparks.

That was another thing she should tell her mother: her hair was not only sparking, but talking to her in several languages. *What IS going on?*, she wondered, deciding that being a ten-year-old was very difficult and confusing at times.

2

Hallowe'en

School had finally finished and Bella, Lucy and Miranda burst into the playground, only to run into Nerdy-Nigel, who had been avoiding Miranda all day since the swarm of bees had given him such a terrible fright.

Miranda glared at him. 'What, the bees got your tongue? Or was it your bum?' she sniggered and added: 'Of course, they're excellent at flying through open windows and down chimneys... if I should-so-happen-to-command-it.'

Nigel went white and made a quick beeline for the exit. Grinning, Miranda turned to Bella and Lucy.

'What was that all about?' asked Bella.

'Oh, I forgot to tell you earlier, he had a run-in with Mimi's bees,' she said, with a cat-like smile on her face.

'Cor! I'd love to have seen that,' piped in Lucy, relishing the idea of the Nerd being chased by a large swarm.

'Have you got your costumes?' Miranda asked, and both Bella and Lucy merrily waved their bags up in the air. Miranda looked around nervously, praying and hoping that Karmela was waiting discreetly around the corner with the pony and trap, instead of gliding through the school gates looking like the *Cutty Sark*, a beautiful sea clipper in full sail.

Thankfully, she was nowhere to be seen, so they headed towards the road. 'That's odd,' said Miranda, looking up and down the street. 'She's never late.' The roar of a motorbike could be heard in the distance. Miranda looked at her friends and said, 'I hope that's not Mimi because, if it is, I'm not sure how we're all going to fit in.'

Sure enough, Mimi could be seen whizzing down the road astride her new mode of transport. Narrowly missing the lollipop lady – who dived into a bush in order to avoid her – Mimi swerved to a halt. 'Yoo-hoo, over here, darlings,' she shouted, dangling three crash helmets. Bella and Lucy's eyes lit up at the sight of Mimi's gleaming bike. Miranda, on the other hand, gave her granny a murderous glare.

'Where's Mum?' she asked crossly, stomping over to the bike.

'Someone from the past has flown in to have a meeting with her.'

Miranda wondered who it was, as Karmela hadn't said anything about it earlier.

Bella and Lucy happily put on their sparkly purple helmets and squeezed into the sidecar, with Lucy sitting in front. Miranda reluctantly put on hers and sat behind Mimi. Grabbing her grandmother around the waist, she shut her eyes and prayed to St Christopher, the patron saint of travellers, all the way home.

Having survived Mimi's hell-raising driving, they arrived to find Karmela, Fortuna and Destina in the kitchen. 'All home in one piece I see,' said Karmela, smiling with relief and busily searching for some glue and silver paper to make some stars and a moon to add the finishing touches to Miranda's pointy hat.

'Just about,' Miranda mumbled under her breath.

Karmela had put out some sandwiches and rock-cakes, and Bella was just about to take a large bite when Miranda screwed up her face and pretended to be sick, causing Bella to put it back hastily.

Miranda was wondering where this person from the past was when she heard what sounded like the loud cry of a seagull. Thinking that slightly odd, as they rarely got seagulls this far inland from the sea, she looked out of the kitchen window and spotted what appeared to be the most enormous gull she'd ever seen. It looked like it was wearing flying goggles and seemed to be running up the garden trying to take off!

Miranda stood, spellbound, as she watched it rise up in the air and fly straight into an electricity pylon that was situated in the field further on. It let out a terrible cry and fell straight down onto its back. Then it got up and let out a series of the most horrendous squawks. Staggering about, it proceeded to take off again, this time narrowly missing an enormous oak tree.

'Did you see that?' she exclaimed, turning around with her eyes popping out and her jaw dropping to her knees.

'See what?' asked Bella.

'That gigantic seagull with flying goggles! Look!' she cried excitedly, pointing outside.

Bella got up and looked out of the window. 'Don't be stupid, seagulls don't wear flying goggles,' she said with a superior air. 'Anyway, there's nothing there,' she added, giving Miranda a searching look.

Miranda was beginning to feel a bit silly; perhaps she was starting to imagine things because not only had she seen it, but she could have sworn that the gull had screamed out: 'Flaming wombats!' She looked at Karmela for reassurance but, as usual, she was busily trying to catch the contents spilling out of the bulging cupboards.

*   *   *

Bella and Lucy loved visiting Miranda's home because they could really let their hair down and relax. Their own mothers were neurotically house-proud and desperately tried to keep up appearances – unlike Karmela, who never seemed to notice things like layers of dust, cobwebs, baskets of laundry or the stacks of dirty washing-up by the kitchen sink.

Bella had wrapped herself in bandages and was dressing up as a mummy from an Egyptian tomb. She was so tall and skinny that Miranda secretly thought she looked like a white stick insect. Lucy, on the other hand, was short and plump. She'd thrown a sheet over her head and was making ghostly noises. Miranda tried to encourage her friend to be a bit more inventive with her costume – after all, anyone could throw a sheet over their head and cut two holes out for eyes. Destina agreed and used some wax crayons to draw a terrifying ghoul's face on the front of Lucy's sheet.

Miranda was painting her own face with thick, green face paint and she smeared a thick layer over her nose in order to hide her freckles. She chose electric blue to apply to her eyelids and piled mascara onto her already thick eyelashes. For the final touch, she applied copious amounts of fake warts to her face and some bright red lipstick to her lips. This made the permanently upturned corners of her mouth – which gave her a naughty, impish grin that constantly got her into trouble at school – even more apparent. She put on her witch's costume and began to hiss and cackle. Mimi draped a long, black velvet cloak with a bright red satin lining around her shoulders and placed her witch's hat on her head.

The three girls went outside and filled a black bin liner with soggy leaves. This was ammunition against those unfortunates who had either forgotten it was Hallowe'en or were too mean to put their hands in their pockets to buy some treats. They were now ready to go and frighten the neighbourhood – and stuff their faces, of course.

Just as they were leaving, Karmela took Miranda aside and told her to avoid going anywhere near Desolation Manor, the old Gothic mansion on the edge of the village because it looked as though it was about to fall down. That, of course, was like waving a red rag in front of a bull. Miranda sensed that this wasn't the real reason and decided that a visit was definitely on the agenda.

Their first trick or treat victim was Mrs O'Keefe, the local gossip and busybody. They gave her door a good loud knock and, even though there was no answer, they knew she was in because the net curtains were twitching. They knocked again, determined to get an answer.

'Trick or treat!' they chorused.

'Go away, you miserable brats! Be off with you, or else!' shouted Mrs O'Keefe, lifting up the flap of her letter-box.

'Or else what?' replied Miranda brazenly, grabbing handfuls of soggy leaves and stuffing them through the letterbox, failing to realise that Mrs O'Keefe was still there. The shrieks that followed were loud enough to wake the dead. The door flew open, revealing Mrs O'Keefe with curlers in her hair, furiously waving a broom in the air as she spat out bits of leaves.

'I'll get you for this, you evil scallywags! I know where you live, Miranda Wyrd. You can expect a visit from the police!' she shouted, pointing a gnarled finger at them. The three girls flew through the garden gate, shrieking in delight. By the time they reached the corner of the street, they were totally out of breath from too much laughter. They fared a lot better after that and their goody bags – and stomachs – were filling up nicely. *Now it's time to have a real thrill*, thought Miranda, remembering the Gothic mansion.

'There's one more place I think we should try. Follow me,' she said, striding off.

When Lucy and Bella saw the mansion that Miranda was talking about they both let out a gasp.

'Mum says I'm never to go anywhere near Desolation Manor!' said a frightened Bella.

'Mine says weird things go on in there and once you cross the threshold you're never seen again,' said Lucy, whose knees were now knocking together.

'Oh that's rubbish! Your mum does have an overactive imagination!' said Miranda bravely.

Both Bella and Lucy refused to go one step nearer.

'You're just being sissies,' snapped Miranda. 'I'm not in the least bit frightened,' she lied, turning towards the bleak mansion.

It did look exceptionally creepy. The filthy curtains were always closed which meant you couldn't see inside, and for some strange reason there was always a dark cloud hanging just above the roof, even on boiling hot days when there were no other clouds in sight. Not even weeds grew in the dusty garden; in fact, all life forms appeared to avoid the place like the plague.

As for the mansion itself, it was enormous, with five tall, Gothic, grey turrets and arched leaded windows. The double-fronted door was huge and a large brass knocker in the shape of a gargoyle hung from the peeling grey wood.

* * *

Miranda's heart was thumping as she slowly tiptoed towards the mansion. *Perhaps this wasn't such a good idea,* she thought. Then she felt a cool breeze whoosh around her head and she heard a young girl's voice whisper in her ear: 'Don't go, Miranda. Don't go in. Danger awaits!'

Miranda nearly leapt out of her skin. She spun around looking for the person who had spoken but there was nobody there. A cold feeling of fear crept up her legs and entered her stomach. She thought she might be sick but it was too late to go back now. She'd given herself a challenge and Miranda never turned down a dare or a challenge.

Shaking like a leaf, she approached the huge front door. 'I'm not scared – I'm not scared at all,' she kept muttering under her breath. Peering around, she raised her hand to grab the gargoyle knocker but, before she touched it, the gargoyle grunted and bared its sharp, pointed teeth.

'What. Do. You. Want?' it asked in a low guttural hiss.

Leaping back hastily and quickly withdrawing her hand, Miranda stammered, her voice quivering with fear, 'T-trick or t-treat!'

'Trick or treat, eh... I'll show you trick or treat,' hissed the gargoyle menacingly.

Miranda turned to bolt... but the door suddenly flew open and it felt as though an enormous pair of invisible hands was yanking her inside. She tried to grab hold of the door frame but the force was too strong and she was sucked into the mansion and flung onto the cold stone floor.

The door slammed shut behind her. Stunned and rigid with fear, she lay for a few moments trying to catch her breath. Glancing around and seeing that she was alone, she quickly got up and lunged for the door, struggling to open it, but it wouldn't budge. With her heart pounding and her terror mounting by the second, she frantically kept trying to pull it open. Tears of panic stung her eyes as Bella and Lucy's stories rang loudly in her ears. She was filled with the most awful feeling of dread and was beginning to wonder if she'd ever see her family again.

She turned around and covered her face with her hands, letting out a huge sob. Peeping through her fingers, she saw a gas lamp slowly light up on its own, creating a dim glow which cast menacing shadows that flickered over the walls of the massive hallway. The place smelled of damp and mildew and the wallpaper was peeling away from the crumbling walls. Everything looked fragile; it was as if the thick layers of dust and cobwebs were the only things holding it all together. What little furniture was there was tatty and crumbling with age. With her heart in her mouth and fighting back more tears, Miranda went to see if she could find another exit.

She entered an enormous living room where most of the furniture was covered with dust sheets. As she crept around, her weight made the old wooden floors creak and groan as if they were moaning to each other and complaining about being disturbed. The room was bleak and lifeless, just like the rest of the mansion, which felt unloved and sadly neglected.

Miranda was suddenly aware of an overwhelming smell of decay as she entered the next room, which was lined with dusty portraits of elderly men with mean faces. This was obviously the dining room, since there was a long, fully laid dining table with two ornate silver candelabras containing half-burnt candles at either end. The table had been set for twelve and the meal had obviously been eaten; the remains of the food were strewn everywhere. Half-eaten, maggot-infested chicken carcasses and sides of beef lay rotting in congealed gravy next to mounds of mouldy vegetables. Miranda realised that the revolting smell was coming from the putrefying food which looked to be at least two weeks old. Wine glasses were scattered everywhere, some still half-full, others on their sides with the spilt red contents staining the once-white tablecloth.

A wooden box – about the size of a tissue box – was sitting in the centre of the table, and Miranda had an irresistible urge to open it. She stood there staring at the box, trying to stop herself from lifting the lid. Miranda had spent her entire life fighting to control her insatiable curiosity and generally failed miserably.

She'd now convinced herself that the box was talking to her. 'Go on, I dare you to open me,' it whispered. She found her hands reaching out and lifting the lid. She was horrified to find it that it was filled with hair... and amazed to see that it wasn't just any hair – it had the same colours and textures as hers! She shivered; as far as she was aware, only she and the women in her family had such hair. But, it couldn't possibly be any of theirs, so whose was it? Impulsively, she grabbed a handful of the hair and stuffed it into her goody bag.

Continuing her search for a way out, Miranda walked back into the hallway and along to the bottom of a large, forbidding staircase. As she looked up the stairs, she froze to the spot. There, halfway up the stairs, was a shadow in the shape of an enormous man. Even though it was still too dark to see him clearly, there was something very sinister about him. Her legs started to tremble and her heart pounded so loudly she thought it might burst!

'SOOO, ye want a tr-rick or a tr-reat do ye, lassie?' he said in a rasping, creepy Scottish accent.

Miranda opened her mouth to scream for help, but nothing came out.

'I asked ye a question, Miranda. NOW YOOO ANSWER IT!' he growled, and started to limp down the stairs. STAMP went his foot, and TAP went his peg leg. STAMP … TAP… STAMP… TAP… The sounds echoed eerily throughout the mansion.

Little did Miranda know that she was facing Nasty MacNoxious… the most evil pirate in the world and little did she know that this pirate was going to be the cause of so much trouble to her in the future.

As he got closer she could smell the salt of the sea on his musty clothes. The reek of stale rum and tobacco from his wheezing breath shot up her nostrils, making her retch. He was now only a few feet away from her and she could see him quite clearly: his black, greasy hair was tied back in a ponytail and he looked and smelt as if he hadn't seen a bath or shaved in weeks. An ugly red scar ran down his right cheek, and his coal-black eyes pierced her with an evil stare while his thin lips formed a spiteful sneer.

Oh my God! It's the pirate from my dreams! And he knows my name! she thought, feeling sick with terror.

He was just about to make a grab for her when she felt the same cool breeze that she had felt earlier whoosh past her towards the pirate. He suddenly tripped over violently and fell down the rest of the stairs, losing his wooden peg in the process.

The front door sprang open and Miranda found herself being catapulted out into the garden. Without a second's hesitation she picked herself up and flew through the garden gate, landing beside a parked car behind which Bella and Lucy were hiding. The three of them looked at each other and, without having to say a word, ran as fast as they could back to Miranda's house.

* * *

They got back in record time and tumbled through the door where Karmela was standing, ready to greet them. The girls were in a very sorry state indeed. Lucy's sheet was ripped to pieces, Miranda had lost her granny's cape and her hat was bent crooked and dangling beneath her chin, while Bella was trailing several metres of bandages behind her.

'What on earth have you been up to?' asked Karmela, with a startled expression. 'And Miranda, where's Mimi's cloak?'

'Oh, some boys tried to steal our goody bags, so we had to run for it and I lost Mimi's cape in the process,' she lied. Miranda didn't dare tell her mother the truth, as she had been warned not to go to that mansion in the first place.

Karmela peered over her half-rimmed glasses and stared at Miranda for what seemed like eternity. Miranda knew that her mother didn't believe her by the way she flared her nostrils – always a bad sign.

'We'll talk more of this in the morning. Bella, your mother's on her way to collect you and Lucy so I suggest you go and clean yourselves up before she arrives. And as for you, young lady,' she said, turning to her daughter, 'it's time for bed.'

For once, Miranda was highly relieved to be sent to her room as she was thoroughly exhausted, confused and feeling rather sick from all the sweets she had eaten earlier. She just about managed to brush her teeth and remove her green face paint before she fell, exhausted, into bed.

As she was drifting off to sleep and wondering how on earth the pirate had known her name, the trapdoor suddenly opened again and off she went, hurtling down the tunnel. But this time she didn't wake up in her own bedroom...

3

The Wilderness

She had landed on a huge bed that was rocking gently from side to side. Out of the corner of her eye, she could see the sea. *I must be on a ship!* she thought in amazement.

'FINALLY!' yelled a deep, gruff voice, with yet *another* Scottish accent. 'I thought ye'd never get here. I even sent Stavros the albatross tae have a word with yer mother.'

Miranda's heart leapt into her mouth. She turned her head slowly and, to her utter surprise, she saw an enormous man sitting at a large desk with a laptop in front of him, lit by an old-fashioned oil lamp. He had bright ginger pigtails which stuck out at right angles above his large, protruding ears. A flamenco hat was perched cockily on the top of his head and he was wearing a white shirt with a large ruffle going down the front, tucked into a wide leather belt that held up his ample pot-belly, and, to top it all, a kilt.

'Y-y-you're the man who's b-b-been flying around my garden in the middle of the night, and this is the old-fashioned galleon from my dreams,' Miranda stammered. 'And I wasn't imagining things when I saw a seagull wearing flying goggles, crashing into an electricity pylon.'

The enormous man snorted with mirth. 'Aye, correct on all counts, and that most definitely soonds like ma good fr-riend Stavr-ros, except he's no' a seagull... he's an albatross. And – welcome aboard ma galleon, the *Wilderness*'.

For once in her life, Miranda was utterly speechless. Slowly, a toothless grin spread across the man's weather-beaten face. 'And I'd just taken ma wallies out, thinking ye weren't coming tonight after all.'

She stared at the colossus in front of her and the only thing she could think to say was, 'W-w-wallies, what are wallies?'

'Och, ma false teeth!' he replied and popped them into his mouth and smiled, revealing one missing tooth. Miranda stared at the gap.

'I thought it made them look more authentic, if ye get ma dr-rift.'

She kept pinching herself in order to wake up, because she was obviously dreaming. But in actual fact, she felt wide awake, and what was happening was all too real. *And how does he know my name?* she thought.

'Oh trust me... I know more aboot yooo, than yooo do.'

Now that IS worrying, thought Miranda, highly alarmed, *and even more disturbing is the fact that he seemed to read my mind.*

'Let me introduce maself. Ma name is Notorious Red MacNaughty and it has been said by many that I'm one of the most feared pir-rates on all the seas and oceans throughout the World… or Universe, for that matter.'

He stared at Miranda, his sparkling blue eyes full of laughter. He glanced around and bent forward with the air of a conspirator. 'But the tr-ruth of the matter is… I'm no' r-really a pirate, but – if people want tae believe such things, I say, let them.'

He let out a thunderous laugh while slapping his thigh. 'And in tr-ruth, I secretly relish playing the role. In actual fact, I'm a philanthropist…'

'What's a philanthropist?' butted in Miranda.

'Oh, someone who goes around giving large amounts of money away tae the poor and needy but generally, in ma case, the money's no' mine, but someone else's. I'm a bit like ma good fr-riend, Robin Hood.'

'Robin Hood didn't exist.'

'Och, that's what yooo think!'

Miranda was slowly regaining her senses and thinking of a number of questions to ask. But just as she was about to begin her interrogation, the giant clicked his fingers and she promptly forgot every one of them. In a state of dazed confusion, Miranda looked around the cabin. The bed was made of beautifully carved wood and was covered in the most luxurious fabrics and cushions. *Karmela would just die for these*, she thought, feeling the different fabrics. The walls of the cabin itself were also elaborately carved, and lying all around were several sea chests of various sizes. Some were locked with enormous padlocks while others had been left open and were filled with pearls, glittering jewels, ornate candelabras, exquisite porcelain vases and mountains of gold coins. One enormous chest in particular caught Miranda's eye, as it was filled with every type of hat and headdress imaginable. The only modern appliance was the laptop, which Miranda thought looked totally out of place.

She suddenly felt an overwhelming tiredness grip her body. Yawning and collapsing back down onto the bed, she let out a heavy sigh, wondering why she wasn't terrified and, for some mysterious reason, why she felt right at home with the giant.

'Well, I don't know aboot yooo, but I'm tired and it's time for ma bed,' he said, bending down as he started rummaging through an old chest. With his head buried in the trunk, he threw out an odd assortment of things over his head: a rubber duck, large balls of string, a tennis racket, a cricket bat, a *Star Wars* light-sabre, a fishing rod and a rugby ball. Eventually, he found the hammock he was looking for and fixed it up on one side of the cabin. In the centre of the room he hung up a curtain to give them both some privacy.

'I'm a wee bit old to be sleeping in a hammock, so I'll take ma bed if ye don't mind.'

Miranda had a terrible time getting into the hammock; she was spun around, tossed onto the floor several times, and ended up completely cocooned. Red tried his best to hide his amusement but failed miserably. He began chuckling, which turned into a full-blown howling laugh.

He gallantly offered to help her, but was met with a clenched fist and muffled growls.

By now, her hair was beginning to light up and fizz with electricity due to her anger and humiliation. Creasing up with laughter even more, Red ignored her stifled threats and disentangled her unruly mop of hair, receiving a few electric shocks in the process.

'Okay, I'll take the hammock,' he sighed.

Miranda, seething with fury and mortification, gave him her deadliest look and stomped behind the curtain, throwing herself onto his huge magnificent bed and hiding under the covers.

'I hope ye dinnae snore, lassie, as I cannae abide the sound.' Red promptly fell asleep, and within minutes the whole cabin was shaking with his snorts, whistles and grunting. Miranda thought that she'd never get to sleep with that racket going on but she was so exhausted by the day's events that she soon fell asleep, wondering if tomorrow was going to prove to be as weird as today had been.

* * *

Miranda woke to unfamiliar sounds and smells. *Must still be dreaming*, she thought drowsily. She turned over and snuggled further down under the covers. *Hang about! I can still smell the sea... and what's that awful grunting sound? It sounds like Farmer Frank's pigs.* She instantly sat up, realising she was still on the galleon and that the grunting noise was actually Red snoring. Her heart sank as she realised that she hadn't dreamt it. She decided to try and go back to sleep, praying a miracle would happen and that she'd wake up in her own bed. Just as she was nodding off, however, there was a loud knock at the door. Nearly jumping out of her skin, Miranda held her breath to see what would happen next.

'HOOTS MA ROOTS... Who's that knocking ma door doun?' Red shouted gruffly, shaking himself out of a deep sleep and nearly falling out of the hammock.

'It's me, Sh-ly... I've brought your breakfast down.'

Miranda slipped off the bed and peeked around the curtain. To her utter disbelief, there stood a giant rat with the biggest pot-belly she had ever seen, and he was carrying a large tray laden with silver dishes. She immediately withdrew and hid behind the curtain. *Good grief! That can't be right; I could have sworn that was a giant rat.* It suddenly dawned on her that he was the very same rat from her dreams. She popped her head around again, just to double check. The cross-eyed, oversized rat was wearing a long, crimson frock-coat, a yellow bowler hat which had two holes cut out for his ears, a tatty blue and white striped T-shirt and stained, white, baggy pants held up with braces. He gave her a beaming smile, revealing two very long, protruding front teeth in the process.

Red looked up and spotted Miranda. 'Och, I forgot all about ye, wee lassie... Miranda, this is Sly – ship's cook. He's a master culinary expert and he can take ye round the world with his different exotic dishes... Och, and he's a bit of a magician on the side,' added the pirate.

The giant rat stepped forward and put out his paw.

'Sh-pleased to meet you,' he giggled, with a distinct lisp.

He was swaying from side to side in the opposite direction to the tilt of the ship, his tail aptly finding places to wrap itself around so that he wouldn't fall over. Miranda got the impression that he was slightly drunk, even though his breath smelled of sweet violets and peppermints.

'Aye... ye'd better come and sit doun and have a bite tae eat,' said Red.

Sly laid the tray on the table and removed the lids from the dishes. The delicious smell of bacon, eggs, baked beans, mushrooms and fried tomatoes filled the cabin. Red pulled out a chair for Miranda, who was still simmering from the night before. Screwing up her eyes, she gave him a filthy look and sat down huffily.

'Did ye sleep well?' he asked.

'NO!' she barked, which wasn't true at all since she'd slept like a log.

'Is anything the matter?'

'YES!'

'Might I enquire as to what the pr-roblem is?'

'I was hoping that I was going to wake up in my own bed!' she said crossly.

'Well, ye'll have to hope some more, as ye're no' going anywhere... just yet!' he replied mysteriously.

'WHO ARE YOU?' she shouted, deciding that she had gone right off this giant, ginger-haired lump.

'I'm yer great, great, great, great... Och,' he said, raising his eyebrows, 'we'll be here all day if I was to get into hoow many gr-reats there are... I'm yer gr-randfather on your mother's side, but Red will do. I thought it was aboot time we met and got to know each other.'

Miranda sat there, totally gobsmacked. Eventually she found her voice and uttered, 'That makes you very, very old then!'

Red roared with laughter. 'Aye, I'm older than you could possibly imagine,' he replied, ruffling her hair.

Miranda felt as if she was in the twilight zone. She knew she should be asking questions, but strangely, she still couldn't think of any.

She picked up her knife and fork and began to eat. An explosion of wonderful flavours erupted in her mouth. *This is, without doubt, the best breakfast ever*, she thought, sighing with pleasure, all her worries slowly evaporating with each mouthful she took. She looked at Red with a satisfied smile. *Perhaps, this isn't going to be so bad after all. I wonder what's on the menu for lunch.*

After breakfast was finished, Red got up, turned to her, and said, 'Ye'd better get dressed and come with me. It's time I introduced ye tae some of ma cr-rew.'

Miranda looked at what she was wearing and explained that she only had her *Lisa Simpson* pyjamas to wear. Red looked her up and down and proceeded to rummage through a chest.

'Noow, me personally, I always preferred *South Park*.'

Miranda was dumbfounded. 'How on earth could you possibly know about the *Simpsons* and *South Park*?'

'Ah! *That* would be telling. All in good time, ma beauty,

everything will be revealed... all in good time.' He found her some leather breeches, a frilly, white shirt similar to the one he was wearing and a pair of shoes. Oddly, they fitted her perfectly and in no time at all she was transformed from a young girl into a young pirate. Red then offered her an eyepatch which she declined, saying that there was nothing wrong with her eyes.

'Ye don't actually think that all those pirates with eyepatches were blind in one eye, do ye? Och, they just wore them for effect. I wear one myself occasionally, when the need arises, but I generally end up fr-rightening myself more,' he said, with eyes full of humour.

He then started to look through all his hats and, to Miranda's surprise, he selected for himself a baseball cap, with *New York Yankees* written on the front. He gave her a three-pointed tricorn pirate's hat to wear which was so big that it completely covered her head. By the time she'd removed it Red had gone, so she ran through the door after him and followed him up to the deck.

* * *

The glare of the sun and the smell of sea salt and oil from the gleaming pulleys hit Miranda as she stepped onto the deck, causing her to shield her eyes from the glare. The galleon was enormous: it had three huge masts, with three sets of billowing sails apiece, that seemed to reach up to the heavens and disappear into the clouds above. At the back of the ship was the bridge, where the enormous wheel was housed. It was painted in bright reds, yellows, blues and greens, reminding Miranda of old-fashioned, beautifully carved and brightly painted gypsy caravans.

To Miranda's amazement, she noticed a large gorilla lounging in a hammock, smoking a pipe and wearing a pearl-encrusted eyepatch, a burgundy smoking jacket and a red fez. He was watching her with a very knowing, self-satisfied grin on his face.

Miranda tugged at Red's sleeve and pointed at the gorilla.

'Och, that's Archibald.'

The gorilla gave her a slow, sinister leer, revealing a set of gold teeth that sparkled in the sunlight. He got out of the hammock and lurched over to her. The smell of expensive aftershave wafted under her nose as he came up to her. Putting out a large simian hand, he grabbed Miranda's and shook it vigorously.

As soon as he touched her, her hair started to murmur and crackle, hissing grave warnings in her ear. Since Miranda had realised that whenever she was in un-desirable company, her hair would let her know, she decided that this was one gorilla she was going to do her best to avoid. A hollow, sick feeling crept into her stomach. Removing her hand as quickly as possible, she gave him a furtive look. *Creep!*, she thought, *I wouldn't trust you as far as I could throw you. And what a STUPID name for a gorilla.*

'Aye... and he's a mind-reading phenomenon,' added Red, as an afterthought.

Miranda's stomach did an about-flip. She gulped and averted her eyes from the gorilla's face down to his large, super-shiny Italian loafers, trying desperately to change her thoughts to something else. *Great! Now you tell me*, she thought. Sneaking a quick look, she saw Archibald was positively sneering at her, thoroughly enjoying her discomfort.

Miranda was beginning to feel a little queasy from the motion of the ship. Looking around, she spotted a large barrel and sat down on it, welcoming the warmth from the sun-drenched wood creeping into her legs.

Suddenly, the barrel began to tilt from side to side and she heard a loud knocking coming from within. She quickly leapt off and, to her surprise, a very cheeky boy's face appeared, grinning from ear to ear. He had the biggest dark brown eyes, sparkling with mischief, and the longest eyelashes Miranda had ever seen.

Red turned to the young lad. 'And this is Mad-Machete-Mo. He's a right Houdini, this one.' Red winked at the young English pirate.

'Houdini! What's a Houdini?' Miranda asked.

'Och, Houdini was the best escape artist that ever lived; he's the equivalent of yer David Blaine.'

'Oh, my Auntie Fortuna thinks he's a real dish.'

'Och… I bet she does,' he said, giving her a knowing look.

The boy got out of the barrel and stood with his legs apart and his hands on his hips. He was very skinny and a little taller than Miranda. He wore a silver hoop in his ear and an emerald in his nose, a bandanna around his head and, to her amazement, pale blue tracksuit bottoms with two black stripes going down the sides, a black T-shirt, and a pair of very trendy trainers. Mad-Machete-Mo was now casually leaning against the ropes, cleaning his nails with the edge of a machete. As well as the machete, he also had a boomerang tucked into his trousers.

'What's Mad-Machete-Mo's talent?' she asked, with a worried expression.

'Och, getting out of tight corners, of course.'

Miranda instantly knew that when it came to getting up to no good, this boy had a lot to teach her. She guessed his age to be about thirteen or fourteen. She also thought he looked very sure of himself and decided that he had the look of trouble written all over him.

Miranda's eyes were darting everywhere, trying to take it all in at once. She looked up at the masts, trying to see where they ended. Halfway up the middle-mast she noticed a small man wearing a top hat with a peacock feather sticking out of the side, sitting in a basket that was being lowered down to the deck.

'Ah, Monsieur Le Grand, I'd like tae introduce ye to ma great, great, great, etc., etc. gr-randdaughter,' Red shouted up to the man.

'Bonjour, ma cherie, I am most honoured to meet wiz you,' he yelled down in a thick French accent.

'Monsieur Le Grand has the good fortune to speak the language of the birds. Which, let me tell ye, is very useful at times – he's the ship's lookout,' said Red, pointing to the top of the middle-mast, 'and he lives way up there.'

Miranda looked up and saw what looked like a tiny tree house perched at the top of the middle-mast, swaying amongst the clouds. She also noticed the flag; it wasn't your usual skull and crossbones, but a picture of a white dove with an olive branch in its beak.

'Wow!' she said, looking up and reeling. Miranda suffered dreadfully from vertigo, which is a terrible fear of heights. Just the thought of being so high up made her stomach turn over. Taking another peep, she felt the contents of her stomach start to bubble and churn. Horrified, she realised she was going to be sick.

Clasping her hand over her mouth, she desperately tried to make her way to the side of the galleon, but instead she found herself looking at her distorted reflection in Archibald's shiny Italian shoes. *Uh-oh! Here it comes*, she thought and she threw up the entire contents of her breakfast all over them.

Mad-Machete-Mo immediately started sniggering. 'Girls!' he spat.

Archibald's face froze with rage. With a look of total disgust, he retrieved a large, snow-white silk handkerchief from the breast-pocket of his smoking jacket and tentatively started to remove bits of regurgitated chewed tomato and baked beans from his loafers. Feeling like a complete idiot and desperately wanting to shrivel up and die, she went to help clean up the mess and slipped on a soggy bit of fried egg.

Looking up from the deck at Red, she mumbled 'It must be the breakfast I ate'. She was by now far too humiliated and embarrassed to admit to the fact that she had a frightful fear of heights, especially in front of that twit, Mad-Machete-Mo.

Sly, who had joined them with a mop and bucket, was highly affronted. 'Sh-nobody has ever got sick from my cooking!' he muttered under his breath.

Miranda now realised that not only had she vomited all over Archibald's shoes and made a complete idiot of herself, but she had also insulted the cook. *Not a good start to the day*, she thought, cringing.

Mad-Machete-Mo sniggered and covered his nose. 'Girls!' he mocked again and, turning to Archibald, said, 'And what is she doing here anyway? This is no place for a stupid little girl.'

Archibald, still wiping his expensive shoes, nodded his head grimly in agreement.

'Did you just call me a stupid little girl?!' growled Miranda. Clenching and unclenching her fists and giving the boy a furious look, she decided that he had *ENEMY* written right across his forehead in invisible ink. Turning to Archibald, she decided that she didn't care whether he could read her mind or not, and gave *him* a deadly glare as well.

Luckily, she was saved from any more embarrassment by Monsieur Le Grand, who strutted over and theatrically removed his hat, knelt down, grabbed her hand and kissed it. Miranda didn't quite know where to look as no one had ever done *that* before and, knowing that she must reek of sick, she found herself blushing furiously.

She couldn't help noticing that he was a very small person indeed. In fact he was so small that she could have rested her chin on the top of his head. He wore his dark, wavy hair tied back in a small ponytail, he had a typically French moustache that curled up at the ends, a pointed goatee beard, a ring through the side of his nose, and two diamond studs in each ear. His roguish, dark brown eyes sparkled with merriment and his right eyebrow appeared to have a life of its own as it danced merrily up and down. His clothes were flamboyant to say the least. Red informed her that Monsieur Le Grand wore a different waistcoat every day of the year.

'You arrr very welcome to come up to my 'ome and I 'ope you know how to play zee chess… non? Or zee poker for zat matter?' said Monsieur Le Grand.

'Monsieur Le Grand!' said Red, glaring at the Frenchman, 'there'll be nooo playing poker with the wee lass.'

Red, seeing the state Miranda was in, told Archibald to take her down and show her where to clean up.

Archibald had mixed feelings about being given such a task. He really didn't like children… but he knew that this child was somebody special. Red, who usually managed to keep his thoughts a secret, had been so excited at her arrival that he'd slipped up and allowed Archibald to read his mind! *So <u>this</u> is Miranda Wyrd*, he gloated. *My chance to make a fortune has finally arrived!*

Miranda was furious at being handed over to Archibald. *Talk about adding insult to injury.* She glared at Red. *He's doing this deliberately to annoy me.* With great dignity, Miranda lifted her arm and wiped her sleeve across her face, hitched up her trousers and, breathing in deeply and with her head held high, she marched gallantly towards the gorilla.

Red averted his crinkling, laughing eyes, thinking, *Och, she's a real bonnie wee lassie... Aye... she's just gr-rand*, he thought, greatly admiring her nerve. *I can see that you and I are going to get on famously.*

After having thoroughly washed her face and rinsed her mouth, she peeked around the door. *Damn, he's still there.* Edging her way out and trying to think vacant thoughts, Miranda did her best to avoid his eyes. She still hadn't found her sea-legs yet and was staggering all over the place. Archibald gave her a withering look and motioned for her to follow.

The deafening sound of music could be heard coming from one of the many cabins. She noticed a door ajar and, peeking around it, she saw a man dressed from head to toe in black leather, with a red and white polka-dot bandanna tied around his head, surrounded by a vast array of musical instruments, CDs, records and different types of stereo equipment. The cabin looked as if a bomb had just gone off. *Blimey! And I thought Karmela was untidy!* she thought, surveying the chaos.

The man looked up and smiled, revealing a missing front tooth and a diamond set in the other one. 'Greetings,' he said in a deep, lyrical West Indian accent, and then got back to the business of choosing his next record.

Miranda withdrew and shook her head, wondering *How come there's all this modern equipment on board, when everything*

else is all so old? Feeling very confused, she decided that this was one very strange ship. *And I'm going to find out all its secrets*, she thought, burning with curiosity. Archibald had gone on ahead, so Miranda decided to have a snoop around. Creeping up to one brightly painted yellow door, she pressed her ear against it. She could hear someone singing *Billy Jean* by Michael Jackson. Just as she was bending down to sneak a look through the keyhole, the door suddenly flew open.

'EXCUSE ME!' he boomed, in an accent similar to Red's. 'Do ye always go aroond spying on people or were ye just picking yer spots in the r-reflection of the brass doorknob?' Stepping forward and tilting Miranda's face up with his hands, he examined it. 'Nooo, I cannae see any zits… sooo ye must be a spy.'

Miranda stood there – mute. The man's blue eyes danced with amusement.

'Let me introduce maself. Ma name is Fearless, and I'm Red's younger and better looking br-rother, which makes me yer gr-reat, gr-reat, etc., etc. uncle.'

He had the same red hair and the same twinkle in his blue eyes, but that's where the resemblance ended. He was of average height, very skinny, and he wore his hair in a knot on the top of his head, with two chopsticks sticking out. His ginger beard was one long dreadlock, which had cotton thread tied all the way around it, and was then wrapped around his neck several times. He had on a pair of red tartan trousers and a T-shirt that said 'GET LOST' written on the front. He wore a black eyepatch, except that it wasn't over his eye, but was placed against his forehead. He also possessed all of his teeth. Miranda kept looking at his eyepatch, wondering why he wore it there. He suddenly flipped it up, revealing a tattoo in the shape of a heart with 'Rita' written across it. Flipping the patch back over the tattoo, he grinned.

'It was done in a moment of madness, when I'd had a touch too much tae drink, but it's no' very manly-like, plus ma missus disnae care for it much as her name is Luscious-Lily,' he giggled. Miranda joined in and decided that she quite liked this one.

Mad-Machete-Mo appeared out of nowhere. 'Red's ordered me to show you around,' he said in an arrogant, offhand manner, and immediately stalked off.

Oh-goody-gum-drops, she thought sarcastically. She waved goodbye to Fearless and reluctantly followed the young boy. Catching up with him, she tried to make polite conversation.

'How old are you?' she asked.

'Old enough!' he shrugged rudely.

'And how long have you been sailing with Red?'

'Long enough!' he mumbled.

'Can he be trusted?'

'CAN HE BE TRUSTED?!' he spluttered. 'There is not a man in this universe that can be trusted more! You're talking about the Notorious Red MacNaughty!'

'Keep your hair on, I was only asking,' she retorted to his outburst.

'Girls!' he hissed.

After asking a few more questions and getting monosyllabic answers, his expression of contempt and boredom was really starting to grate on her nerves.

'Listen! I don't give a flying fan-dan-go if you show me around or not, 'cos I can find my own way… thank you very much!'

Looking at her as if she were something to throw into the garbage, he replied, 'Don't you get it? I said, Red ORDERED it.'

'Do you always do as you're told?' she challenged.

'Oh my days!' he exclaimed. 'Now you listen to me. Red's Cap'n of this ship, and when he says jump – you jump. Do you understand?'

With a strained silence between them, Mad-Machete-Mo continued to show Miranda around the *Wilderness*. Miranda was bubbling over with curiosity about her new surroundings and decided to try and get on his good side. 'Why are you called Mad-Machete-Mo?'

'Why do you think?' he replied, giving her a self-important look.

'Well if I knew, I wouldn't be asking, would I?' she said sarcastically, with her hands on her hips.

The young pirate raised his eyebrows and tried to hide the grin that was slowly spreading across his face. *Ooh, she's right feisty this one,* he thought, deciding that any girl with that much nerve had to be half all right.

'Well, are you going to enlighten me, or what?'

Mad-Machete-Mo started to strut up and down and, with his arms flailing about and trying to act cool, he rapped:

I'm lean. I'm mean
I'm Mad-Machete-Mo
Watch out if I'm about
Yer better get below

If it has a blade
It was made
For me to throw
That's why I'm called
Mad-Machete-Mo.

Miranda stared at him, thinking he was a complete wally and an arrogant little show-off. 'What do you mean – if it has a blade?'

'Well, when I was a kid, I ran away from home and joined a travelling circus. *Barry the Blade and the Cutting Edge Troupe*, a knife-throwing act, took me in, like, and taught me everything I know. There was also Johnny Too Sharp and Noah the Knife. Barry was the best knife-thrower I ever met.'

'What! A real travelling circus?' she asked, highly impressed.

'Of course it was real, what d'ya think? Now me... I don't need to make things up, 'cos I've seen and done it all. Been there, done that!'

BIG HEAD! she thought, giving him a condescending look.

Mo could see that his bragging did not impress her one bit and decided to change tactics.

'Follow me,' he said, and swaggered off.

'Where are we going?'

'To see Chow Yen; he's my martial arts instructor and he's *really* special.'

Knocking on a door which had a large, round, black and white Yin and Yang sign on the front, he barged in before he heard an answer and beckoned Miranda to follow. An ancient and wizened Chinese man wearing sunglasses was hunched over a table, painting a picture with oil paints. The room was dark and smelt of a mixture of linseed oil, turpentine and incense.

Looking up from his work, he peered at Mad-Machete-Mo and said, 'Mo... Confucius says, do not enter the room until invited.'

Mad-Machete-Mo looked slightly shame-faced. 'Sorry,' he mumbled, looking down at the floor.

'So! Are you going to introduce me to your new friend?' Chow Yen asked.

'Umm... this is Miranda,' he said, pushing her forward slightly.

Chow Yen got up and, standing in front of her, he put his hands together and made a little bow. Miranda stared at him, wondering how he could possibly teach martial arts as he looked far too ancient to even *lift* a leg. *And how on earth can he paint in this dim light?* she wondered.

'Very pleased to meet you,' he beamed, wiping the paint off his hands with a rag. Turning to Mad-Machete-Mo, he asked if he'd been practising his karate movements.

'Yup,' replied the boy, full of himself.

'Good, you can show me later.' Chow Yen then looked at Miranda, asking if she liked to paint. She nodded and he told her she was always very welcome to knock on his door and join him.

Once they'd left and were out of earshot, Miranda gave Mad-Machete-Mo a look and started giggling. 'Martial arts expert indeed; he looks at least two hundred years old!'

Mad-Machete-Mo couldn't believe what he was hearing and rounded on her. 'You think you know it all, what with your fancy education an' all. Let me tell you something, Chow Yen trained with your original Ninjas in Japan.'

Miranda burst out laughing. 'Ninja, my foot! They were around thousands of years ago!' she exclaimed.

'Fourteenth century, to be exact,' he stated proudly.

'Well then, he can hardly have been trained by them.'

'That's what you think,' he grinned knowingly, 'and another thing – he's *blind!*' he added dramatically.

'BLIND?!'

'Yup, that's what I just said, didn't I?'

'But he was painting a picture!'

'I told you he was special.'

Miranda shook her head in disbelief. 'If he's blind, how come he knew it was you?'

''Cos he's very sensitive to people's vibrations and once he's met you he never forgets your vibes… ya get me?'

'Can I call you Mad-Mo, or Mo, for short? Mad-Machete-Mo is a bit of a mouthful,' she explained.

'Safe.'

Miranda took that to be a 'yes' and they carried on exploring the ship. Every door was completely different in appearance; some were sombre and conservative, whilst others were brightly coloured. Some even had mysterious symbols etched on them.

'What's behind there?' she asked, looking at a very eye-catching door which had eagle feathers, beads, bits of shell and a dreamcatcher pinned on the front.

'Oh, that's Soaring Eagle's cabin,' he shrugged.

'Who's Soaring Eagle?' she asked, imagining a giant bird.

'He's a Native American Indian; he's away at the moment.'

'Oh!' she said, wondering who else was on board. *This is one strange ship*, she thought.

Miranda ran her fingers along the wooden panelling, feeling the aged smoothness from years of waxing and polishing. As she touched the wood, she was sure that she could detect a pulse and could hear faint sighs coming from the walls. She shivered and quickly withdrew her hand. The galleon moaned, her bow creaking and whispering to the sea, the ocean replying as it crashed against her hull. The eerie sound sent shivers up her spine and she kept getting the feeling that she was being watched but, every time she looked around, there was nobody there.

Miranda wanted some time alone and told Mad-Mo that she was going to Red's cabin to have a rest.

* * *

Once she got back to the cabin she sat down to try and figure out what was going on. Suddenly she heard a loud sigh, followed by moans and groans. Miranda had thought she was alone in the cabin and let out a piercing scream... just as the rolled-up carpet she was sitting on began to wiggle and squirm.

'Mmm, mmm,' said a muffled voice. Leaping up in alarm, Miranda gave the carpet a good prod.

'Om, mmm, mmm...' it mumbled back angrily.

Gingerly, Miranda began to unroll the carpet. Suddenly, a head popped out. 'Did yooo really have to scream like that? I've already got a stinking headache and I really dooo need to get some fresh air.'

Once the carpet was fully unrolled, Miranda let out a gasp; not only did it have a face, but it had hands with very long nails as well.

'You're beautiful,' she exclaimed.

A Persian carpet rose up in the air, fluttering almond-shaped, brown-black eyes rimmed with thick black lashes, and cooed, 'I knooow!'

This is totally bizarre, thought Miranda, *a vain, flying carpet*. 'Do you have a name?' she asked.

'OF COURSE!' it boomed. 'All carpets have names, silly, and mine is SHEEEEBA.'

'You weren't named after the Queen of Sheba, by any chance?' asked Miranda, with awe.

'Oh! The impertinence of it – of course not, *she* was named after *me*. After all, I was around long before she was – and my beauty far surpasses hers.'

Miranda sat down on the bed and wondered how many more surprises were in store.

At this point Sheba rolled herself up, asked Miranda to open one of the windows and then gracefully flew out. Miranda was about to follow the carpet when Red walked in.

'Gosh, I've just met Sheba!' she enthused.

'Och, rather you than me,' he replied.

'Why, don't you like her?'

'Nae... she dr-rives me mad... chat, chat, chat– and her vanity knows no bounds. As far as I'm concerned, she's just a conceited old bit of r-rag.'

'Where did you get her from?'

'Some sailor called Sinbad gave her tae me... I was most flattered at the time but after two days I realised why he'd given her up... she obviously drove *him* nuts as well. I've been trying to get rid of her ever since but she keeps flying back. She's about as useful as a hole in a lifeboat and she's never around when ye need her. What's more, her r-real name's Nora.'

'NORA!? That's not a very Persian name.'

'Aye, and Archibald isn't yer average name for a gorilla... But, as ma good friend Will would say, there's nowt stranger on Earth than there is in Heaven.'

'*Shakespeare* wrote something like that,' said Miranda, with a knowing look.

'Aye, as I said, ma good friend Will.'

'What! You knew William Shakespeare?'

'Aye, I did, and still do.'

'But he's dead!' she exclaimed, 'Everyone knows that.' Miranda was by now starting to get very confused.

'Aye… whatever ye say, lassie. Ye knoow, he based one of his characters on one of ma previous wives and called the play…'

'Don't tell me, let me guess… *Romeo and Juliet?*' she said, grinning from ear to ear.

'Nae, it was *The Taming of the Shr-rew.*'

'You're pulling my leg,' she replied, her eyes dancing with merriment.

'I kid ye not,' he said, winking at her.

'How many wives have you had?'

'More than I care to r-remember,' he mumbled, slightly shamefaced.

'Oh, and one more thing, who's the man with all the records?' she asked.

'Och, that's Vincent, better known as Ress-up,' replied Red, relieved at the change of subject. 'He has the gift of music and can beguile, transfix and hypnotise with just one note from any of his musical instruments'.

'Why's he called Ress-up?'

'Well, he's from Dominica in the West Indies and they have a lovely, gentle, relaxed attitude to life – which Vince has taken to extremes. In other words, he's dead lazy and he likes to live life in the slow lane and… *rest-up* a wee while. Aye, ye cannae hurry Ress-up. He also plays a mean electric guitar!'

Red went on to inform her that Ress-up would spend one month of the year in Ibiza working as a disc jockey, calling himself 'The Ress-up Crew'. He was a huge fan of modern technology and was delighted with his new iPod, as it meant he could now carry his entire collection in his pocket instead of lugging thousands of records around. It must be said that Red was also secretly delighted because the *Wilderness* couldn't have carried any more records without sinking. As it was, Ress-up took up two large cabins just for his musical instruments, which he'd collected throughout his travels.

Miranda was still eager to catch up with Sheba, so she excused herself and ran up to the deck to find her. As she was tearing around on the deck, she had the misfortune to bump into Archibald. Her hair instantly crackled in warning.

* * *

Archibald was an unhappy gorilla. He didn't want Red to discover that he was intending to send on the news of Miranda's arrival on the *Wilderness* to his brother, Douglas. Douglas was a crew member on the pirate ship, *Scavenger*, and his Captain had been waiting for this news for a very long time. He had promised to make the gorilla extremely wealthy if he could pass on useful information about Miranda. However, Archibald would have to wait until Red wasn't around to read his mind... and he was getting increasingly frustrated and angry at the delay. Seeing her standing in front of him now just made him even angrier. He grabbed her, causing her blood to freeze in her veins. Frantically wrestling herself free, she leapt back. With their eyes locked in deadly combat, they stood staring at each other. Tiny sparks were shooting out of her hair as it stood on end, bristling with electricity.

Red had returned and was behind the enormous wheel on the bridge, watching the scenario unfold. Wondering whether he should intervene, he decided to wait and see how Miranda would handle herself. *Aye lass, don't let him get to ye*, he thought, feeling a twinge of anxiety creeping up his spine.

Miranda realised that some sort of power struggle was taking place. *If you think I'm going to look away first... you're wrong*, she thought with steely determination.

Archibald slowly lowered his eyelids until they were mere slits. His top lip curled up at one corner of his mouth, revealing a hint of gold. Miranda winced at his menacing expression; she could feel waves of hatred pouring from the gorilla, causing her to shudder involuntarily. Still, she *wasn't* going to give in. There was a hushed silence on board as everyone stopped what they were doing and watched the scene develop before their eyes. Only the wind rustling the sails and the roll of the ocean could be heard. Miranda could feel all eyes on deck studying her intently.

Red nodded his head and glanced at Fearless. *Aye, she's the one all right*, he conveyed telepathically to his brother.

Aye, she is indeed, thought Fearless, smiling and signifying his agreement.

Hovering up above, Sheba had witnessed the whole event and in that moment she thought, *Hmm... you know,*

I have never liked that great big hairy oaf and to try and intimidate one so young… THAT'S JUST NOT FAIR!' Shaking herself down, she took a deep breath, rolled herself up and hissed, 'Now for some fun…' and accelerated at full speed, heading straight for Archibald.

4

Stavros sticks his beak in it!

Monsieur Le Grand could see that Miranda was visibly shaken by her encounter with the gorilla. *Good ol' Sheba*, he thought, grinning at the expression of horror and disbelief on Archibald's face as Sheba dive-bombed him. The sound alone was horrendous as she whined and whistled through the air like a deadly missile.

Archibald flung himself face down onto the deck. Sheba, skimming over his head, hissed into his ear: 'Next time, pick on someone your own size – BUSTER!'

Archibald heaved himself up. His face was smouldering with rage and all the veins in his neck were throbbing and looking fit to burst. He slowly and methodically dusted himself down. Looking at Miranda, he whispered between clenched teeth, 'Keep out of my way, brat. Or else!' and stalked off.

Monsieur Le Grand strutted over to Miranda. 'You are a very brave young lady to stand up to 'im like zat; I think eet's time you came and visited mon petit 'ouse up in zee clouds, and we shall play a game of chess – non?' He whistled to Sheba, who flew over and joined them.

'My brave and courageous Sheba, would you be zo kind as to take us up to my 'ome?'

'Of course, daaarling, hop on,' she cooed, lapping up the flattery. She unrolled herself and Miranda and the Frenchman jumped on. Off Sheba flew but, before she took them to Monsieur Le Grand's home, knowing that Miranda had never ridden on a flying carpet before, she took them for a quick spin. Miranda was totally delighted and soon forgot her run-in with Archibald – until her vertigo kicked in and she became the colour of pistachio ice-cream. Noticing this, Monsieur Le Grand whispered to Sheba, asking her to drop them off.

By now, the sky was darkening and drops of rain were beginning to fall. Miranda literally fell off Sheba onto Monsieur Le Grand's little balcony. The wind was picking up and the galleon was swaying from side to side.

Miranda lurched through the door – which reached just past her head – and collapsed onto a small armchair. She looked up and saw a cloud pass by the window, causing her to let out a groan and slump down even further in the chair.

Monsieur Le Grand strutted over to her. 'Open your mouz,' he ordered.

'Huh?'

'You know . . . zee gob.'

Miranda did as she was told and Monsieur Le Grand popped a couple of tiny pills into her mouth.

'Voilà! In a coople of zeconds, you will feel magnifique. Non?'

Miranda sat up and, to her surprise, discovered she was starting to feel a lot better. 'What was that?' she asked.

'Ah, juste a petit omeopatique remedy.'

'Don't you mean homeopathic?'

'Oui... zat wot I juste say... omeopatique. I know a vertigo sufferer when I zee woon.'

Looking around the hideaway, Miranda felt as though she was in a doll's house. She could see that everything had been custom-made to fit Monsieur Le Grand. It suited him perfectly, from his two armchairs, his dining chairs and gingham-covered table (with matching gingham curtains) to the beautiful patchwork quilt on his bed. He even had a little bath up there. It reminded her of a house in the south of France which she had visited with her Granny when she was little.

On the walls was a number of framed black and white photos of Monsieur Le Grand standing next to various people. Miranda got up to study the photos and realised that some of the people were famous. 'That's Frank Sinatra, and there's John Lennon. Oh my goodness, that looks like Elvis Presley! Did you really get to meet these people?'

'Of course!' he replied. 'Zey are all good buddies of mine.'

'Crikey, Granny Mimi would be so jealous; she's a huge fan of Sinatra and Presley,' she said.

'Ah, Frank... Now 'ee's *so* naughty!'

'Don't you mean *was*? He's dead, you know.'

'Maybe to you, but not to me!' he replied.

Miranda looked at him quizzically. Monsieur Le Grand smiled and put on a record, winding the handle of the old gramophone. 'Ave you everrr 'eard of Edith Piaf?' he asked, getting his chess set out and beginning to place pieces on the board. 'She was zee most amazing singer; I met 'er when she was a young maiden, singing in a circus… she woz like a petit bird,' he added.

'Oui,' said Miranda, showing off her limited French. 'My granny is a fan of hers and I grew up listening to her.'

Miranda wasn't too impressed with Edith Piaf; she thought she warbled rather than sang and much preferred pop music.

He stopped and listened to the music. 'Ah, c'est magnifique… You know, I was in loove with Edith for a long time… But I'm a sailor and we cannot be tied down so it woz doomed to fail from the beginning… C'est la vie, non?' he lamented, moving his bishop and placing her in checkmate.

'MONSIEUR LE GRAND… were you *born* difficult? Or have you just worked at it?'

'Pardon?' he said, his roguish eyebrow dancing up and down.

'Well, what's the point of playing chess if you put me in checkmate before the game has hardly begun? Where's the fun in that?'

'I can't 'elp eet if I'm a geenious.'

They were interrupted by a loud tap at the window. Miranda looked up to see an enormous bird. 'Good grief! It's the albatross,' she exclaimed.

Monsieur Le Grand gave her a feather and told her to stick it behind her ear. Letting the bird in, he explained that the feather was magical and that it would enable her to understand the language of the birds.

The albatross was soaked through and looked very dishevelled. He strutted in and threw himself into one of Monsieur Le Grand's armchairs. 'Lager…' he demanded.

'It'll 'ave to be rum.'

'Done,' squawked the bird.

Monsieur Le Grand got two tiny glasses off a shelf and poured them both a drink.

'Where's mine?' asked Miranda.

'You are un peu too young to drink ziz stoof,' said Monsieur Le Grand.

'Phff… sheilas are always too young to drink… that's a man's occupation!' said the albatross lazily in an Greek-Australian accent. He turned to Miranda and aimed a beady eye at her. 'Let me introduce myself… I'm Stavros the Albatross from Mykonos via Melbourne and I hear you're here to save the day!'

Save the day?! What was he talking about? thought Miranda, highly alarmed. Monsieur Le Grand gave Stavros a furious sideways look which said, 'Shoot oop, now ees not zee time.'

Stavros puffed up his chest, ruffled his feathers and swivelled his head around, focusing his other beady eye on her. 'Phff… Can't see how that wisp of a thing could possibly heal the world; after all, that's a man's job!'

'HEAL THE WORLD?!' she exclaimed, fear forming a knot in her stomach.

'Ooooo, 'ee doesn't 'alf exaggerate... Take non noteece ov 'eem,' snapped the furious Frenchman.

Miranda sat rooted to the spot. She could feel goose pimples forming on her arm and the hairs on the back of her neck stand up on end. *This is going to be BIG!* she thought, *I'm on the verge of discovering why I'm here!*

There was an awkward, stony silence, with nobody daring to be the one to break it. The words 'Heal the World' kept swirling around Miranda's head. *Stavros is right... how could I possibly heal the world? For a start, I'm far too young and another thing – where would I start? And why me?*

She got up slowly in a very dignified manner. 'I think it's time I had a chat with Red,' she announced solemnly.

The other two sat there in grave silence. Monsieur Le Grand gave Miranda a sombre nod. Stavros, not knowing where to look, started to groom his feathers.

Miranda opened the door to find Sheba listening at the keyhole. Nearly losing her balance from surprise and embarrassment, the carpet gave Miranda a meek smile and offered her a lift back down.

Monsieur Le Grand looked at Stavros and said, 'Well! Zat is juste typicool of you… always steeking your beak where eet's not wanted.'

'Flaming Galahs!' exclaimed Stavros. 'How was I supposed to know that nobody had bothered to inform her of her destiny?'

'Shhh, keep your noise down. Zings are very difficile and dangereuse at zee moment...'

* * *

Miranda found Red standing at the wheel and, by the expression on her face, Red realised she was serious and that some questions were going to have to be answered. But how much should he reveal?

'I've just met Stavros,' she said.

'Oh, that old sticky-beak, he never knows when tae keep his tr-rap shut.'

'Yes… he mentioned something about *me* – healing the world?!' Miranda slumped down beside him. In that moment she felt that the weight of the whole universe was on her shoulders and suddenly all the joy and excitement she had been feeling had completely disappeared.

Miranda could see by Red's expression that this was no joking matter. Tears started to well up in her eyes as the apprehension mounted in her stomach. Red put his arms around her. 'It's all going to be fine, you'll see.'

'What's going to be fine? And what's this all about?' she asked, dreading the answer.

It had been some time since Red had had to look after a child and he didn't know where to begin explaining to Miranda what was really going on, as he didn't want to scare her half to death.

'Aye, lassie, this is very difficult for me… I guess I'll have to start at the beginning, won't I?' he said.

'Yes, you will…' she replied crossly.

'But, I dinnae want to explain what is going to happen – not here – not on the *Wilderness*.'

Miranda was wondering where else they could talk, when Red asked her if she liked sticky almond pastries, dripping with honey. She thought that a very odd question, considering the gravity of the situation. He told her that, later on, he was going to take her out somewhere for a mint tea and cakes but until then she was to go and help Sly prepare lunch.

* * *

The cooking galley was filled with hanging copper pots and pans, plus a few very modern gadgets such as a blender and a cappuccino machine which, of course, thoroughly baffled Miranda.

Sly was slouched on a chair, fast asleep and snoring loudly. His tail was wrapped around his belly and the chair, acting as a seatbelt so that he couldn't fall off.

'Sly…' she said. No response.

'Sly!' This time she said it a little louder but there was still no response so, bending over and grabbing his ear, she yelled, 'SLY!' The rat toppled backwards in fright and landed on his back.

'Sh-what is happening?' he cried, highly confused.

Seeing him lying there with his skinny little legs up in the air and a look of complete bewilderment on his face, Miranda couldn't contain herself and fell about laughing.

Sly got more and more irate by the second, eventually saying, 'Excush me! Do you always wake people up in this mosht unfortunate manner?' Wriggling and trying to rock the chair back and forth to free his tail, he continued,

'And do you generally make fun of other people's mishfortunes?'

Sly finally managed to unwind his tail and staggered to his feet. Reeling over to a cupboard, he bent down and got out a tiny bottle from which he took a few sips. He then proceeded to slide down to the floor with one paw over his heart and the other fanning his face.

'You shouldn't do that... could've given me a heart attack.'

'Sorry,' she said and, looking at the bottle, asked what he'd just taken.

'Reshcue Remedy, of cour-she,' he replied grumpily.

'Oh, my mum gives me that when I've had a shock or something.'

'Exactly!' said Sly.

'My mum says the flower remedies are wonderful.'

Sly was very partial to a nip of rum and Red had ordered him to keep away from it. However, as Rescue Remedy was *brandy*-based, he'd taken to drinking copious bottles of it whenever he had a good excuse. He twitched his whiskers angrily and gave Miranda a very cross look, asking her what she wanted.

She explained that Red had sent her to see if she could be of help. Sly nodded and fetched his apron. Making her way around the kitchen, she asked, 'What's a blender and a cappuccino machine doing on a sea galleon?'

'Well, Red does like a smoothie from time to time... As for the rest of us, sh-we can't begin the day without a cappuccino!'

'But that doesn't answer my question: how did Red get hold of them?'

'Well, your great, great, great etc. grandfather is a thoroughly modern adventurer on sh-ome levels and, when he's cruising through the twenty-first century, he sh-likes nothing sh-better than to pop into London for the ideal home exhibition. He likes to keep abreast of things and just sh-loves modern gadgets.'

What on earth is he talking about? thought Miranda who was getting very confused by now. 'What do you mean, when he's cruising through the twenty-first century?' she asked.

'Sh-didn't Red tell you? This is a time sh-travelling galleon; Red and the crew are time sh-travellers and can hop from one dimension to another.'

Miranda was totally gobsmacked. *I must still be sleeping, this just can't be happening to me!* she thought. *A time-travelling, dimension-hopping grandad... wicked!*

Looking around, she noticed Sly's tail darting about.

'Sly, why do you wear a bow on your tail?' she asked.

'It's to remind me that I have one,' he replied.

'How can you possibly forget that you have a tail? It would be like me forgetting that I have an arm or a leg.'

'Can you sh-keep a sh-ecret?' he whispered, having a quick glance around, peering under the table and into a few cupboards.

'Absolutely,' she conspired.

'I think I'm a sh-amster.'

'A what?' she asked.

'A sh-amster!' he replied.

'Don't you mean hamster?'

'Ye-sh, that's what I just said,' Sly said, rolling his eyes, mystified as to why she was having problems understanding him. 'You see,' he continued, solemnly clutching his tail and swinging it around in circles, 'I've never felt comfortable being a rat! I'm convinced I sh-lould have been born a sh-amster. And as sh-amsters don't have long tails, and I feel more sh-amster than rat, I sometimes forget that I possess one.'

Miranda stood, wide-eyed, not quite believing what she was hearing.

'And not only that, my tail has a mind of its own,' he continued, 'so the bow helps me to locate it quickly, because it has the habit of sh-wrapping itself around my legs and tripping me up.'

'Well, you definitely look like a rat to me, even if you are a giant one.'

Helping herself to a bunch of grapes, she carried on looking around the galley. Enormous sides of ham were hanging from the ceiling, along with chillies, peppers, dried herbs, garlic and onions, plus a few other vegetables that Miranda had never seen before. There were bowls of exotic fruits and several caskets of rum, which Sly would walk up to, shake his head at, and then walk away from.

Sly was really very lovable; he seemed to find everything amusing and giggled all the time. Emptying the bottle of Rescue Remedy, he started to sway from side to side but, luckily, his long tail managed to wrap itself

Stavros sticks his beak in it!

around the legs of the chopping bench to keep him from falling over.

Miranda was just wondering how he was going to prepare lunch when he said, 'Ash I'm running late, I'm going to have to cheat a little.' He hiccupped twice and then proceeded to wiggle his tail and, before you knew it, the entire table was covered with a load of flapping fish of every description – including an enormous octopus.

'Oh!' said Sly, totally mystified, 'sh-not quite what I had in mind.' He passed his paws over the table and the fish disappeared. He twitched his tail again and the table was now covered with hundreds of fairy cakes. Miranda threw back her head in delight and promptly stuffed one in her mouth.

'Oooo...' she exclaimed, licking the crumbs from her lips. 'They're yummy,' she said, taking a bite out of another one and slipping an extra one into her pocket.

Sly was scratching his head, 'That was sh-not supposed to sh-happen, either.'

'But they're delicious!' she cried, alarmed that they might suddenly disappear.

Wiggling his tail again, he shouted, 'Shwacker-macca-widdeldy-do!' Suddenly, the table was covered with the most glorious assortment of food. There were pies, flans, salads, roast chickens, sides of beef, curries, trifles, biscuits, exotic fruits and, of course, the fairy cakes. Miranda looked on in amazement, wondering how they could possibly eat it all.

'That's better, I'd thought I'd losht my touch,' said Sly, hiccupping three times.

'How on earth did you do that?' asked Miranda, madly shaking her bottom and fervently making wishes.

'Well, I once met a witch called Samantha who used to wiggle her nose and all sorts of magical things would happen. It was she who instructed me in the art of magic – much to her husband Darren's annoyance,' Sly replied.

'You don't mean Samantha from the television series *Bewitched*, do you?'

'The very one,' he said with conviction.

'But she's just an actress on the telly.'

'That's what you think,' the giant rat smirked.

While all this was going on, Sly kept nibbling at the food and sneakily sipping another bottle of Rescue Remedy. It didn't matter how much he ate, there seemed to be a never-ending supply. He looked at Miranda and said, 'I only use magic in emergencies, as I truly love to cook and magic takes all the pleasure out of it.'

Miranda wasn't so sure about that because she'd just *love* to be able to wiggle her backside and have any wish granted. Gosh, she could even alter the way her mother, Karmela, dressed – no more hippie clothes, a normal mother at last!

5

The Truth is finally revealed

Later on that afternoon, after the enormous lunch, Red found Sheba snoozing in his cabin. Shaking her awake, he asked her if she fancied a delicious coffee in the local bazaar.

Raising her head, Sheba rubbed her eyes and, not quite believing what she'd heard, she asked, 'Did you say coffee?'

'Aye, I thought ye might like a change of scenery.'

Sheba couldn't believe her ears. *At last!* she thought, getting all flustered, *Red and I can finally be alone.* She fluttered her eyelashes and said, 'I know, you're thinking of that romantic little café at the bazaar, aren't you? Of course, I'd be delighted. I'll be up in a jiffy.'

After Red had left, Sheba dabbed on copious amounts of perfumed oils and delicately flicked herself all over with a wicker carpet beater. 'At last, a date with Red!' she enthused. She peered into the mirror and added a touch more kohl to her already dark, flashing eyes. She blew a kiss to her reflection in the mirror and sang, 'Perfect-o-mon, I'm utterly irresistible.'

She arrived on deck full of anticipation and smelling like a perfumery, and then saw Miranda. *Blast!* she thought, *I hope she's not coming.*

When Red asked Miranda to get on, Sheba fell flat onto the deck and whimpered with frustration; she'd been hanging out for a date ever since she'd met the Notorious Red MacNaughty. Then, Chow Yen appeared and got on as well. *Oh, charming,* she thought and, once Red had embarked, grudgingly lifted herself up and sped off.

Whilst all this was going on, Archibald was pretending to be asleep in his hammock. Even though Red and the rest of his crew could shield their thoughts from mind-readers, Sheba was far too excited and forgot to protect hers. Miranda hadn't yet learnt how to shield her thoughts so it was easy for Archibald to deduce where they were off to. At last! Red was leaving the galleon and he could finally contact his brother, Douglas, aboard the *Scavenger*! He slipped down to his cabin and telepathically sent him not only the news of Miranda's presence but also that she would be going to the bazaar. He knew that this was just the information that Douglas's evil Captain had been waiting for!

* * *

In no time at all, the ocean had been left behind and Miranda was completely awestruck by the landscape passing rapidly below. The huge sun hovered above the tall, weather-beaten mountains which loomed up in jagged edges and sharp peaks. The snow-laden caps glittered in the sun, causing them all to shield their eyes from the glare.

Soon, the mountains were replaced by a lifeless barren desert that stretched for miles and miles. Sheba, wheeling and swooping like a bird, began to descend. The sun was beginning to set, casting a glorious orange glow across the horizon. A tiny dot appeared in the distance. As they flew nearer, they saw a large, bustling oasis.

They landed in the central square where the busy market traders were packing up their stalls, helped by their children. People were sitting at the numerous cafés, drinking mint tea and thick, cardamom-scented coffee, whilst nibbling on little cakes made of honey and almonds. Lamps and candles were dotted everywhere, giving the place a magical, luminous quality. Sheba was getting giddy from the intoxicating smell of the local flowers, which only release their scent at night to entice passing lovers. *If only Red and I were here alone...* she thought. *How could he possibly resist me in a place like this?*

Long, flowing robes covered the people from head to toe as they stood under the palms, fanning themselves and fighting off the never-ending flies. Camels stood chewing and gleefully spitting at passers-by and donkeys brayed, knowing their work was done for the day.

Red led them to his favourite corner coffee shop which gave them an excellent view of the marketplace. After they'd finished their drinks and nibbled on some delicious pastries, Sheba, still sulking, decided to go and catch up with some other carpets and Chow Yen went for a wander.

* * *

'So Gramps, why *am* I on your ship?' Miranda asked, the minute they were alone.

'Aye, I was just going to get to that. Hmm… ye see… hum… ah… mmm… Och lassie, this is *sooo* difficult for me, I really dinnae know how or where tae start.'

'You said you'd start at the beginning,' said Miranda, wondering what on earth he was trying to tell her.

'Och, that'll take far too long.' After shuffling around in his seat, he finally began. 'Mir-randa, ye knoow how ye've never really felt like ye've fitted in? Well, there's a reason fer that… You're no' fr-rom Earth… You're from the Pleiades.'

'What on earth are the Pleiades?!'

'They're a cluster of stars in the constellation of Taurus.'

'Stars?! Are you trying to tell me that I'm an *alien* or something?' she asked, completely thrown.

'Hmm… From *ma* point of view, ye come fr-rom an extraordinary and noble lineage,' he replied.

Miranda burst out laughing, more from shock than anything else, but Red's expression remained serious. A sick feeling began to creep into her stomach and the hairs on her arms stood up on end. Instinctively, she knew her life was about to change radically.

'Are you from there as well?' she said slowly.

'Aye, I am indeed,' he stated proudly.

'So, could you explain to me how, exactly, *my* family fits into this "noble lineage"?' she asked, totally bewildered.

The Truth is finally revealed

Red took a deep breath and began to explain: 'Well, as you now know, Earth is not the only inhabited planet in the universe. There are planets with civilisations that are much older than Earth's. The Pleiades are, in fact, the oldest inhabited group of planets and the Pleiadians are some of the most evolved beings in the cosmos. Thousands of years ago, it was observed by the Grand Pleiadian Council that in every generation of your family a set of female triplets had been born... these triplets were always highly gifted and displayed great wisdom, compassion and foresight. So, with special training, the privilege of spinning and weaving the destiny of humans befell to the triplets within your family – and they've been doing that ever since the beginning of man.'

Miranda sat motionless, feeling utterly stupefied by the revelation.

'WHAT?! My mum and aunties spin and weave the destiny of humans?' she exclaimed, incredulously. 'Don't be ridiculous – Mum can't even bake a cake! As for toast, she manages to burn every single slice. She's totally hopeless at housework and rides around in a pony and trap! How can Karmela and the rest of my dotty family *possibly* help weave the destiny of mankind?'

'Perhaps it's because they have gr-reater things on their minds that they're not as domesticated as you would like.'

Miranda sat in complete wonderment, now looking at her family from a *totally* different perspective.

'Ye see... it's all in yer hair,' said Red.

'My hair?!' she said, puzzled.

'Each strand of your family's hair contains the interweaving souls of millions and millions of people who are waiting to be born. And when a filament of hair falls out naturally, Karmela and her sisters know that the time has come for the souls contained in those strands to be released... and this takes place when Karmela and your aunties weave the hair onto the magical loom. Aye, and the fabr-ric on that loom is the very tapestry of life, because it contains the history and all the choices made by every person ever born.'

Red paused and asked Miranda if she was following him so far.

'Sort of,' she replied. 'Now, I understand why she never throws our hair out. I thought she was just being neurotic!'

Wanting to get back to the subject, Red cleared his throat and carried on: 'Right, well... Sarakuta and I represent the Pleiades on the Inter-Galactic council; this is the council which rules all the inhabited planets in the cosmos. It is made up of the most knowledgeable and wise leaders from each planet and they decided that the people of Earth were to have free will. In other words, humans had tae learn from their own mistakes and take responsibility for their actions. No one was to interfere, unless of course, mankind was heading towards the brink of destruction.' Red rubbed his eyes and continued. 'Precautions were, of course, taken in case this happened. And those precautions came in the form of thirteen crystal skulls...'

The Truth is finally revealed

'Karmela's got one of those!' Miranda interrupted.

'Aye, indeed she has. Noow, would ye please let me finish. This is r-really important,' he said, sternly. 'These skulls can only heal the planet if they're all together. But, as they are so powerful and can be used for both good and evil, it was decided to split them up for safety. So, nine of these skulls were entrusted to the three generations of Wyrd sisters that were alive at any given time. But, they had tae earn them by passing various challenges in order to be considered worthy. In other words, your grandmother Mimi and her two sisters, Esmeralda and Vivienne have one each, as do your mother and aunties, Karmela, Destina and Fortuna. Noow as yer sisters, Scarlet and Wilde, died at birth, I am looking after theirs. There's the People of the Crystals... And as fer yours... Well, ye've yet tae earn it.'

'Earn it?!' she gasped.

'We'll get tae that bit later.'

'OK, you said that you also had one... then who has the other two?'

'Sarakuta has one...'

'You mentioned him earlier. Who's he?

'He, ma' dear, is yer gr-reat, gr-reat, etc, etc, grandfather, on yer father's side. He is also is one of the greatest sorcerers that ever lived.'

Miranda sat open-mouthed, wondering how many more surprises were in store. 'And the last skull?' she said.

'Ah, ma twin brother, Nasty MacNoxious, had one…'

'Your *twin*! You've never mentioned *him* before!'

'Aye, that's because the less said aboot him, the better. Anyway, over time, ma twin allowed power and greed to corrupt him – and he became highly dangerous. Because of this, he was deemed unworthy to possess his skull, so the Inter-Galactic council confiscated it and gave it to me to look after.

Red paused and then carried on: 'After you were born, and your sisters tragically died, it changed *absolutely* everything! We knew Nasty was even more desperate to get his skull back. So Gideon was given the task of hiding it away somewhere where only he would know its whereabouts.'

At the mention of Gideon, a sad expression fleetingly crossed Miranda's face.

'I have no memories of my father. Mum says I would have adored him and that he's a wonderful man. She says she'd know in her heart if he wasn't alive and is convinced that he'll return one day. But I'm not so sure... so many years have passed with no news of him...'

Red gravely nodded, and smiled sadly.

He put his arm around her and, as she snuggled up to him, she said: Tell me more about Sarakuta. I take it he's dead.'

'Far fr-rom it, he's alive and kicking.'

'Then he must be ancient like you, and how come I haven't met him yet?'

'Well, ye *did* meet him but ye were only six months old at the time so ye're hardly likely tae remember him. At present he's on a spaceship hovering above Earth with the People of the Crystals.'

The Truth is finally revealed

'A spaceship!' she gasped. 'How cool is that? And *who* are the People of the Crystals?'

'The People of the Crystals are not of this world but were star-seeded from a distant galaxy.'

'Cor!' she exclaimed.

'They once lived on Earth,' he continued, 'but they were persecuted for being different.'

'Do they still live there?

'Nae, they couldn't tolerate the cruelty and prejudices of humans. The People of the Crystals are a loving and peaceful race and are great healers. They came tae teach the inhabitants of Earth how to love unconditionally and heal themselves. But humans are a warring people and weren't ready to hear such teachings. They reacted by hounding and torturing them. Finally, the People of the Crystals could take no more and left. They will continue to live on their spaceship until such a time as humans will be ready to receive them.'

'That's so sad!' cried Miranda.

'Aye, indeed it is,' Red lamented. 'Noow, getting back to Gideon's task... As a precautionary measure in case something happened to him, we – Sarakuta, maself, your family and a few of the People of the Crystals – held a ceremony when you were six months old. This ceremony enabled you to be aligned not only with your own skull but with all the others too. This was done in case Nasty's or any of the other skulls were lost or stolen. Your skull would then be able to *sense* their location. Now we're getting to the heart of the matter. The Inter-Galactic council has observed that Earth is in deep trouble and on the verge of collapse. The time has come to bring all of the crystal skulls together in order for the planet and its occupants to be saved. So, tae cut a long story short, we now need ma twin's skull so that the healing can begin.'

Suddenly, it all fell into place and Miranda's heart skipped a beat in terror.

'So... in order to do that,' she said solemnly, 'I need to earn my skull, which has been aligned with me and Nasty's, so that I can go and find it.'

'Aye! Ye've got it in one,' said Red.

'Did Gideon have the ability to dimension-hop and time-travel as well?'

'Aye, he did.'

'So, that means, he could have hidden it absolutely anywhere!' she cried, totally dismayed by the task. 'And how on earth am I supposed to do those things?'

'Ah! Your skull will empower you to do that, plus, much more. But, I'm afr-raid, lassie, you have tae work that out for yourself.'

'Oh great! And how exactly am I supposed to earn this skull?' she asked, morosely.

'You have to show that you possess five virtues: Courage, Faith, Forgiveness, Compassion and Generosity. Take Courage, for example. Noow, that's a virtue as far as I'm concerned. Then there's Faith, did ye knoow that a mustard seed of faith can move mountains?'

'Oh, Karmela's always coming out with sayings like that,' said Miranda, feigning a yawn.

The Truth is finally revealed

'Aye, your mother is a very wise woman. Ye should listen to her sometimes. Forgiveness, noow that's a grand virtue; aye, nobody can move forward in life if they can't let go and forgive. Life is too short tae hold a grudge, don't ye think?'

Miranda nodded her head meekly.

'Och, then of course there's Compassion,' continued Red. 'Where would we be without compassion? Last but not least, Generosity. I mean generosity of spirit. Caring about people and helping them when you see that they're in trouble – now that, Miranda, is a virtue that's really worth having, is it not? And did you know that the more you give, the more you get?'

Miranda slouched further down into the chair, by the challenges of the task facing her.

'I'll never be able to display all those! For a start, I'm not that courageous and, secondly, I find it very hard to forgive. Take my nerdy neighbour, Nigel, for example; Mum says I should forgive him because he can't help being a nerd. That's a lame excuse if ever I heard one. He's utterly *beastly*, you know,' she said, poking Red's knee to emphasise the point. 'And thirdly, why should I show an ounce of compassion, when everyone is so horrid to me?'

'Are ye referring tae school?' asked Red.

'Yes, I hate it! I've only got two friends, Bella and Lucy, and sometimes they can be horrible too. It's this dreadful hair of mine; it sets me apart from everyone else. Do you know what it's like to be called weirdo or freak-show every day? Mind you', she said, staring at Red's attire, 'I guess you know exactly what I mean.'

Red nodded his head solemnly. 'Aye, only too well, but ye're no' tae fash with what people think. True freedom means not caring about people's opinions. Take me fer instance; I don't care what people think aboot me, because I knoow who I am and I live ma life accordingly.'

'And lastly', added Miranda sulkily, 'why should I be generous, when everyone I know at school has *heaps* more than me? Some of them even have a television in their own bedrooms! *I'm* only allowed to watch, occasionally, old films and nature documentaries with Mimi – and it's not even a colour television.'

'Och, why waste yer time sitting in front of a telly when ye've a life tae lead.'

'Life – what life?' she grumbled. 'I'm not allowed to do anything. I'm beginning to realise I've had a very sheltered upbringing compared to everyone else at school.'

'Well *that*, lassie... is all aboot tae change.'

'And how am I to be judged? And who's judging me?'

'Sarakuta and maself will be judging.'

'Well, considering he's stuck on a spaceship, how's he supposed to do that?'

'The People of the Crystals have satellite technology that is far more advanced than Earth's. Come tae think of it, he's probably watching right noow.'

Miranda was thoroughly dismayed to think that her ancient great, great, great etc., etc. grandfather – who she couldn't even remember – was observing her. She looked up to the sky and gave a little wave. 'How long has he been spying on me?'

'Well, I wouldn't call it spying, more keeping an eye. Anyway, since ye were aboot six months old.'

Miranda covered her face with her hands. 'Oh God!' she moaned, dramatically. 'He must know me better than I do.' A horrid cringing sensation enveloped her as all the naughty things she'd ever done came to mind and – until now – thought she'd got away with.

'Och dinnae fash, he was once young and naughty and he has a gr-reat sense of humour. Anyway, he only checked in occasionally – unlike noow, of course.'

'I still don't get how I'm supposed to prove that I have these virtues.'

'Well, Sarakuta decided to make it into an adventure. All I knoow is that we're to go back in time to different places, where various situations will be presented. It's up tae you as to hoow ye respond. Sarakuta has kindly given us clues in the shape of poems. After ye pass each test, ye'll receive another poem.'

He delved into his large sporran and retrieved a piece of parchment paper. 'This is the introductory poem,' he said, and cleared his throat:

If your love be true
And you're pure of heart,
You're off to a cracking start.
You might sway along the way
To lend a helping hand

*But dinnae fash wee lass
For it's all part of the plan.
You will be tested
When ye least expect it.*

*So remain calm and alert
Listen to your feelings as they'll lead you true.
Three tests you'll have to go through
You won't know where
You won't know when
But five virtues you must show
Before you can reach the end.*

'So', Red continued, 'we know Courage and Faith are the first virtues that ye'll have tae show. I'd imagine that Sarakuta will create a situation where ye'll have tae show those virtues. Noow... don't fer one minute think that this is going tae be easy, because it won't be. You will be challenged in many different ways. And, there's a twist...'

'A TWIST?!' said Miranda, her heart sinking even lower.

'Aye... listen, just because you might have overcome some gr-reat challenge, it might not mean that ye've passed the test. Because, in reality, ye might have missed a tiny opportunity that ye thought insignificant and ignored it and *that*,' he uttered sternly, 'might have been the true test. In other words, I think it is best ye display all the virtues at all times. Then ye cannae go much wrong. D'ye get ma dr-rift?'

The Truth is finally revealed

'I think so,' said Miranda, morosely.

* * *

The sun had finally disappeared and the sky was filled with a million twinkling stars. Suddenly, out of the corner of her eye, Miranda saw Red stiffen. Her hair began to crackle and murmur, and she felt the same breeze swirling around her head as she had at the Gothic mansion. Her heart quickened as she sensed that something was very wrong.

Red had suddenly sensed the presence of his twin. He scanned the square casually, as a tourist might, so as not to arouse suspicion. He then leant over and told Miranda not to panic, but they had undesirable company. He quickly sent a telepathic S.O.S. message to Sheba and Chow Yen. Sheba was too busy to notice, but Chow Yen tuned in straight away. He knew he'd be quicker jumping over the rooftops than winding his way through the busy alleyways of the oasis, so he shimmied up the wall of the nearest building and sprang onto the roof with feline grace. Taking giant strides, Chow Yen quickly made his way along until he reached the roof of the café where Red and Miranda were sitting. He tuned into a group of people below and instantly realised that five of them were members of Nasty's crew.

Sheba was still nowhere to be seen. *Where is she?* thought Red, drumming the table. *If she's not here in twenty seconds I swear, on the breath of Zeus, I'll cut her up into a thousand pieces and feed her tae burn in Hades.*

Sheba was holding court and hadn't stopped gossiping since she'd got there. At last, she paused for breath and Red's telepathic S.O.S. finally managed to get through.

'Oh my Gaaad!' she exclaimed, 'I must fly, Red neeeds me,' and promptly shot out of the door of the carpet shop.

As she entered the square, she slowed down and began to float casually towards Red and Miranda, as if she didn't have a care in the world. Red was chatting to Miranda pretending that he was totally unaware of the presence of Nasty's men.

'When Sheba gets here, I want you to get on her as if ye were just going for a bit of sightseeing or something. Act r-real natural like, and hold on tight, because Sheba is going tae fly like the wind. And when Chow Yen and I have dealt with this lot, Sheba will come back and pick us up.'

Sheba arrived, flopped over a chair and fanned herself with an ornate Japanese fan. Red made some secret signs with his fingers and Sheba said in a very loud voice to Miranda, 'I have just seen the most divine dress at the other end of the bazaar. It is sooo totally you, I suggest we have a quick look,' she uttered, winking madly at Miranda.

As Miranda began to climb onto the carpet, Nasty's men were instantly alerted and began to walk rapidly towards them, all taking out their previously concealed swords. Sheba accelerated at full speed and shot off over their heads.

Red got up, drawing his sword, becoming bigger and bigger until he blocked out the bright light of the moon.

Suddenly, all the lights and candles that lit the place fizzled out, shrouding it in darkness. Chow Yen pounced down from the roof as silent as a cat stalking its prey.

Within seconds, one of the assailants was down; Chow Yen had rendered him unconscious just by touching a specific spot on the man's neck. The other four began to back away as Red, towering above them, eyes blazing, slowly advanced, his sword hissing and slashing the air.

Once Sheba and Miranda were away from the square, Sheba swooped down into one of the many dark, twisting alleyways. Sheba knew that Nasty also had a flying carpet and she, Salome, was just as vicious as he was. Sheba had no intention of bumping into her; she couldn't afford a confrontation, especially as she was carrying Miranda.

They flew stealthily through the alleys until they came to a dead end. There, waiting, was Salome... The smell of stale tobacco and the sea wafted around them. Miranda recoiled; the smell was eerily familiar. Her hair began to fizz and hiss. Sheba knew instantly that Nasty was very close by. She also knew that she was no match for him; she had to get Miranda out of there – quickly.

In a whisper, Sheba told Miranda to lie down and hold on very tightly. Then she shot straight up in the air, with Salome in hot pursuit. But it didn't matter how hard she tried, Sheba couldn't shake off the other carpet. She knew her only chance was to put Miranda down somewhere safe so that she could face Salome alone. She spotted a hiding place on one of the rooftops and dropped her off.

Miranda edged her way over to a corner and hid in the shadows. The temperature was dropping and shock was setting in. She huddled up, shaking with fear and cold. A shrill, piecing scream rang out, echoing down the alley.

Miranda crawled along and peeked over the edge of the roof, hoping and praying that Sheba was okay. All she could make out was a blur of swirling, swooping, whirling colours, moving at lightning speed. Again, Miranda caught the familiar smell of the sea and stale tobacco. Suddenly, it came to her where she had first smelt that odour – it was at Desolation Manor! Stricken with terror, her limbs turned to lead as she realised it was the pirate with the peg-leg. In the distance she could hear STEP... TAP... STEP... TAP slowly approaching. Her hair began to rise and fizz, whimpering with terror.

Sheba had managed to corner Salome by a cart; they were now both covered in scratches and utterly dishevelled. Sheba's normally beautifully groomed hair was now loose and a mass of tangles. She spotted a piece of metal sticking out of the cart. *If only I could push her onto it, it might snag her and enable me to escape*, she thought, noticing a basket of over-ripe figs to her right. Quick as a flash, she swooped down, picked up a handful of the fruit and started bombarding Salome with them. Salome, being as vain as Sheba, was horrified by the sticky mess covering her and edged backwards towards the cart. Realising she was cornered, she shot up and the jagged piece of metal caught in her weave and ripped her almost in half. She screamed and flopped down to the ground, unable to fly.

Miranda was so relieved to see that Salome had been beaten she let out a huge sigh of relief and moved out of the shadows. Suddenly a very large, smelly, leathery hand covered her face. She couldn't breathe. Fighting and struggling with all her might, she tried to wriggle out of her assailant's grasp.

Clutching his hand, she felt fur. *That's not a human hand! It's Archibald!* she thought. Her hair was fizzing with fear and multi-coloured sparks were shooting out and singeing the gorilla's fur, but his grip held fast. With one almighty effort, she tried to struggle free, but then a very *strange* thing occurred. Suddenly, an enormous surge of energy shot out of Miranda, flinging the gorilla backwards.

Then, something even more mysterious happened. The gorilla was suddenly shrouded in a blanket of fog and she heard a young girl's voice urging her to run. It was the same voice that she'd heard at the Gothic mansion! Turning around, Miranda wondered where to run to, when she heard a terrible voice ringing out behind her. She spun round and saw the silhouette of a giant man with a peg-leg.

'Ye can r-run, but there's nowhere tae hide,' he sneered, limping towards her.

Miranda opened her mouth to scream but nothing came out. She spun around again and saw Sheba hovering in wait by the roof's edge. Without hesitating, Miranda ran as fast as she could and leapt off the building onto

Sheba. They flew back to the café where they found Red and Chow Yen, tying up the last of Nasty's crew.

'Och, what happened to yooo, Sheba?!' asked Red as he realised that she was flying in a most haphazard way.

'We were cornered by Salome,' she whimpered feebly as she landed.

Red rushed over and grabbed Miranda, lifting her off the flying carpet.

'Are ye all right, lassie?'

Miranda nodded numbly and buried her head in his chest, promptly bursting into tears.

'Och, ye're safe noow,' he murmured, stroking her tousled hair. 'Sheba, are ye fit tae fly us home?'

'No doubt I'll rise to the occasion,' she answered.

'What aboot Salome, is she still a danger tae us?'

'Salome won't be a threat for some time to come, seeing that she is more or less ripped in half,' Sheba stated, with a note of pride in her voice.

'Och Sheba, ye're a real trooper; what would I do without ye?' he said, patting her weave. 'Right, I think it's time tae be getting back to the *Wilderness*.'

They climbed on, and Sheba slowly made her way back towards the galleon. Miranda was beginning to recover from the shock of nearly being caught. She suddenly sat bolt upright.

'Of course!' she exclaimed. 'I've just realised who that vile, smelly, old pirate is!'

Miranda, stared at Red, open-mouthed and slowly whispered, 'He's your twin! Nasty MacNoxious!'

'Aye! Sadly, you're right!'

'Oh my God! We've already met!' she wailed. 'He's the man from Desolation Manor in my village! OH MY GOD! He can't be, he's detestable,' she spluttered.

'I know, which is why ye're on the *Wilderness*. Ye see, Nasty not only wants his skull but he wants yooo – and *your* skull too. If he achieves that, then he can find all the other skulls as well.'

'But why?' she asked.

'Because, if he has all thirteen skulls and you under his control, he would be in a position to weave an even more terrible and bleak destiny for mankind.'

'In other words – I'm stuffed, and I might as well go home now because I'm most definitely not up to the job!' she howled. 'I'm really beginning to appreciate my dull life in Stillwater Lane and I want to go home!'

'Mir-randa, it's yer fate and there's no avoiding it!'

'It's so unfair, I didn't ask for this destiny...'

'Aye, I bet Prince William said the very same thing, but, like yooo, he just has tae grin and bear it.'

'Well, at least he gets to be a *Prince*,' she huffed.

Red pulled her close and gave her a hug.

'And another thing, how did Archibald get to the bazaar before us?' she asked.

'Archibald? What do ye mean? *He* was there...?!' asked Red.

'Well, some great big gorilla tried to suffocate me on top of the roof! At least, I think it was Archibald, although he didn't smell like him. You know how he always *stinks*

of aftershave? Well this one just stank... and he was dressed very shabbily.'

'Sheba, did ye see the gorilla?'

'No, I couldn't see properly, it was too dark.'

'This is very interesting news. I wonder if this is a relative of Archibald's – who he has conveniently forgotten tae mention... Maybe that's how Nasty knew we were going tae be here; Archibald must be communicating telepathically with this other gorilla. Right, we'll all have tae keep an eye on him from noow on. Maybe I'll be able tae use this tae my advantage.'

* * *

Miranda stared ahead and saw an eagle flying towards them. 'Look, there's an eagle heading straight for us!'

'Och, that's Soaring Eagle, he must be back from the plains of the Mid-West in America. He likes tae go back to a time when foreigners hadn't yet arrived in the Americas.'

'I thought he was a Native American Indian.'

'Aye he is, but he's also a shape-shifter.'

Red hailed the approaching bird of prey. 'It's gr-rand tae see ye, Soaring Eagle, and what brings ye here? Ye must be exhausted from yer travels.'

'Greetings, Red, I'm glad to see you are all in one piece. Fearless picked up your S.O.S. just as I arrived back and I thought you might need a little help.'

As the eagle landed on Sheba, he began to tremble and slowly change into a Native American Indian.

The Truth is finally revealed

Miranda stared open-mouthed at the apparition in front of her.

Soaring Eagle was truly amazing. He wore his grey hair in two long plaits, with brightly coloured feathers threaded through them. Attached to his beautiful soft leather jerkin were shells, beads and more feathers. Tied to a leather thong around his neck were various pouches and he wore deer-skin moccasins on his feet. He had piercing eyes that bored right into Miranda and she could feel his power surging through her like a bolt of electricity. She felt her hair crackling with static, highlighting all the different colours and making it sparkle.

'That's gr-rand of ye', replied Red, 'but they were no match for the likes of us. Although, as you can see from her appearance, our weary, war-torn, magnificent, brave Sheba courageously took on Nasty and his shrew of a flying carpet and managed tae pr-rotect the wee lass as well!'

'It was nothing!' said Sheba, coquettishly rolling her eyes. She was cooing with pleasure at the compliments and managed to speed up a little.

6

Red's Island

The journey back to the *Wilderness* seemed to take forever. She was covered in little rips and holes, which made it very hard for her to fly. By the time they reached the galleon, she was totally exhausted. Chow Yen immediately administered some foul-tasting herbal remedy to her and sent her to bed. Fearless said he was going to try and darn her weave in the morning. Sheba was horrified by the thought but was too tired to argue.

'I'll let you darn me, as long as Red takes me back to Persia to be rewoven as soon as poss, because I cannot possibly be seen looking like *this!*' she sighed.

'It'll be ma pleasure,' said Red.

The rest of the crew stood by, shocked by their appearance and wondering what could have happened.

'Och, we're all OK,' Red told them. 'We just had a run-in with ma odious twin. I'd forgotten that the oasis was his favourite watering hole and I should have been more careful.'

* * *

In the meantime Archibald lay in his hammock; his heart pounding as he wondered whether or not Red had sussed him out yet. Unfortunately, Red's mind was impossible to read so he had no idea what was going on. Yet, Red seemed jovial enough and he couldn't detect any changes in his attitude towards him so Archibald began to relax.

Miranda wanted to get as far away as possible from the gorilla and went downstairs to Red's cabin. She sat on Red's gigantic bed with a blanket wrapped around her, trying to read a book but, due to the day's events, she was having trouble concentrating.

There was a tap at the door and Sly popped his head around with a slice of delicious cake and a mug of steaming hot chocolate. 'There's sh-nothing better than some warm lemon drizzle cake and a cup of cocoa laced with Rescue Remedy to ease your sh-nerves,' he said, wobbling through the door.

Miranda gratefully took the beverage and cake. After having a bite and a sip of chocolate, she decided that they must be magical, because with every bite and sip she took her fears faded a little and, by the time she'd finished, she was feeling wonderful; all her worries had mysteriously vanished.

Red marched in and plonked himself down on the bed next to her. 'How are ye feeling, lass?' he enquired tenderly.

'Considering what I've been through – fantastic,' she answered chirpily.

'Och that's grand.'

'Red, I know this must sound a bit strange, but every time I'm anywhere near Nasty, I feel this breeze swoosh around my head and I hear a girl's voice.'

'Och, that'll be Orphia... I guess now's the time to introduce ye.'

'Who's Orphia?'

'She's yer angel-ling.'

'Angel-ling?' she asked, looking thoroughly baffled.

'Aye, she's an angel-in-training and is there tae keep an eye on ye and tae give ye a helping hand when necessary.'

Red looked up and said, 'Orphia, I'd like tae introduce ye tae Miranda.'

Miranda felt Orphia brush her cheek and, in a hushed and gentle voice, she whispered in her ear, 'Salutations, Miranda, now that we have been formally introduced, you and I can communicate verbally from now on.'

'We can? Why couldn't we before?'

'Normally, in the case of angels, we're not allowed to interfere or help unless asked. But – as you're special – I was allowed to help when necessary which, in your case, was quite often. But I wasn't allowed to introduce myself until Red had formally introduced us.'

Miranda was thrilled to think she had an invisible friend and helper. 'So what happens now?' she asked.

'We're off tae ma island,' replied Red.

'Did you just say your – island? Do you mean to tell me that you own an *island*?'

'Aye, I do.'

'Where is it?'

'It's situated in the Bermuda Triangle.'

'The Bermuda Triangle!' she gasped. 'But people disappear when they travel through there.'

'Aye, don't I knoow it. They all end up living on ma island and refuse tae go back, because it's heaven on earth.'

'What are we going to do there?'

'I want ye tae look at yer stay on there as a training camp.'

'Training camp!' she gasped. 'What sort of training?'

'Fer a start, Chow Yen will be teaching ye various different forms of martial arts. Ye'll start with ta'i chi.'

'YES!' said Miranda, imagining running up walls and giving Nerdy-Nigel a few choice karate chops.

'Chow Yen will also teach ye hoow tae meditate,' added Red.

'Boring!' said Miranda. 'I'd love to learn martial arts, but meditation... borrrring. I've done that and I generally fall asleep or I can't stop my mind from chattering. So I think I'll give that a miss, thanks.'

'Nae ye won't; every member of ma crew has tae meditate and practise ta'i chi every day. Also, Soaring Eagle will teach ye hoow tae manipulate the weather.'

'Whoa! This just gets better and better. I could hang a permanent rain cloud above the Nerd.'

'Hopefully ye'll find a better use for it than that.'

With those words, Red went off to issue instructions to the crew to set sail for his island.

* * *

Red's island finally came into view and as they drew nearer Miranda could hear music playing. It sounded like a full orchestra performing the Death March by Wagner, which always reminded Miranda of funerals. She shivered and gave Red a nervous glance.

'Why the music, Red? Is it a sign of bad things to come?' she asked, with a twinge of apprehension creeping into her stomach.

'Och nae... I know who that'll be... He's quite harmless, really.'

Red ordered the enormous anchor to be dropped. The sound of the great chains rattling whilst being lowered was deafening. With a loud splash, the anchor hit the water and disappeared.

Miranda was looking over the side of the galleon when she spotted a mermaid frolicking about with two dolphins.

'I don't believe it!' she yelled. 'I can see a mermaid.'

'That's Lucille,' said Red, striding over to join her. 'Oh, and how fantastic –Dolphus and Delilah are here as well!'

'Who are they?' asked Miranda.

'The dolphins, of course. They've been sailing the seven seas with me for a very long time.'

Miranda waved at the dolphins and the mermaid.

'I bet ye never thought that ye'd get tae meet a real mermaid?'

'No, not in a million years, but then again, neither was I expecting to meet a giant *rat* and a mind-reading *gorilla*.'

Red chuckled, 'Aye, well Lucille's one of the last of the great mer-sirens.'

'She is?' said Miranda, totally awestruck. 'I thought sirens were supposed to lure sailors to their death if they should hear them sing.'

Lucille let out a laugh that sent the waves crashing against the sides of the galleon, the ocean's spray shooting into the air showering both Red and Miranda with tears of amusement.

'Oh, I only harm those with a treacherous heart,' she murmured silkily, casually flapping her tail and stroking her hair.

'So I don't have to block my ears when you sing then?'

'Why, child, are you dark of heart?'

'No… well… er… I don't think I'm that bad, really,' said Miranda, desperately trying to think of some really horrid people she could gauge herself against.

'Then you have nothing to worry about,' said Lucille.

Phew! That's a relief, thought Miranda, smiling ever so sweetly at the mermaid.

Red leant over the side and shouted: 'Lucille, it is grand tae see ye. Hoow was yer holiday with the Mer-people?'

'Wonderful,' she sang. Her silken, honeyed voice sent delightful shivers up Miranda's spine.

* * *

The longboat had been lowered by now and the crew had rushed off to visit their friends and families, leaving Red and Miranda on the beach. She spotted a parrot sitting on a branch of a tree up ahead. The music was still playing but there was no sign of an orchestra.

Red raised his hand and the music stopped. He turned to the parrot and said, 'Ludwig, it is gr-rand tae see ye 'n'all... but do ye have tae play that damn piece of music? It's scaring the wee lass here. Ye could've chosen something a little more cheerful-like.'

'But it's my favourite piece and anyvay, if I had something to be happy about, I vould... but as the Vorld is coming to an end...,' wailed Ludwig.

'Hush yer mouth... it's no' coming to an end.'

'That's vot you think. Varicose-Vera read it in my tea leaves...'

'Och... you're no' tae listen tae that old crone.'

'Anyvay... I can feel it in every feather on my body.'

'Well, I can see yer honeymoon cheered ye up nae end... Its gr-reat tae see ye so happy! Anyways, hoow's yer good wife Jakeeta?' asked Red, trying to change the subject.

'Considering that ve are all about to die, she's very vell,' the parrot replied, bobbing his head up and down.

Whilst all this was going on, Miranda was watching a giant turtle slowly make its way to the sea, leaving little mounds of sand behind it. She noticed something sparkly half-hidden in the sand. Hoping it was some buried treasure, she casually sauntered over. It turned out to be a small bottle with something in it. She stuffed it in her bag, deciding she would have a closer look at it later.

Hiding behind some bushes, Archibald smiled. *Perfect!* he thought as Miranda picked up the bottle; he quietly slipped away. 'I can't believe how easy this is going to be,' he snickered. 'And I can't believe how stupid Red is. He hasn't even clicked that I'm in constant touch with Nasty's lot!' Nasty had promised him riches beyond his wildest dreams if he helped to catch Miranda and by now Archibald was practically delirious with greed: 'I'm going to be RICH, RICH, RICH!'

* * *

Ludwig flew on ahead and, once he was out of earshot, Miranda asked Red why the parrot was called Ludwig and how on earth he produced the sound of a full orchestra?

'Well, ma old fr-riend Ludwig is a genius; he can copy any musical instrument he wishes. And not only that, he can play all of them at the same time.'

'Wow, that's amazing!'

'He was the musical brains behind Beethoven,' Red continued. 'He'd sit on his shoulder composing the most fantastic symphonies and Beethoven, who wasn't a bad composer himself, used to write down all Ludwig's music. How d'ye think Beethoven ended up deaf? It was like having the London Symphony Orchestra sitting on his shoulder!'

'I don't believe you,' she chortled. 'Is he always so gloomy?'

'Aye, he never got over the fact that Beethoven got all the credit and glory but I really think he should have got tae grips with it by noow. After all, unlike Beethoven, Ludwig is still alive and kicking... Mind yooo, I think Ludwig was born a pessimist; he's been predicting the end of the world for the last five hundred years or so. Every day he tells me it's ma last. I don't know how his new wife stands it; she's the most cheerful, optimistic, sunny-natured parrot you'll ever meet. Luckily for me, his missus disnae like sailing much so he's decided to stay on the island.'

As they started to move away from the beach, they met Fearless, with a very buxom blonde on his arm. She wore her hair in bleached-blonde ringlets, piled high on her head, with a red hibiscus pinned just above her ear. Her throat was adorned with a necklace of sweet-scented frangipani. Her eyes were deep emerald-green, with long, dark, curling eyelashes which almost disappeared amidst a ray of laughter lines when she smiled.

'Miranda... this is Luscious-Lily, the most heavenly creature ye're ever likely tae meet,' said Fearless, with the look of love in his eyes.

Lily immediately clasped Miranda to her ample body and hugged her. Pushing Miranda away, she looked her up and down.

'She sure is peachy. I'm pleased to meet ya, kiddo. Fearless has told me all about ya. I'm always around if ya need me; ya'll find me at my saloon in Sovereign Street,' she said, in a Mid-West American drawl.

Lily picked up her long skirt, revealing layers of brightly coloured petticoats and, whipping out a lolly. Lily then slapped Fearless on his backside and let out the most raucous laugh, making Miranda giggle at Fearless's pained expression. Instantly liking her, Miranda smiled and thanked her for her lolly.

Fearless told Red that Jimmy, the driver, was waiting with his coach and horses in the town square. Red and Miranda found the coach with Jimmy up in the driving seat. He wore an old grey string vest, a rather tatty kilt and a beret with a great big feather in it.

'Hey Jimmy, how are ye doin'?' asked Red.

'Fine!' he drawled.

'And how are yer two brothers, Jimmy and Jimmy?'

'Fine and fine,' he mumbled.

'That's grand,' uttered Red, rolling his eyes.

He and Miranda got into the coach and made themselves comfortable.

The coach reminded Miranda of the old swashbuckling movies of highwaymen on misty moors. They sat patiently, waiting to get going. Five minutes went by and they still hadn't moved.

Red eventually popped his head out of the window and said, 'We'll be moving then...'

'Fine!' Jimmy picked up his whip and lashed the ground. The four dapple-grey horses reared up and leapt forward, galloping off at speed. Their hooves were thundering along the cobbled street while Miranda and Red held on for dear life.

'He thinks he was a Roman charioteer in his last life,' shouted Red above the din of the squealing wheels and clattering hooves. Eventually, the horses slowed down to a gentler pace, giving Miranda time to take in the view. As they trotted through the town centre, Miranda noticed an extraordinary array of different architecture. There seemed to be old-fashioned Tudor houses alongside very modern ones. She also spotted a huge glass pyramid with the word 'Library' written up above the doors.

Not only was the architecture in a variety of styles but the inhabitants looked as though they, too, had stepped out of every century imaginable. People in Elizabethan dress walked daintily alongside men in World War One flying gear. There were others who looked as though they'd just stepped out of a futuristic science fiction movie.

As they passed Luscious-Lily's tavern, she could hear an Elvis Presley song being sung. Glancing through the window, she saw what she assumed was an Elvis lookalike singing his heart out.

'That Elvis impersonator sure looks like the real thing,' observed Miranda.

'Who said he's an impersonator?' said Red, winking at her.

* * *

Earlier, Miranda had been under the impression that this was a tropical island, with its pure white sand and gracefully-arching palm trees. She had noticed beautiful coral reefs with shoals of brightly coloured fish swimming around. By now, however, the landscape was changing dramatically. The higher they went, the more it began to resemble the Scottish highlands with rolling hills covered in pine and spruce, topped with snow.

Miranda was looking excitedly out of the window when she suddenly spotted a small figure on a pony galloping towards them. The rider, wearing a large black floppy hat and a white handkerchief around the face, was pointing two pistols at the coach.

'RED!' exclaimed Miranda, 'I think we're in trouble now!'

He looked out of the window and let out a laugh.

'Yer money or yer life!' ordered a girl's voice.

'Och... Musket-Marie, I've no' the patience for this, so go and hold up someone else, ye wee cataran.'

'What's a cataran?' asked Miranda, surprised that the rider was a young girl.

'Och, a bandit of course,' Red replied.

Musket-Marie removed her hanky from her face and, giving Red a murderous glare, she promptly dismounted and climbed up to the door, sticking her head through the window of the carriage.

'Who's she?' asked Musket-Marie roughly.

'This, Musket-Marie, is ma great, great, great etc., etc. gr-randdaughter, Miranda.'

Musket-Marie gave Miranda a scathing look, got back on her pony and rode off.

'Who was that?' Miranda asked.

'That's Dick Turpin's gr-randdaughter.'

'Who's Dick Turpin?'

'What! Ye've never heard of Dick Turpin? He was one of the most famous highwaymen in England. He was forever holding up carriages and robbing the occupants. 'Stand and deliver!' was a famous phrase of his and Musket-Marie is determined to carry on the family tradition. She drives us all crazy... but she means well.'

They drove on and then, in the distance, Miranda saw an extraordinary castle situated next to a large loch.

'Is that your home?' she asked in awe.

'Aye... it is indeed.'

'It's fantastic,' she gasped. 'It's straight out of a fairy tale.'

Finally, they drew up at the castle where two men were waiting. Miranda guessed they were the other two Jimmies, as they all looked pretty similar to one another.

Further up the stone steps leading to the vast front door stood a woman, frantically waving at Red. She had a silvery-greenish tint to her skin and her face was covered in warts. Her hair was a mass of multi-coloured dreadlocks that sprouted out in every direction. For one horrific moment, Miranda thought she'd come face to face with Medusa, and decided that it might be safer to stay put and avoid looking into her eyes, in case she was turned to stone.

'Who's the old crone?' whispered Miranda in Red's ear, sliding across the seat and hiding behind him.

'Och, that's Varicose-Vera, ma housekeeper,' he replied, grinning at Miranda's expression of horror.

'She looks like an old witch!'

'Aye, she *is* an old witch, but she's no' as bad as she appears. She makes a tidy living from selling love-potions and face creams.'

Miranda stared at the witch's green, pallid skin and wondered what horrendous ingredients she put into her lotions.

'She looks as if she should create a cream to banish warts!'

'Och, dinnae tell her that, she's under the impression that she's a real bonnie lassie. And for a witch, the more warts the better – they are a sign of gr-reat beauty.'

Red opened the door of the coach and climbed down, with Miranda cautiously following. The three Jimmies carried Red's luggage into the castle without uttering a word. Varicose-Vera threw herself at Red, cursing him in the process for not giving her enough time to prepare for their arrival.

'Och, I thought being a witch, ye'd have somehow managed tae divine it,' responded Red.

Varicose-Vera then laid her waspish eyes on Miranda, sending nervous shivers up the young girl's spine. Miranda got the distinct impression that the old witch disliked her intensely. *That's not fair, she doesn't even know me*, she thought, deciding that she liked the wart-ridden old bag less and less.

* * *

Miranda followed everyone into the castle and gasped as she entered the great hall. It was gargantuan! She arched her head up so far that she nearly fell over backwards as she slowly turned around, trying to take everything in. She could see now that the circular hall was lined with intricate latticework balconies which were set at different levels around the walls. What seemed to be metal vines hung down from each tier. It reminded her of the inside of a shell, the way that the hall spiralled up to reach the roof. Inset in the roof were oddly shaped, multi-coloured windows which cast rainbows of light to dance in the air above her and, looking down at the floor, Miranda could see that it was covered in tiny mosaic tiles which continued up the walls to create a picture of a magical forest. She'd never seen anything like it – it was all *so* beautiful!

In the centre of the hall was a huge wrought-iron staircase but she was confused when she realised that the stairs seemed to reach only the first balcony. *How on earth do people reach the other levels?*, she wondered. There were six passageways branching off from the hall, leading to the other towers and she could hardly wait to explore the rest of this amazing castle!

Miranda looked at Red. 'I never thought you'd have a castle like this,' she exclaimed. 'I thought it would be more traditional.'

'I may be a Scottish-Pleiadian, but I tend to view myself as a citizen of the universe, sooo I don't really feel I'm from anywhere in particular… if ye get ma dr-rift. I was most taken with Antonio Gaudi's architecture when I visited Barcelona in the year 1920, and he agreed to design ma home here.'

'The year 1920? That doesn't make any sense at all,' said Miranda, getting more and more confused. 'When was the castle actually built?'

'Aboot eight-hundred years ago,' he replied.

'Eight-hundred years! But he couldn't possibly have been alive then.'

'Aye, true enough, but as I'm a *time*-traveller, I just skipped forward in time and brought him back.'

'Of course, I never thought of that... and who *is* Antonio Gaudi exactly?'

'Och, have ye no' heard of him? He's one of Spain's most celebrated architects.'

Hanging off the walls on either side of the staircase were the heads of a large moose and an enormous brown bear. To Miranda's surprise, the moose greeted them both, but his accent was so broad that she couldn't understand a word. The bear let out a thunderous laugh and told Red he was delighted to have him back. Red introduced them to Miranda: the bear was called Boris and the moose was called Mac.

He then led her into his library. It was vast. A bronze spiral staircase led up to the balcony, which went all the way around. The room doubled in height with an arch vaulted ceiling covered in thousands of tiny dark blue tiles which displayed a map of the cosmos with a million fairy lights that twinkled like real stars. The multitude of shelves were crammed with thousands and thousands of books, both old and new, music CDs as well as vinyl records.

Varicose-Vera appeared, zigzagging her way across the floor like a drunken crab. She had plastered her face with make-up, highlighting all her warts with black kohl, hoping to turn them into beauty spots. She smelled of cheap air freshener; her false eyelashes were so long and thick she could hardly keep her eyes open, and her mouth had become a brilliant, bright-red gash.

Red asked Varicose-Vera to show Miranda to her room so she could have a bath. Then she was to prepare some food as they were both hungry. Vera cocked her head and uncurled a gnarled finger, beckoning for Miranda to follow. Swallowing twice, Miranda crossed her fingers, praying that the old hag wouldn't turn her into a frog.

As they walked back into the hall, one of the metal vines which she had seen hanging from the balconies earlier unfurled to form a staircase. It stretched out to meet them and Varicose-Vera leapt on and grabbed the handrail, hailing Miranda to follow. The stairs slowly reversed and started moving up, depositing them onto one of the tiers. A strangely shaped door opened automatically as they walked, leading them into a bedroom. Miranda followed Varicose-Vera inside and was instantly captivated. It was perfect. A large, wooden four-poster bed stood in the centre of the room. Small ivy leaves were carved into the four posts which were hung with soft, pale-yellow silk curtains fluttering gently in the breeze. A brilliant white duvet, all clean, puffed up and inviting, lay ready. *Oh boy*, she thought, staring longingly at the bed. *It's been a while since I slept in one of those!* A roaring fire crackled in the fireplace and the bookcase was miraculously filled with many of her favourite authors.

After having a quick glance around, she walked up to the large, arched glass doors, opened them and stepped out onto a delicate balcony of wrought-iron latticework. It looked so frail she thought it might tear and fall like autumn leaves. Looking out over the loch and the snow-capped mountains, she greedily soaked up the magnificent scenery. Turning to leave, she detected a strange shape swimming in the loch. *Mmm, I think I might have to investigate that later*, she thought excitedly.

A glorious smell of lavender oil wafted under her nose and, looking to see where the scent was coming from, she noticed a door leading off her room. Popping her head around it, she found an en-suite bathroom with an old-fashioned roll-top bath in the centre. It was filled with steaming water and loads of bubbles that cascaded over the sides. Varicose-Vera cleared her throat loudly and let out a cackle, revealing one green, grimy, mossy tooth that had seen better days.

Miranda winced when she saw it, wondering whether if she cleaned the plaque off it would fall out, because it looked as though the plaque was cementing it to her red, swollen gums. *Oooo yuck*, she thought. *Now I know why Karmela insists that I brush my teeth twice a day.* Not wanting her teeth to end up like that, she made a mental note to brush her teeth at least three times a day from then on.

'There's a towel over there,' said Varicose-Vera, in a rumbling cackle. As she bent down by the bath to test the temperature of the water, her dress rose up, revealing a snakes and ladders board of varicose veins on her legs.

Vera caught Miranda's look and misread her expression of horror as being one of awe. Promptly lifting up her dress, with great aplomb, she gave Miranda a better view. 'Where I come from, these are a mark of great beauty,' she said, pointing to the multitude of writhing red and purple rivers that entwined her wrinkly white legs. 'And who needs fancy stockings, when you've got legs like these?' she stated with pride.

Desperately trying to keep a blank expression on her face so that she wouldn't offend the old crone, Miranda silently thanked her lucky stars that she wasn't a witch. She was starting to feel very uncomfortable as Varicose-Vera scrutinised her, paying particular attention to her hair.

'There's a pretty dress over there for you to change into,' she said, pointing her withered hand to a white frilly dress laid over a chair.

Miranda was horrified and refused point blank to wear it – after all, she was a *pirate*, wasn't she?!

Shrugging her shoulders, Varicose-Vera screeched, 'Well, I'll be off then...' and shuffled out of the room. Just as she was leaving, she whipped around, giving Miranda a reptilian sneer. 'Oh, by the way', she hissed, 'there's something you should know about me... I don't care for children! Boys are bad enough... but girls! Oh, how I *detest* little girls.' Closing her eyes until they were mere slits, she added, 'Especially ones that are close to Red!' With that she left, slamming the door behind her.

Miranda, shaking from Varicose-Vera's venom, sat on her bed wondering how she could win the old witch over. She had enough enemies and certainly didn't need any more. She decided to get into the bath, hoping it would ease her anxiety. After a wonderful soak, she looked in the wardrobe and, to her delight, hanging there was a large array of different types of clothes that were all in her size. She grabbed a pair of jogging bottoms and a jumper since she didn't feel like dressing up.

She scanned the bookcase hoping to find something to read at bedtime. 'Ah,' she sighed with pleasure. '"The Lion, the Witch and the Wardrobe", one of my favourites.' She opened it up and ran her fingers gently down the page. A warm memory of Mimi sitting on her bed at night reading it to her came flooding back.

Suddenly, a voice boomed out: 'Miranda, now is not a good time, I'm afraid. I'm in the middle of a meeting.' Jumping with surprise, she looked at the page and saw a picture of Aslan, the lion, smiling up at her. 'But if you pick the story up tonight, I'm sure we'll all be ready,' the lion continued.

Next on the shelf were all the Harry Potter books. Miranda absolutely adored Harry Potter. She was just about to pick one from the shelf but quickly decided against it, thinking *If the last book could talk, goodness knows what these are capable of. What if a spell escapes and I end up growing a pig's tail?*

Noticing a dark blue book that didn't have a title, she pulled it out and opened it.

'Go away,' it wailed. 'I'm depressed. I've got the blues and I want to be alone.'

'Oh dear, whatever is the matter?' asked Miranda sympathetically.

'Life!' the book moaned, 'What's the point of it all? Everything is grey. Grey, grey, grey,' it bleated on and on.

Deciding to change the subject, Miranda asked what the book's title was.

'Ten Steps to Happiness and Positive Thinking,' it replied miserably.

'Crikey! Well, I can see it's working, then,' she said, promptly shutting the book, thinking that it should have been called 'Ten Steps to Misery'.

On the bedside table she noticed a button and pressed it to see what would happen. Red's voice boomed out, causing Miranda to nearly jump out of her skin.

'Red, where are you?'

'Doun in ma library… I had the tannoy installed so we could all keep in touch as ma castle is sooo big,' he replied.

'Have ye found the telly yet?' he asked.

'No.'

'Look in the drawer of yer bedside table and you'll find a remote control. Press the red button.'

Miranda did as she was told and instantly a television screen appeared, hovering in front of her bed. 'WOW!' she shouted.

'Cool, eh? I skipped forward to the year 2020 and I just couldn't r-resist it. If ye pr-ress the gr-reen button it'll make the screen bigger and if ye pr-ress the yellow it will make it smaller.'

Miranda pressed the green button until the screen was nearly touching the walls, floor and ceiling.

'This is wicked!' she shrieked with excitement.

'Aye… ye can pick up programmes throughout the galaxy. Talk aboot extra-terrestrial television!'

Miranda settled down to explore the various channels. Choosing one that featured lizard-like creatures working in a futuristic hospital, she found herself being caught up in the drama when Varicose-Vera's voice crackled over the tannoy. 'Dinner will be served in ten minutes and if ye're a minute late you can – LUMP IT!'

Miranda was in two minds whether to turn up or not; she didn't fancy eating Varicose-Vera's cooking, but her stomach had other ideas and was growling with hunger.

This time, as she opened her bedroom door, instead of the stairs being there, a very large, flat, metal vine leaf appeared and a high-pitched voice told her to step aboard. She placed her foot gingerly onto the leaf and sat down. Once seated, she was instantly encircled by tendrils which acted as a safety belt. The leaf gently twisted down to the ground and unfurled itself, allowing Miranda to step off. She was just wondering which way to go when Boris the bear came to her rescue, pointing her in the direction of the dining room.

She found Red sitting at the head of an enormous wooden table, having a one-way conversation with one of the three Jimmies. The strain of trying to have a chat was starting to show on his face. He looked up at Miranda with an expression of relief.

'Mir-randa, come and join me, I was having a wee chat here with Jimmy…' He turned his head and gave her a cross-eyed look as he said this.

Miranda grinned and sat down.

Jimmy got up, muttering 'Fine,' and promptly left.

'Phew! Och they're awfy hard work, the three Jimmies.'

'Why are they all called Jimmy?' asked Miranda.

'Well, they've got eighteen older brothers, and I guess their mother must have run out of names by the time she had the last three. Anyways, in Scotland, Jimmy is a very popular name.'

'Red, there's a very strange book in my room and it's most depressing.'

'Aye, let me guess, it's no' *Ten Steps to Happiness and Positive Thinking*, is it?'

'How did you know that?'

'Och, the book dr-rove me mad. What a misery!'

'You can say that again.'

'I picked the book up for Ludwig, thought it might cheer him up. Believe it or not, the book was thoroughly joyful and optimistic when I first brought it back. But after a week with Ludwig, the book was suicidal and was forever trying to jump into the nearest log fire.'

Red's eyes danced with mirth. Miranda gave him a questioning look.

'It's the tr-ruth!' he said. 'Anyway, I asked Varicose-Vera to remove it from ma library; I coudna stand its constant whinging.'

Varicose-Vera meandered in, pushing a trolley laden with food. She eyed up Red, giving him a flirtatious, one-fanged grin. She tried to flutter her false eyelashes at him, except that one was now hanging off, and the others kept getting stuck together every time she blinked, giving her a very lopsided look.

Well, Red certainly has a way with horrid old crones and carpets, thought Miranda, as she observed Varicose-Vera in action. The old witch then turned to Miranda, giving her an icy smile that sent shivers down her spine.

Red clapped his hands together and said, 'Aye, it's gr-rand to see that you two have hit it off.' Miranda gulped and wondered how someone so wise could be so blind.

Varicose-Vera was wearing a crown of small inter-woven branches, with a cuckoo perched on top in a nest. Her long, floating dress looked like a scene from a forest. The smell of damp earth and grass filled the room and Miranda could hear the wind rustling the leaves on the branches that were shooting out of Vera's outfit. Bees could be heard buzzing amongst the wild flowers and frogs croaked. Tiny butterflies and dragonflies flew back and forth.

Varicose-Vera lifted a silver lid from one of the dishes and a tiny frog jumped onto a plate, then hopped across the table. Ignoring the frog, Red tied an enormous purple napkin around his neck. 'Aye... something smells delicious,' he said, sniffing the air and rubbing his hands together in anticipation. Vera laid a large bowl of big black mussels in garlic butter in front of him.

'Och… ma favourite, a bowl of clappy-doos in fragrant butter, what more could an old pirate want? Vera, ye're a wonder,' he added. Miranda watched the old crone melt with pleasure at the compliment, and wondered how she and Sheba got on and whether or not there was any rivalry between them.

Glancing at the bowl of mussels, Miranda found herself gagging. Just the thought of eating one made her retch. *Ooooo, how anyone can eat those is beyond me*, she thought, cringing and making a sickened expression.

Varicose-Vera gave her a scornful stare and produced a plate of fish and chips. Giving the old crone her best smile, Miranda had a quick sneaky prod about, in case any slugs or creepy crawlies had fallen off Varicose-Vera's dress into her food. Finding nothing untoward, she tucked into her meal enthusiastically. *Not bad! Not bad at all*, she thought, highly relieved. As she looked at Red with a pleased smile, he told her that Varicose-Vera had cooked for kings and queens. However hard she tried, Miranda could not imagine royalty hiring Vera to cook for them. She was just about to take her last mouthful when she noticed something wiggling on her fork. On closer inspection, she realised it was a maggot. Coughing and spluttering, she spat the remainder of the food out and eye-balled Varicose-Vera with as much venom as she could muster. The old witch gave Miranda a knowing, caustic smile and scuttled out.

* * *

After the meal had finished, Miranda asked to be excused so that she could go and explore and, deciding that the loch was her first port of call, she made her way down to the edge of its banks. She sat down near the water and, just as she thought she detected some movement, a very large head appeared out of the water, covered in weeds, minuscule crabs and eels, followed by a tremendously long neck.

Miranda quickly crouched down, then scurried away on all fours and hid behind a tree. She held her breath, thoroughly mesmerised, wondering what the creature was going to do next. She didn't have to wait long.

With a rush of cascading water, the monster heaved its huge prehistoric body out of the loch. The ground shook, causing the trees to lose their leaves and the chirping birds to flee. Cracks appeared in the earth where the creature trod. Coming to a standstill, the monster opened its cavernous mouth, uttering terrible rumbles and gargling sounds.

The creature's violently vibrating neck began bobbing up and down and suddenly, with a tremendous belch, a small rowing boat burst forth, followed by a lifebuoy, half a chewed-up oar and a small man covered with pondweed and green algae, clutching a fishing rod.

'There'll be nooo poaching tr-rout from ma loch,' the prehistoric monster bellowed. 'Next time, fish somewhere else or it won't be ma mouth that ye come out of.'

The terrified little man scurried away as fast as he could, spitting out tiny fish as he went.

Letting out another large burp, the creature swung his head in Miranda's direction.

'And as fer yooo… ye'd best be stepping oot fr-rom behind that tr-ree,' he growled.

With her heart beating rapidly, Miranda timidly edged her way into the open and stared wide-eyed and open-mouthed at the colossus in front of her.

'And who might yooo be?' he grumbled.

'M-M-Miranda Wyrd,' she quavered.

'Och, are yooo the wee bairn that Red's been yabbering on aboot?' enquired the monster, his manner softening instantly.

'Wee bairn… I'm not a baby, thank you very much; I'm ten years old,' she snapped, breathing through her mouth to avoid the stench of his rank, fishy breath.

'Well, compared to me, you're a wee bairn.'

'And who are you?' she asked.

The monster was so taken aback by the question that he sat down with a tremendous thud.

'Och… who dooo ye think I am? I'm famous all over the world! People travel far and wide tae come and see if they can spot me,' he said in a superior voice. 'I cannae think why, as I'm very rarely there – though I do go back home and pop ma head up aboot every hundred years or so, just tae keep the myth alive. Ye know, everyone needs something to believe in, do they no'?'

Miranda stared at him blankly.

'I cannae believe it! I'm as famous as Sean Connery or Ewan McGregor!'

It suddenly dawned on Miranda who he was. 'You're the Loch Ness monster!' she cried. 'So you do exist, how brilliant!'

'MONSTER... Charming! Hoow would you like it if someone called you a monster? Of course I exist and, r-remember this, there's a grain of tr-ruth in most myths...'

'So how come you're here, instead of Loch Ness?' she asked.

The beast cocked his head to one side and gave her a very woeful look. 'Well, I'm camera shy... every time I pop ma head up, a hundred flashbulbs go off as people try to catch me on camera, and I'll be having noone of that noow. And, no' only that! If yer scientists got a hold of me, they'd take me away and do hundreds of tests on me. And I just hate being prodded and pushed about. *Plus*, they would want tae keep me in some confined area and make loads of money from my captivity.'

The monster suddenly had an air of vulnerability and Miranda could quite understand his reluctance to let the scientists get hold of him.

He shook his body all over, spraying water everywhere, and, rolling over onto his back, he stuck his short stumpy legs in the air. Having totally drenched Miranda, he turned and barked, 'Well... whit ye waiting for?'

'Pardon?' she said, wondering what he wanted.

'Och, it's not only dogs that like having their stomachs scratched, ye knoow,' he huffed.

Miranda approached the giant beast cautiously and began to scratch his vast underbelly.

'You'll have to do better than that, I can hardly feel it.'

Looking around, she spotted a decent-sized broken branch and, dragging it over, she rubbed it back and forth.

'Ooo… ooo… doun a bit, to the r-right… a bit more... Aye, that's it… ye've hit the spot… Hmmm… HEAVEN!' he sighed, rolling his eyes with pleasure. The ground trembled as he giggled and gurgled whenever Miranda hit a particularly ticklish spot.

'So I presume you're called Nessie?'

The monster gave her a filthy look and, with surprising dexterity, quickly rolled over and stood up. Towering over her, he reared back and shook his head in horror, sending Miranda flying backwards, where she landed on the ground with a thump.

'NESSIE?! NESSIE! Dinnae ever call me by that name. I mean, do I look like a *Nessie* tae yooo?'

'Uh… No-no… I-I guess Nessie is a bit of a sissy name.'

'Aye… tooo r-right it is. Ma name is Fr-rank... Fr-rank Ness of Loch Ness.'

'Frank! That's an odd name for a monster.'

The monster couldn't believe his ears. *The cheek of it!* he thought, with great indignation. He lowered his head right down until he was looking straight into her eyes. 'Well… rumour has it that *I'm* a wee bit frank – a wee bit short on diplomacy. Obviously I'm not the only one!'

'So, what's your gift then?'

'Avoiding the paparazzi of course... Oh – and surviving for as long as I have.'

Miranda could hear Mad-Mo calling out for her. She looked up and saw him with Chow Yen walking down to the loch.

'Och, if it isn't double-trouble and ma favourite philosopher. Hoow are ye doing, Chow Yen? I've really missed our philosophical conversations,' shouted Frank Ness.

'I'm well and pleased to see you too' said Chow Yen, bowing. 'I've come to give Miranda her first ta'i chi lesson; after that we shall sit down and put the world to rights.'

Frank Ness made his way back into the loch. Once he was fully submerged, he popped his head out of the water.

'If ye come across Monsieur Le Gr-rand, tell him I'm ready for ma next French lesson …' he hollered and disappeared.

* * *

Chow Yen was demonstrating the forms of ta'i chi when the sound of galloping hooves could be heard. Miranda looked up and her heart sank; Musket-Marie was heading in their direction.

The pony stopped a few feet away from Miranda and reared up. Musket-Marie gave Miranda a disdainful look, dismounted, and rushed over to Mad-Mo, slapping him on the back and sending him tumbling.

Staggering to his feet, he said, 'Aw! Marie! Do you have to hit me *that* hard?'

'Just glad to see ma best mate,' she said, eyeballing Miranda once more.

She's welcome to the twit, thought Miranda, disliking the girl intensely.

Chow Yen, ignoring Musket-Marie, told Miranda to copy him.

This should be a doddle, thought Miranda. But it wasn't, even though Chow Yen made it look so easy. Both Musket-Marie and Mad-Mo found it hilarious every time Miranda made a mistake, causing her to make even more, until she was burning with embarrassment.

Mad-Mo was giving a running commentary on her failings. He just couldn't help himself, and kept shouting out instructions, jumping in and demonstrating how it should be done. Chow Yen told Miranda to ignore Mad-Mo, especially as he wasn't even practising ta'i chi but karate.

One of Mad-Mo's greatest weaknesses was showing off at every available opportunity. In order to get rid of him, Chow Yen decided to make an example out of him, and told Miranda that he and Mad-Mo were going to give a kung fu demonstration. They both stood opposite each other, moving around in a circle. Mad-Mo was making the most peculiar noises. He sounded like a tomcat being tortured, while madly kicking out his feet and flinging his arms about. Musket-Marie sighed and looked on with a dreamy expression at Mo's antics. Miranda tried to suppress her giggles; she thought he looked like a complete wally with ants in his pants.

Chow Yen, who usually looked so old and feeble when he was stationary, moved with incredible grace and fluidity. Suddenly, he sprang forward, and before one could utter, 'Kung Fu Charlie', he made some rapid moves, leaving Mad-Mo lying in a heap on the floor.

Mad-Mo gave Miranda a sheepish grin and admitted that that's how it should really be done. Miranda burst out laughing and Mad-Mo joined in heartily, leaving Musket-Marie seething with jealousy.

Miranda decided that anyone who could make a complete idiot of themselves and laugh about it must be half okay, and she began to warm to him a bit more. *Hmm, and if I was to become great friends with Mad-Mo, it would TOTALLY rile Musket-Marie, who obviously has a huge crush on him.* Miranda suddenly felt a great deal better; the gloves were off and she wasn't going to be intimidated by the galloping goon. In fact, she relished the challenge so, after that, whenever they all hung out together, every time Mad-Mo cracked a joke or was particularly stupid, Miranda would roll around laughing and tell him he was the funniest boy she knew. This, of course, was music to Mad-Mo's ears and he lapped it up. On the other hand, a jealous, brooding anger was smouldering in Musket-Marie's heart.

7

Secret Passages

The days on Red's island rolled into each other. There wasn't much time for play as Miranda was put through her paces by Chow Yen and Soaring Eagle.

Chow Yen was relentless with Miranda. He had her training in various forms of martial arts for at least six to eight hours a day until she could hardly walk from muscle fatigue. Chow Yen also taught her how to free-climb sheer rock faces with no safety apparel at all – all she had were her fingers and toes to help her up. As long as she had a good supply of Monsieur Le Grand's homeopathic remedies to keep her vertigo at bay, she grew to thoroughly enjoy the climbs. Chow Yen, of course, could nip up in no time at all. With his strong fingers intuitively finding places to hold on to and with his toes balancing on the smallest of ledges, he'd shimmy up like a spider.

Chow Yen also taught her about her *chakras* – the spinning wheels of energy situated down the centre of the body which are invisible to the naked eye. He told her to focus on each one of the *chakras* spinning when she was meditating. After a while, Miranda could see great changes in herself. Apart from her body getting stronger and more supple, there were other things. Sometimes, when she was outside and sitting under a tree meditating, she could hear flowers talking to each other. She could understand the wildlife scuttling around her. Even with her eyes closed, she could sense someone approaching long before they saw her. One day, when she was standing outside Luscious-Lily's saloon with Red, two Japanese fellows walked out, chattering away in their native language. To Miranda's great surprise, she understood every word. Later that day, she bumped into Ricardo, the Portuguese gardener, who was talking to his plants and she understood him perfectly as well. Miranda was delighted with these new-found abilities, but her intuition urged her to remain silent and not tell anyone except Red, Soaring Eagle and Chow Yen. Towards the end of her stay, she rarely had time to play with Musket-Marie and Mad-Mo. She would see them in the distance, frolicking around, and she felt a little jealous, envying them their freedom.

Miranda had spent the last week with Soaring Eagle, and he had been teaching her how to manipulate the weather. She was a keen student; she found the whole idea absolutely thrilling; her mind was working overtime with the thought of the tricks she could get up to... except that she was finding it very difficult. This was proving to be her greatest challenge so far. It didn't matter how hard she tried and how often Soaring Eagle patiently explained, she just couldn't get it. Once or twice she managed to conjure up a gentle breeze and a few rain drops, but that was all.

Soaring Eagle knew that Miranda was extraordinarily powerful. She herself just didn't know it. He knew that if she could learn how to harness her energy and control it, she was capable of raising a howling storm. The medicine man realised that something would have to trigger it and in the end he decided to wait until that occasion happened. Forcing her could prove dangerous, as she needed to be able to control and contain her power, and so he concentrated on her psychic and healing abilities.

They were sitting on a hill, overlooking the loch and castle.

'Did you know that there is a healer in all of us?' he said.

'If that's the case, why is there so much disease on the planet?' Miranda asked.

'Like you, man has no idea of his true power or nature. A long time ago humans drifted off course, becoming spiritually lost, and they've been trying to find their way back ever since. If man knew his true nature, there would be no need for wars or acts of aggression. Heaven would indeed reside on Earth. There would be no hunger or illness and the peoples of the planet would work as one, for the good of all. This is why the skulls are *so* important; they will help to reawaken humans from a long, long slumber and help them to remember their divinity and connection to the Divine. They will realise that, although everyone is separate, they are also all one.'

Miranda sat deep in thought, imagining Heaven on Earth.

'Of course, you come from a long line of healers,' added Soaring Eagle.

'I do? How come I'm not a healer?'

'Oh, but you are, as are your mother, aunts and grandmother.'

'I never knew that,' she said, her family history surprising her once more. Thinking about it further, she realised that she'd never in her life had a day off school through illness; none of her animals had ever suffered from illnesses either. From then on, whenever Miranda came across an injured or sick animal, she would lay her hands over it and imagine a beam of white light radiating from her fingers. Sure enough, she could feel the healing energy pulsating through her hands and the injured creature was slowly healed.

The medicine man also knew that Miranda was psychic. Miranda had been having prophetic dreams for as long as she could remember, but she had never thought anything of it. Soaring Eagle told her to keep a dream diary and that she should always keep it next to where she slept so that the minute she woke up, she could write them down. Miranda wondered what her dreams of her dead sisters were about; she'd been having those more and more recently.

Miranda's time on the island was drawing to a close. Luckily, she had managed to avoid Varicose-Vera most of the time – Red had given Vera a laptop and ever since then the walking wart had spent a lot of her time secretly joining internet dating agencies.

Red, Chow Yen and Soaring Eagle were delighted with Miranda's progress. She had surprised them all with her willingness to learn, her intellectual and intuitive insights, and with how quickly she grasped difficult concepts.

Red decided that Miranda could finally have some time off and told her she was free to roam the island and play... He also told Mad-Mo to keep an eye on her and not to lead her astray.

* * *

In the meantime, Archibald's patience was running out. Miranda had been nowhere near the underground passages in the castle and there were only two more days to go before they all left. He didn't know if she had even taken the treasure map out of the bottle. He sat, deep in concentration, sending Miranda telepathic pictures of the bottle.

Miranda and Mad-Mo were sitting down by the loch, skimming stones across the water. 'Wha' d'ya fancy doing?' he asked. 'It's got to be something special.'

'Dunno, I can't think of anything...'

Suddenly, the bottle she'd picked up off the beach sprang to mind. 'Oooh! I'd forgotten all about it . . . when we first arrived I found a bottle on the beach. I think it had a piece of paper in it... Maybe it's a message!'

'Or a map!' said Mad-Mo, his eyes lighting up. He immediately got up and swaggered off in the direction of the castle. Without turning around, he shouted, 'Well, wha' ya waiting for?'

In Miranda's excitement, she'd forgotten to shield her thoughts. Archibald now realised that she'd finally remembered the bottle and he slipped down to the underground passages to wait for her. Miranda went up to her room and fetched the bottle. Upon returning, she found Mad-Mo skulking about in one of the corridors off the main hall, wearing a thoroughly guilty expression.

'Mo, why is it that you always look like you're in the middle of, or about to get up to, no good?'

'Well, we are, aren't we?'

'I s'pose so,' she said, handing him the bottle.

'Not so obvious,' he said, nervously glancing around. 'I swear these walls have eyes.'

'Don't be ridiculous, how can walls have eyes?'

'Trust me, this isn't your average castle.'

Putting the bottle into a shaft of light from one of the many windows and squinting, he tried to see what was hidden in it.

'Looks like a piece of paper,' he said excitedly.

'Do you know, your insight and powers of deduction never cease to amaze me, Mo,' she said sarcastically. 'Of course it's a piece of paper! We already know that! I just want to get it out without breaking the pretty bottle,' she added impatiently.

Giving her the evil eye, he removed a bit of wire that was hidden up his sleeve. Uncorking the bottle, he fished out the yellowing piece of parchment.

'It looks like part of a map,' said Miranda, her excitement mounting.

'Told ya!' he said, grinning from ear to ear. 'Yeah, and it doesn't half look familiar…' His enormous dark brown eyes lit up. 'It's a map of the underground passages, and look here, there's a drawing of a treasure chest. Wicked! There's treasure to be had! Right, we're definitely going down,' he whispered, trying to contain his exhilaration.

As Miranda watched Mad-Mo stealthily creeping along, cautiously looking around and keeping his body pressed firmly against the wall, she had an uncontrollable urge to giggle. Shaking with mirth, she stuffed her fist in her mouth to stop her laughter.

'Wha' ya laughing at now?' he hissed over his shoulder.

'Anyone would think you were a spy, the way you're *slithering* against the wall,' she giggled.

'Shush, we've got to get past Red's library and I don' want him to see us.'

'Why ever not?' she asked.

''Cos, he'll ask twenty questions, won't he – stupid!'

'I'm not stupid,' snapped Miranda, giving him a filthy look.

Mo put his finger to his lips, motioning her to be quiet. As they came to Red's door, Mad-Mo looked around carefully and saw Red with his back to them. *Phew!* he thought. 'Luckeee!' he mouthed.

As he was tiptoeing past, Red cleared his throat: 'Her-hum… Is that yooo, Mo?'

Mad-Mo froze and, with sagging shoulders, he gave Miranda a look which conveyed that it was all her fault.

'Come in, laddie, come in.'

They both entered and found Ludwig trying to convince Red that they only had seven more days to go before a giant asteroid hit the planet and flattened it. Red had given up trying to explain to Ludwig that that was not about to happen, suggesting instead that as the parrot only had a week left, perhaps he should go out and live a little. Ludwig, deciding this was sound advice, went to ponder on what he'd like to do before his time was up. In fact, he seemed positively cheered by the thought.

Red turned to the others and said: 'Do ye know, I was really looking forward to coming hoome tae put ma feet up, like. But I've had Varicose-Vera nagging and fussin' around, telling me I'm looking peelie-wally... Honestly! How on earth, can a pirate look peelie-wally when he spends most of his life at sea... I ask ye.'

'What does peelie-wally mean?' Miranda asked, looking thoroughly baffled.

'Pale and unhealthy looking,' he answered, and continued to moan. 'What with Ludwig spreading his doom and gloom... I tell ye, I'm definitely ready tae go back tae sea.'

Miranda and Mad-Mo made sympathetic noises and asked him if they could take a look around the castle. They conveniently forgot to tell him about the map and the secret passages in case he said no. Red nodded his head, but gave Mad-Mo a look that said: 'Stay out of trouble... or else.'

They crept under Mac the moose and Boris the bear, who both appeared to be sleeping. Suddenly, a snort could be heard coming from above. Looking up, Mad-Mo saw Mac the moose eyeballing him with one eye.

'Och, it's the wee English blatherskate. Whit ye up tae, laddie?'

'We're out to terrorise Varicose-Vera.'

'Oh, in that case be ma guest! She's a miserable old tr-rout who insists on shaking her feather duster oot r-right oonder ma snoot, knowing full well that I'm allergic tae dust!'

Miranda was delighted to know that she wasn't the only one who disliked the walking wart.

Slipping around a corner, Mad-Mo ran his fingers over the mosaic-covered wall, searching for something. Finding a little indentation, he pressed it and the panel slid open, revealing a dark passageway. He turned on his torch and they quickly eased their way in. Miranda wondered how Red managed to get through since there was very little room.

The walls were slimy from the damp and smelled of mildew. It was so dark that, even with a torch, it was still very hard to see. After navigating all the twists and turns, they came to a dungeon, where Miranda let out a piercing scream.

'What d'ya do that for?! Trying to give me a heart attack or something?'

'Mo, there are piles of skeletons lying around the place!' she said, her throat constricting in fear.

'There not real, they're plastic! Red imports them from some teaching hospital. He uses them as a deterrent.'

Miranda let out a huge sigh of relief; she really couldn't imagine Red starving someone to death. 'How do you know that?' she asked.

'Because he threw me down here, when I had been really naughty, to teach me a lesson.'

'Did it work?'

'You bet... I'm not much fatter than a skeleton, and I didn't think I'd last too long. It was only after my punishment that Red told me that they were plastic and that he'd had no intention of keeping me locked up for long.'

'Why did Red throw you in here? What did you do that was so bad?'

'I threw a fire-cracker under Varicose-Vera's skirt when she was bending over in her herb garden,' he answered, grinning from ear to ear.

'You didn't?' she chuckled, her face lighting up with glee.

'I did!'

'What did she *do*?' she squealed, her eyes now the size of saucers.

'Trust me, you don't wanna know.'

'Oh, I most definitely do,' she replied, eagerly waiting for an explanation.

'It was horrible, it was!'

'Well, go on then, don't keep me in suspense.'

'All her varicose veins slid off her legs and crawled along the grass.'

Miranda burst out laughing, 'Oh yeah, likely story!'

'They did, I swear on Red's dentures! *Then*, they wrapped themselves around my legs, tripping me up, and *then*, they pinned me to the ground! I felt like that bloke from Gulliver's travels.'

Miranda thought she was going to be sick and felt herself squirming all over. 'Urgh, that's totally and utterly *disgusting*!'

'Yeah, tell me about it!'

Recovering from their feelings of revulsion, they carried on exploring. Miranda found herself being a little disappointed with the underground secret passages until they came across an enormous cave with a large underground lake, which was surrounded by stalagmites and stalactites. It was stunningly beautiful and Miranda felt as though she'd stepped back to the beginning of time. The still water suddenly began to stir, forming a circle of ripples and, lo and behold, Frank's head popped up.

'Och, it's yous... Whit ye's doin' doun here? Does R-Red know ye're sneaking aboot?'

'Well, we did ask permission to have a snoop around,' replied Miranda.

'Aye, but did ye ask tae come doun *here*? Because R-Red disnae like people coming doun; he says it's dangerous and ye could get lost.'

Both Miranda and Mad-Mo shuffled around, not quite able to meet Frank's eyes.

'As I thought, ye shoudna be here but, fer once, I'll keep ma tr-rap shut.'

Relaxing, they both let out a sigh of relief.

'How come you're here and not in the loch, and how did you get here?' asked Miranda.

'Och, there are loads of underground r-rivers that lead to the loch, and I come here to pr-ractise ma singing ye knoow, as nobody can hear me doun here.'

'Singing, what kind of singing?' she enquired.

'Opera, of course! But apparently, it's no' to everyone's taste. I cannae think why, because I just love it.'

'Give us a demo, then,' asked Miranda.

Well, the noise that erupted from Frank's mouth was unbelievable. The sheer volume was deafening as it echoed around the cave, causing the place to moan and tremble. Miranda and Mad-Mo put their hands to their ears, trying to soften the ear-splitting din. Frank was obviously tone deaf. In other words, he sounded diabolical.

'That was lovely,' Miranda lied.

Mad-Mo was desperately trying to muffle his giggles; tears were beginning to stream down his face. Not wanting to hurt Frank's feelings, Miranda gave him a quick sharp kick to shut him up, leaving Mad-Mo hopping about on one leg and squealing like a piglet.

'Well, I guess we'd better be going; Red might be wondering where we are,' she said, waving farewell.

They both made their way towards the maze of tunnels, still hoping to find the treasure. But, after thoroughly searching every nook and cranny, they slowly came to the conclusion that the map had sent them on a wild goose chase and they were starting to feel a little scared. Deciding to turn back, they slowly retraced their steps. Miranda was convinced they were totally lost and her intuition was *screaming* for her to get out.

'I'm sure this isn't the way, Mo,' she whimpered. 'We seemed to have been walking for ages. I'm positive we should have turned right, further back.'

'Look... I've been down here loads of times, and I know my way around like the back of my hand.'

'Well, if that's the case, where are we? Because I wanna get back.'

'It's all right, I've just temporarily lost my bearings.'

'So, got any of your knives on you then?'

'Of course, never without them,' he replied.

And that's a point! Where's my angel-ling, Orphia? I haven't felt or heard her since I landed on the island, thought Miranda, trying to keep her fear at bay.

* * *

Red was sitting in his library, listening to Bach, when he felt a shiver run up his spine. Something was wrong; he could feel it in his bones. He got up and went into the hall.

'Have ye seen Mir-randa and Mad-Mo?' he asked Mac the moose.

'Aye... some time back,' he said. 'They were off tae terrorise Varicose-Vera.'

'Och... that Mo, always up tae something. Well, keep an eye oot for them; I'm a little worried. Orphia had to go to the Chief Angel for a progress r-report and she won't be back fer a while.'

Popping his head around the kitchen door, he found Varicose-Vera dancing the salsa around a bubbling cauldron. Spotting Red, she pushed out her chest, pulled down her shoulder straps, and shook her shoulders at him, beckoning him to join in. He hastily withdrew before she could grab him and whisk him around the kitchen.

'Where the blazes are they?' he grumbled, making his way to the loch. But all was quiet there and even Frank was absent. He tried to put himself in Mad-Mo's shoes and think what they could be up to.

'And why does Nasty MacNoxious keep popping into my mind? And where is Archibald?'

He sent a telepathic message to Fearless, telling him to join him and to bring Chow Yen.

Red was still pondering by the loch when Frank popped his head up.

'Och, Red, I was wondering when you'd show yerself. How have ye been doin'?'

Then he saw that Red had a very troubled expression on his face. 'What's the matter, is anything wr-rong?' he asked.

'Aye, I cannae find Mir-randa and Mo, and I'm getting awfy worried. Have ye seen them by any chance?'

Now Frank wasn't one to break a promise, and he *had* said that he'd keep quiet about seeing them down in the cave but, if he remembered rightly, he hadn't actually made any *promises* as such...

Red was eyeing Frank while all this was going on in the monster's head. He knew by his expression that he had some idea as to the whereabouts of Miranda and Mad-Mo.

'If ye're keeping something from me, Fr-rank, I'd be most obliged if ye were to share it.'

'OK, OK… I found them doun in the cave where I practise ma singing but they left some time ago, so they should be back by noow.'

'Och, the wee tyke…! When I get my hands on that braiggart, he'll regret ever having met me… Listen, go back to the cave in case they show up. Let's just hope they're lost and not in any danger.

Red made his way back to the castle, hoping they would be there. When he arrived, Fearless, Chow Yen, and Sheba (who'd given them a lift from Luscious-Lily's) were waiting for him. There was still no sign of Miranda and Mad-Mo.

'Fearless, have ye seen Archibald? I feel he's up tae something, but... what?'

'Cannae say that I have.'

'From noow on, I want that gorilla under constant surveillance. Chow Yen, I want ye to go into the secret passages and see if ye can find them, because if anyone can, yooo can.'

Chow Yen quickly made his way into the passage, his sixth sense guiding him. He emptied his mind in case Archibald was lurking about; he didn't want him to pick up on his thoughts.

* * *

Archibald lay in wait. He knew it wouldn't be long; he could hear Miranda and Mad-Mo squabbling about which way to go. If he could just separate them, it would make it so much easier. He didn't want to have to kill Mad-Mo but if the boy put up a fight, he might have no choice.

Miranda and Mad-Mo were wandering around in circles and didn't seem to be getting anywhere. Mad-Mo suggested that Miranda have a rest and he would go and find the right exit.

'Are you mad?' she exclaimed. 'Leave me here on my own? Not likely.'

'Shush... I thought I heard a noise.' He crept silently towards the direction of the sound. 'Wait there, I'll be one moment.' But before Miranda had time to reply, he'd vanished.

'Oh great... thanks a lot, Mo,' she cried out. Since he'd taken the torch, she was now in complete darkness and feeling very cold and frightened.

Mad-Mo crept along stealthily; he could feel the hairs on his neck prickle with foreboding. Archibald squeezed his body against the wall, silently waiting. The unexpected blow was so heavy, it instantly rendered Mad-Mo unconscious. Dragging his limp body into a cell, Archibald locked the door and went to look for Miranda.

Miranda heard scuffling and something being dragged along the floor, and she rammed her fist into her mouth to muffle the screams.

'Mo, where are you?' she whispered. 'Are you all right? *Please* come back.' Only a deathly silence responded.

The squeaking of rats broke the quiet as they scuttled past, brushing her ankles with their tails. 'Arrrrrrgh!' she screamed and started jumping up and down. 'Orphia… HELP!' she whimpered, in between great sobs. Swamped by dread, she lunged forward and got entangled in a huge spider's web.

In that instant, her hair began to hiss and crackle. Instinctively, she knew someone was following her. Brushing away the web, she crept along as silently as she could, desperately trying to control her rapid breathing. She thought she detected the sound of muffled footsteps but, every time she stopped, the footsteps stopped.

Her hair was now standing on end with fear as the familiar smell of aftershave floated by. Miranda tried desperately to remember Chow Yen's advice on how to empty her mind, when a hand suddenly grabbed her from behind. Struggling with all her might, she twisted and turned, trying to free herself, but Archibald's powerful arms were firmly clasped around her waist. Even her electrically charged hair – which had badly singed his fur – did not deter him. She felt something cover her mouth and then her legs went weak. Collapsing unconscious onto the floor, she was dragged roughly into a cell.

Mad-Mo was now regaining consciousness. He sat up, feeling dizzy, and realised his hands were tied behind his back. He had a splitting headache and was feeling sick from the throbbing pain in the back of his head. If he could just get to his knife he could cut himself free but, as it was strapped to his ankle, this was going to be very awkward.

Luckily for him, one of his better qualities was perseverance... and Red didn't call him Houdini for nothing.

Slowly, Mad-Mo moved his arms down his back and, easing them under his bottom and legs, he brought them up, finally managing to get at his knife. Cutting his ankles free, He then held the knife between his trainers and cut the rope that tied his hands. He immediately felt his head and found an enormous bump and gash, his hands getting wet and sticky from his blood. He blindly felt about the floor, praying he would find the torch. 'YES!' he shouted, his hands finding what he was looking for.

He turned on the torch and shone it around the cell; what he found alarmed him greatly. There were maps of the underground passages, plus all the different entrances. He also found bags of food, a couple of torches, rope, under-water diving gear, a pistol and a bottle of ether for putting people to sleep. It looked as though someone was expected, but who? And why was he knocked out in the first place? He suddenly remembered Miranda, and his stomach sank to China and back. Silently, he prayed she was all right.

He tried the heavy door but it was firmly locked. Then he remembered the sturdy piece of wire he always carried up his sleeve in case of emergencies; he got it out and started fiddling with the lock. Barry the Blade had not only taught Mad-Mo how to throw knives – he had also shown him how to pick locks and open safes, something which had often proved very handy. Sweat was starting to trickle down his face as he concentrated on the task in hand. Eventually, he heard a click and the door creaked open. He stuck his head out to see if anybody was there, and when he was sure that he was alone, he slipped out silently and went to find Miranda, hoping that whoever had knocked him out hadn't found her yet.

* * *

Chow Yen crept along the passage. He could sense someone up ahead and stopped to feel who it was. 'Ah… as I thought, Archibald is sneaking around.' He tiptoed on, preparing for combat.

Rubbing his singed fur, Archibald felt a surge of excitement rush through him as he anticipated Nasty's pleasure when he informed him that he'd managed to trap the snivelling brat. He was imagining spending his reward, when, quite unexpectedly, he felt a sharp pain in the side of his neck and then another in his kidneys. Before he had a chance to regain his composure, he was being bombarded by agonising blows all over his body. His legs began to buckle underneath him, and he felt one last stab of pain in his temple and then remembered nothing more as he fell in a heap on the floor.

'Serves you right!' said Chow Yen, continuing his search for the others. Mad-Mo heard the commotion and knew that someone had taken a good beating; he prayed that it was his assailant.

'Mo, is that you? It's me, Chow Yen.' Mad-Mo stepped out from the shadows, relieved to see his karate master, his confidence now returning.

'Red is very, very angry with you.'

Mad-Mo's new-found relief disappeared in a flash. 'Oh!' he muttered meekly.

'Ah, I've just knocked out Archibald…'

'So it *was* Archibald… CREEP… he's up to something, that's for sure. We'd better find Miranda as fast as possible!'

As they crept forward, Chow Yen would periodically stop to see if he could sense where she was. Soon, he was picking up her vibration.

'We are going in the right direction… please keep the noise down.'

Miranda was starting to regain consciousness; she felt sick and ached all over. 'Where am I?' she shouted as loudly as she could.

Chow Yen and Mad-Mo ran in the direction of her voice. They found the cell that Miranda was in; luckily, in Archibald's arrogance, he had forgotten to lock the door. Miranda let out a huge sigh of relief and promptly burst into tears. Mad-Mo, who had always hated to see girls cry, decided to get back to Archibald to make sure he hadn't regained consciousness and was securely tied. His heart sank when he got there. The gorilla had gone… and so had everything else in the cell. *Now, I'm really in for it!* he thought. He returned to find that Miranda had calmed down and, taking Chow Yen aside, he informed him of the gorilla's disappearance. They decided to get back up to the castle as quickly as possible. Following Chow Yen, they safely made their way back.

As they slipped through the secret door out into the hall, Red grabbed Mad-Mo by his ear and dragged him into his library.

'Mir-randa, go to yer room. I'll be up soon enough.'

Fleeing onto the moving stairs, she made her way to her bedroom and jumped straight under the duvet.

Red turned to Mad-Mo with a furious expression. 'I THOUGHT I TOLD YE TAE STAY AWAY FROM THE SECRET PASSAGES!' he exploded. 'HOOW CAN I TR-RUST YE IF YE KEEP GOING BEHIND MA BACK?!'

Red's eyes bored into Mad-Mo's, making him feel very ashamed. Red had placed more trust in him than he probably deserved.

'We nearly lost Mir-randa! Do you have any idea what could have happened if we had? The course of mankind could have changed forever. I'm beginning to wonder why I ever invited you along in the first place. So what's your EXCUSE, laddie?!'

Mad-Mo stood silently with his head down, mute with regret and fear.

Red had originally met Mad-Mo when he was on one his excursions into the twenty-first century. He had bumped into him while he was strolling up the Portobello Road Market in London, one Saturday morning. Mad-Mo had tried to pick Red's pockets which, considering Red knew all the tricks of the trade, was a fatal mistake. Red picked him up, turned him upside down and proceeded to shake the living daylights out of him, emptying his pockets in the process. After Red had put him down, he looked into Mad-Mo's eyes and saw his potential; potential for many things: naughtiness, humour, rebelliousness, loyalty, intelligence, cunning, compassion and daring. He was a boy after his own heart and was in need of some guidance. So, in that moment, Red had decided to enlist him as one of his crew. Later that day, he made him an offer he couldn't refuse and Mad-Mo found himself on the *Wilderness*, training to be a special pirate.

Red was still standing, waiting for an answer from him. As he didn't have one, it was a lengthy wait. Eventually, Mad-Mo told him about the bottle with the map inside it.

'Och, and it never occurred tae ye tae ask me aboot it? Are ye really that stupid? Do ye think I wadne be aware of secret treasure doun in ma underground passages? What were ye trying tae do... scare her half tae death?'

'The only truly scary thing was Frank's singing. Apart from that, I knew I could handle it,' Mad-Mo said, with more daring than he felt.

'Is that right? So ye think ye're a fair match for Archibald and Nasty MacNoxious... Wake up, Mo, ye've a lot tae learn, laddie. Well, ye've one last chance before I send ye back to London. Still, having heard Fr-rank's singing, I guess ye've been punished enough fer noow.'

Highly relieved, Mad-Mo made a very quick exit.

Miranda lay in bed, dreading Red's fury, but she was also bursting with questions as to what had just happened.

There was a knock on the door and Red appeared.

He found her hidden under her duvet. 'Och, ye can come oot noow, I'm not cross with you, but that little scallywag, he should know better than to take ye doun there.'

Feeling highly relieved, Miranda popped her head out.

'How are ye feeling, lassie? Not too bruised, I hope. I'm sending Varicose-Vera up with some tea for ye. After that, I want ye tae go and meet Chow Yen doun by the loch to do some ta'i chi; it will help calm yer nerves.'

Red went downstairs and found Chow Yen with a very worried expression on his face.

'Sooo what exactly happened ma fr-riend?'

'You were right, it was Archibald. I knocked him out but by the time I got back, he'd gone! Mad-Mo says he found maps, food, diving gear and pistols.'

'Och... this is terrible... Luckily, Miranda has more or less finished her training, sooo we'll pr-robably be safer on the *Wilderness*... Go doun tae the loch and I'll send Miranda to join ye.'

Varicose-Vera arrived and handed Miranda a murky cup of tea and a squirming, lumpy sandwich. When she had gone, Miranda promptly watered a houseplant on her bedside table with the tea and threw the sandwich over the balcony. Turning to go down to the loch, she noticed that the plant lay withered and dying over the side of the pot. Miranda wondered if Red had any idea of his housekeeper's treatment of her, or whether it was all part of her training, and the old witch was doing it to keep her on her toes.

Down by the water, she found that Frank was back

from his singing practice and was now watching Chow Yen doing ta'i chi, his long neck gracefully swaying in time to Chow Yen's movements. They were discussing Taoism. Well, Frank was discussing Taoism as Chow Yen silently went about his daily practice, always calm and smiling, occasionally nodding his head in agreement.

Miranda sat down and watched Chow Yen complete his movements. She always found herself feeling very tranquil in his presence, since nothing seemed to worry or annoy him. He took everything in his stride and stayed constantly placid – except when it was time to move, when he astounded everyone with his speed and agility.

Chow Yen greeted her when he was finished and told her to go through the movements. Enjoying them more and more each time she practised, Miranda found she had improved beyond recognition and looked as if she had been studying it for years.

'Sooo is Taoism a religion or a philosophy?' enquired Frank.

'Tao – which is pronounced 'Dow' – started off as a combination of philosophy and what Westerners would call psychology. It eventually evolved into a religion in 440 BC, so is, as you can see, very old.

'But what exactly does it mean?' asked Miranda.

'It's very different from Western faith. Tao, simply put, means the Path or the Way. We believe that it is a force of energy that flows through everything.'

'Do ye pray, fer example?' enquired Frank.

'No, we look for the answers within ourselves; we

meditate, observe and ponder on life. We seek to practise compassion, moderation and humility.'

'Sounds good tae me; we could all learn to be more humble and compassionate.'

'Miranda, why do you think it's good to practise ta'i chi?' asked Chow Yen.

'It makes me feel good. It gives me more energy.'

'Very good, but it is also good for your health – because illness is caused by energy which is blocked. Ta'i chi is a very good way to get energy moving. It has many good qualities.'

'Chow Yen, you're blind... so how *do* you see?' she asked, hoping this was an appropriate time to ask this question which had been bothering her.

'Good question. I see with my aura.'

'My mum's always going on about people's auras. But what are they exactly?'

'Everyone is made up of energy and your aura is the energy-body that surrounds you. It looks like a luminous egg that spreads out around your body.'

'You mean to say that I look like an egg?'

'From my point of view, yes. I can tell if someone is happy or sad, ill or healthy, good or bad.'

'Neat! I wish I could do that.'

'Soon you will,' said Chow Yen, beaming.

Back at the castle, Red had gathered everyone together to explain what had happened. Mad-Mo kept his head down; he still felt so awful for getting Miranda into trouble. Red gave him a sideways glance and said, 'Och, dinnae fash, Mo. In a way you've done us a favour by catching Archibald oot. Imagine if he'd got hold of her, and you *weren't* there to help her.' This left Mad-Mo feeling slightly better.

'But,' continued Red, 'as Archibald is on the loose, it might no' be safe here at present. I think it's best we go back to the *Wilderness*.'

Red turned to Mad-Mo and told him he was to keep an eye on Miranda and under NO circumstances was he to lead her astray.

8

Circus Maximus

The crew were all seated on deck with Red while he was looking for the clues in the first of Sarakuta's riddle-poems.

To Rome we go
There's a race to be won
Only Faith and Courage will see the deed done
A creature of burden will appear
With a rickety old cart he will steer

Around the circus you will run
In Maximus, surely faith will come
Understand this riddle
And thy will be done.

'Och, it looks like we're off tae Ancient Rome tae visit Circus Maximus!' Red declared triumphantly. 'And, from what I can deduce, it looks as though a chariot race is on the cards. I think it's time tae send for Jimmy.'

Everyone nodded in agreement because they all knew Jimmy spent most of the day tearing around Red's island, pretending to be charioteer.

'Sheba, I want ye to go home and pick him up,' ordered Red.

Sheba groaned. 'Oh no, not Jimmy! He's about as interesting as a dead duck. Let's just hope I don't die from an overdose of thrilling conversation.'

She lifted herself up reluctantly. 'I'M EXHAUSTED! All I do is fly around, carrying you lot – and it's not as if you're all lightweights either,' she said, glaring at Sly.

'Sheba, you know that we cannae heal the planet without yooo,' soothed Red. 'After all, yooo are one of the most important players on this mission.'

'That's true,' she agreed. 'Well, I suppose there's always room for one more martyr,' she sighed, fluttering her hand and gracefully flying off.

Miranda was so excited that she was hopping around the deck. 'A CHARIOT RACE?' she screeched. 'What, like the one in *Ben Hur*?'

'Aye,' laughed Red.

'Oh my giddy aunt, this is just brilliant! I just loved *Ben Hur*, I thought it was the *bestest* movie *ever*.'

The excitement of the moment was interrupted by a loud thud, followed by a terrible squawk. Stavros had fallen to the deck, landing on his back. Staggering to his feet, he let out another great squawk and said, 'Flaming camels! When did that mast appear?'

'Stavros, this is a galleon and the mast has always been there for, withoot it, we coudna sail this ship,' Red said, rolling his eyes.

'Aw, strange... I never noticed it before. So, where are you off to?'

'We're off to the chariot races at Circus Maximus in ancient Rome,' said Miranda, full of excitement.

'The races?' gasped Stavros. 'Aw, ripper!' he exclaimed. 'I just love the races! Boy, I'd better get going. See ya there.' Stavros immediately ran up the deck and took off, narrowly missing the billowing sails.

* * *

Turning to Miranda, Red said, 'Now that you're aboot tae embark on an incr-redible odyssey, maself and the crew all have wee gifts for ye.'

He whipped out a baseball cap from his sporran. 'Here,' he said, planting it upon her head. 'This cap is magical. If ye fancy a chat, just put it on and think my name and I'll always hear ye.'

'Wow! Thanks, gramps.'

Fearless stepped forward and handed her an ordinary, small stone. Feeling a little disappointed, Miranda looked at it and wondered what it was for.

'That, lassie, is the Stone of Courage. They're very rare and precious, so guard it well. If ye're full of fear and need a helping hand, just squeeze it tight and you'll find the strength and courage tae go on.'

Miranda squeezed it tightly and popped it in her pocket.

Soaring Eagle followed Fearless and handed Miranda a storm rattle to help her manipulate the weather. Ress-up gave her a magical flute. He explained that when she played it, it would send everyone in the vicinity into a trance. Miranda nodded her thanks and thought the small flute would be very useful. Sly waddled forward and gave her a lunchbox, which would mysteriously fill up with all her favourite foods. 'Sh-after all, the sh-aviour of the world needs to be well fed,' he chuckled, patting his enormous belly.

Chow Yen stood before Miranda and bowed slightly. He placed two meditation balls in her hands. 'These will help to calm and focus your mind, allowing you to listen to your intuition.'

Mad-Mo sidled up to her and gave her a small knife. 'This is one of me most favourite little numbers. You'll find it cuts through more or less everything.'

Miranda, beaming from ear to ear, thanked everyone for her gifts and Fearless handed her a small rucksack to carry her gifts in.

'Before ye disappear, Lucille asked me to give ye this,' said Red, passing her a large conch shell. 'Apparently, if ye blow it, the Mer-people will come to yer rescue.'

Miranda rubbed the beautiful shell and leant over the side of ship, calling out her thanks. Lucille laughed and sent a shower of seawater up in the air.

Miranda was exhausted and could hardly keep her eyes open. Yawning and stretching, she excused herself, said goodnight to everyone, and went to the cabin.

'I'm going to bed, Orphia. I'm bushed.'

'Me too,' said the Angel-ling, who had returned from her meeting.

Just as she was about to fall asleep, Red popped his head around the door. 'I've one more gift for ye,' he said, coming in and handing Miranda a small, beautifully-made wooden box. 'It's from yer father, Gideon.'

Taking the box, she tried to open it, but couldn't find the lid. 'Mum reckons he'll come back one day. I think he's been abducted by aliens.'

More likely by ma twin, Nasty, thought Red. He took the box and, touching a certain spot, a secret door popped open. Inside was a beautiful pendant made of platinum, gold and quartz. Around the base of the pendant were two serpents' heads, their bodies twisting around the base of a crystal.

With great reverence, Red placed it in Miranda's hand. She felt gentle waves of energy heating her palm and pulsating up her arm. Long-lost memories murmured in her mind, evoking the strong smell of pine needles. Feeling her eyes filling with tears, she uttered, 'It's beautiful.'

'It was made by Sarakuta and he passed it down to your father. It's a talisman and it will warn you when Nasty's approaching.'

Miranda undid the clasp and Red tied it around her neck. 'I'll never take it off,' she declared.

* * *

Stavros had been flying for about an hour when he realised that he'd lost his bearings and had no idea where he was going, or even the direction he was flying in. He also had absolutely no idea where Rome actually was.

He spotted a ship further on and made his way over to it, landing on the mast and beginning to groom his feathers. He always did this when he was lost, which was most of the time. He was convinced that it helped his inner navigational system. Little did he realise that he'd landed on Nasty MacNoxious's ship, the *Scavenger*, and that Nasty happened to be sitting directly below him.

'Now, where in flaming Florence does Rome lie?' he wondered out loud. 'Strewth! I've always wanted to go to a chariot race. And I could do with a steam. I wonder if they let albatrosses into the ancient bathhouses?'

Continuing to pluck at his feathers, he realised he'd forgotten the name of the race track. 'Flaming macaroni!' he screeched. 'What was the name of the racetrack? Was it Circus Marvellous? No, no, that wasn't it. Circus Maximus... yup, that's the one. If only I'd asked Red for directions.'

At the mention of Red, Nasty's ears pricked up. *Circus Maximus, eh? I wonder why they're going back to Ancient Rome? Well, no' tae worry as I'm aboot tae find oot*, he thought, changing the course of the *Scavenger*.

Stavros was still wondering which way to go when a deep, rumbling voice came out of nowhere and told him to fly to his left and keep going. Stavros thought it must have been God that had spoken and flew off to his left. *Strewth! Who'd have thought that God would have a Scottish accent?* he thought.

Nasty chuckled; he'd sent Stavros in the direction of the Antarctic.

* * *

That night, Miranda dreamt of a huge arena, where thousands of people were shouting and screaming. She saw beautiful chariots gleaming in the sunlight, and powerful horses neighing and stamping their hooves. She also saw Nasty and his crew laughing and jeering at Red, and she was so angry that it woke her up.

Miranda found Sheba lying in a heap on the floor of the cabin.

'Are you all right?' she asked.

'That Jimmy is about as chatty as a ton of mulch. I'm absolutely exhausted ever since you came on the scene, and I haven't had a minute to myself. I've been trampled on, stamped on, sat on and I've stretched myself beyond the call of duty. And what do I get for being a martyr – absolutely nothing!' Sheba let out a groan and blew her nose.

Miranda lay down on the floor next to her, gently stroking her. 'Ah, you'll feel brand new after a soak in the Roman baths,' she soothed.

'That's true,' Sheba whimpered mournfully.

* * *

The road into Ancient Rome was long and dusty. Red and the crew were getting excited at the thought of soaking in the magnificent Roman baths. Sheba had dressed Miranda like the locals and she quite liked her simple tunic. Red had thrown a toga over his kilt and was carrying Sheba, rolled up over his shoulder, whilst Monsieur Le Grand kept tripping over his own toga.

Miranda wondered why they bothered trying to dress like the locals and fit in. Sly had yards of fabric wrapped around his waist, making him more rotund than ever, and he insisted on wearing his bowler hat and frock coat. Fearless was wearing his Dr. Martens boots under his toga but Mad-Mo was having none of it. He was still wearing his tracksuit, customary trainers and his jacket, hood up covering most of his face. Miranda was straggling behind Mad-Mo, wondering why he was walking with a limp.

'Got a pebble in your trainers?' she asked.

'Na.'

'Pooped your pants?'

'NO!'

'Then why are you walking with a limp, **with your trousers drooping under your bum?**' she asked, thoroughly unimpressed.

'Because it's the fashion, innit,' he said, looking at her as if she was a complete idiot.

'So, in order to be trendy, you don't mind looking like a plonker with exceedingly short legs,' she said, giggling, thinking that boys were really daft at times.

Suddenly a terrible 'Eeeee–aaawww' resounded in the air, and Miranda spotted a young man with a donkey on the side of the road. The man was brutally beating the donkey with a long stick, screaming and shouting abuse at the poor half-starved creature which was obviously too exhausted to take another step.

Well, that was it! Miranda immediately ran up to the man and gave him a fearsome karate chop. The abuser was so taken aback that his jaw practically dropped to the ground, during which time Miranda had managed to grab the whip and give him one sharp whack on the back of his knees. The man fell to the ground and prayed for mercy, believing that a mad spirit was punishing him for his sins. The donkey couldn't believe his good fortune and in that moment he gave his allegiance to this magnificent creature with the wild, crazy hair, making an oath to be faithful and serve her in whatever capacity he could.

Red and the rest of the crew were rolling around with laughter and shouting out words of encouragement. This, of course, started to annoy the man who was still cowering on the ground. His anger took hold. *No girl is going to show ME up*, he thought, and started to rise, readying himself for his retaliation.

Miranda had her back turned to him because she was tending to the donkey, but she could sense his approach. Without needing to turn around, she shot her leg back and caught him on the knee.

Where did she learn to fight like that, I wonder? thought the man, dropping down to the ground in agony.

'Miranda, that is no' very ladylike behaviour,' shouted Red. 'I can see yer training is coming along splendidly!'

Nudging Fearless in the ribs, he said, 'Och she's a bonny wee lass, is she no'?' Wiping the tears of laughter from his eyes, he turned to Chow Yen and Soaring Eagle.

'Ye've both done a gr-rand job; she can most certainly look after herself noow.'

Miranda returned, wondering what they were going to do with the donkey; they couldn't possibly leave him there. The donkey happily trotted behind her; his hope had returned, giving him a new-found strength. Miranda fetched some water and got out her magic lunchbox, wishing for some hay and oats. She then fed and watered the donkey, who was famished and gasping with thirst.

Red was deep in thought. *Didn't the poem say a creature of burden will appear?* He looked at Miranda with a huge smile.

'The donkey stays. I think this was fate,' he said.

Miranda was thrilled since she was most taken with her new friend. 'What shall we call him?' she asked Red.

'My name is Brian,' brayed the donkey.

'OK, Brian, you're now one of the gang. Welcome,' she said.

They carried on into the city, and Sheba and Miranda went to the ladies' baths whilst the rest of the crew went to the men's.

Sheba was getting more and more excited by the minute because one of her favourite pastimes was to be pampered. 'Daaarling, by the time they've finished with you, you'll feel brand new and sparkling clean. My weave comes out so bright that I'm positively dazzling and even more gorgeous. My dear, I even have to wear sunglasses until my eyes adjust to the glare of my beauty,' she gloated with vanity.

Stepping into the *thermae* – which was the Roman name for the baths – Miranda was amazed by the activities taking place. There were art galleries, cafés, reading rooms, libraries, hairdressers, steam rooms, saunas and exercise areas.

'Cor, this is fantastic,' said Miranda, very impressed. 'Why can't we have places like this?'

'Yes, daaarling, I quite agree. The ancient Romans really were highly sophisticated and left the rest of Europe way behind, especially when it came to cleanliness,' replied Sheba.

Glorious mosaics covered the walls and huge marble columns stood towering above them. Sheba led Miranda to the *uncturium*, which is the place where the citizens were covered in oil. The word comes from the word unction, which means to anoint with a special salve. Instead of going to the exercise yard, which was the norm, Sheba led her straight to the *tepidarium*, which was the warm room. Miranda now understood where the word tepid came from. Sheba ceremoniously lay over the seating area, thoroughly enjoying the warmth.

The place was filled with women chattering and laughing while their servants tended to their every need. After a while, they were taken to the *caldarium* which was hot and steamy, just like a Turkish bath. Sheba fanned her face, which was getting redder by the second, and her elaborate hairstyle was beginning to droop. It was so hot it was hard to breathe and Miranda thought she was going to pass out. Sheba began to scrape the oil off Miranda's body with a curved instrument called a *strigil*, and this helped to clean and remove all the dead skin.

At first, Miranda felt embarrassed being undressed in front of so many women, but everyone appeared so unselfconscious and relaxed as they chatted and nibbled on sausages and pies and she soon found herself really enjoying the occasion. After she had been scraped clean, she jumped into the hot bath, followed by a quick dip in the freezing *frigidarium*. Spluttering and choking from the cold, she leapt out and wrapped a warm towel around herself.

Finding Sheba already outside and sunning herself in a courtyard, Miranda plonked herself down next to her. 'That was fantastic,' she said.

'Mmm,' said Sheba lazily, 'I really think all females should have this experience at least once a week.'

'I must say I wish I could join in,' lamented Orphia in Miranda's ear, envying their indulgent pleasure.

However, on the other side of the courtyard, Salome was also sunning herself, but Miranda and Sheba hadn't yet noticed her.

Sheba was thinking about the upcoming thrill of the Circus Maximus. Turning to Miranda, she said: 'Red really can't expect that donkey to run in the chariot race all by itself . . . plus we don't have a chariot yet. If we don't win the race, we don't get Sarakuta's next poem. So how will we know where we're going next?' She continued: 'Mind you, I love the races. You wait! It will be one of the most exciting events you'll ever witness.'

Whilst Sheba was babbling on about the races, a small serving-woman, who had overheard their conversation, slipped over to Salome and whispered in her ear. Delighted with the information she had received, Salome made haste to find Nasty MacNoxious, but not before Miranda caught sight of her leaving.

Sitting bolt upright, Miranda told Sheba who she'd just seen exiting.

Sheba whipped up her head and gasped. 'Oh for goodness sakes! One can't even have a decent steam these days without some lowlife ruining it all. We'd better hurry up and inform Red.'

As Sheba hovered in the air, waiting for Miranda to get dressed, she asked, 'How did the flying strumpet look?'

'As though she'd never been ripped in the first place,' answered Miranda truthfully.

That, of course, was not what Sheba wanted to hear. Bristling with anger, she rushed out, with Miranda hastily following.

At the front of the baths, Mad-Mo and Brian were patiently waiting for them. 'Cor, take all day, I've been waiting ages. I could have swum the channel in the time it took you two to wash,' moaned Mad-Mo.

'Why didn't you go in with the others?' asked Miranda.

'What with all those naked men washing each other – not likely,' he spluttered, turning bright red.

'Listen, Salome's in town,' interrupted Sheba, 'which means Nasty's around somewhere.'

In no time at all the crew had assembled.

'Right, it's time we got to Circus Maximus before ma disgusting twin gets there. Brian may be part of the plan, but we need a team of four in order to take part in the race, so we'd better find the rest of our winning team,' said Red.

Pushing their way through the hordes of people who were milling around, Red led them towards the Circus Maximus.

Miranda felt the crystal around her neck start to heat up, and when she looked down she saw the snakes moving slightly, both their tongues flickering in and out. 'Red, look at my crystal!' She lifted it up to show him.

'Och, as I thought, my evil twin isn't too far away.' Turning to the others, he told them to keep an eye out. *How in Hades did he knoow we were coming here?* thought Red, his spirits sinking slightly.

* * *

Circus Maximus was built in a long valley between two hills, the Aventine and the Palatine. When it was originally used as an arena it was just a sandy track with no buildings, and the spectators sat on the grassy slopes of the hills, instead of on seats. By the time Red and his crew had arrived in the time of Augustus, 6 AD, the Circus Maximus had grown to six hundred and twenty metres long and about one hundred and fifty metres wide.

They managed to locate the stables where the horses were being kept before the races, but, to their utter horror, Nasty was already standing there, grinning from ear to ear, malice positively radiating from him.

Red's heart sank as he looked at his brother's expression of triumph. *What has he gone and done noow?* he wondered, with a sinking heart.

'Sooo, you'll be looking for your own team of horses, if ye want tae win the gr-reat r-race?' Nasty jeered. 'Tough, for I've procured every single one, plus all the chariots,' he added jubilantly.

The crew stood stock still; they were all utterly speechless, disappointment invading their hearts like molten lead.

However, they hadn't taken into account the fact that Brian wasn't your average donkey. For a start, he had travelled the world and witnessed some extraordinary and life-changing events. He had outlived all his peers and had forgotten his age a long time ago. All he knew was that the older he got, the younger he became. And, unbeknown to Red and Miranda, Brian was an Olympic athlete, winning the ten thousand metres Donkey Race in record time.

Being a sensitive donkey, Brian immediately grasped the situation, feeling that his true vocation had finally arrived. Ever since dropping Mary and Joseph off in Bethlehem, he had known in his heart that he had a special destiny to fulfil and his old bones told him that this could be it!

He nudged Miranda on the arm, but she was in no mind to respond, feeling thoroughly depressed by the turn of events. He nudged her again, and muttered something.

'Excuse me, did you just say something?' she asked.

'At last!' brayed the donkey, vigorously nodding his head. 'I think I can be of service to you all.'

Miranda was so taken aback that she just stood there gaping.

'You may not believe it,' continued Brian, 'but I was once an Olympic athlete.'

Yeah – in your last life, thought Miranda, looking at his spindly legs and mangy appearance.

'And I do believe that I can help win the race.'

'How so?' she asked sceptically.

'Follow me and find out.'

Miranda walked up to Red and informed him that Brian had spoken, and that he had told her he was going to win the race.

'Fantastic!' he roared, 'Aye, he might just be able to help.'

Miranda stood there, thinking the whole world had gone mad. She leant over and whispered, 'You don't seriously believe him, do you?'

'Of course… there's something aboot that donkey… I'm sure we've met before. I have a feeling that he was the donkey that dropped Mary and Joseph off in Bethlehem. In fact, I'm sure of it.'

'You were never there!' she ribbed, poking his belly.

'Excuse me, I was most definitely there but as I'm no' one to stick out in a crowd, I blended in with everyone else.'

'Why, what were you wearing?'

'Ma kilt of course!' he answered. 'I was one of the three wise men.'

Miranda burst out laughing. 'Yeah!' she giggled. 'Likely story – not.'

Brian trotted over. 'I thought you looked familiar.'

Red patted his back. 'Aye, it is grand tae see ye. Well done for getting them both to Bethlehem. Noow that was a night tae remember, was it no'?'

The donkey nodded his head enthusiastically and Miranda looked on in amazement.

'Miranda tells me that you can help,' continued Red. 'Well that would really be appreciated; we need all the help we can get.'

Brian explained that he had to get to the other side of Rome as he might be able to provide Red and Miranda with a winning team.

Imagining gleaming black stallions, Miranda began to feel a lot better. Red told Mad-Mo and Monsieur Le Grand to accompany Miranda and Brian.

But, when they saw that they had arrived at a home for geriatric donkeys, Mad-Mo let out a loud groan and sank to his knees in despair. 'Oh my days… oh my days,' he wailed. 'We're never going to win this race.' Even Monsieur Le Grand was scratching his goatee in disbelief.

'Well, zee poem did zay a creature of burden and a lot of Faith woz needed' he muttered.

Orphia floated by and tutted: 'I say it's not looking too good, I suggest we pray for a miracle.'

Miranda's heart sank even lower. Just then, Brian leapt gracefully over the very high wall of the home and disappeared.

'Zat, my friends, was a mightee leap for zuch a old creature, don't you zink?'

Miranda had to nod her head in agreement, because not even a huge horse could have jumped *that* wall.

A few minutes later, Brian jumped back over, followed by three more decrepit donkeys. Miranda was aghast and whispered to Mad-Mo: 'So, if this is the "winning team", I might as well give up and go home now.'

'Innit… I think I'll join you,' muttered Mo.

'Come, come now, where eez your Faith?' said Monsieur Le Grand, unconvincingly.

Miranda decided that she needed to have a chat with Red. She took the magical hat out of her rucksack, and stuck it on her head.

'Testing, one, two, three – can you hear me, Red?' she said out loud, not quite understanding how it worked, as it was her first try.

'Loud and clear, lassie – except ye dinnae have to shout, it's done telepathically, like. Anyway, hoow's things going?'

'I'm at a home for old donkeys on the outskirts of Rome and, you'll never guess what – Brian is under the impression that he and three other mangy old donkeys can win the race. Red, I don't want to burst his bubble but, if you could see the state of the four of them, we don't stand a chance in Hades... Trust me!'

For some strange reason, Red found this hilariously funny and told her to come back as quickly as possible, not forgetting to bring the three extra donkeys.

Red's mood had lifted considerably. Nodding to Fearless and giving him their secret sign for a silent chat, he strolled away from the stables. Fearless caught up with Red, and was highly intrigued as to what the next stage of the plan would be, since Nasty had foiled them all so far.

'Fearless, we need a cart. Forget yer shiny chariots, they've all gone. We need something that will last five laps. I dinnae care what it looks like as long as it has got wheels... that go round that is... if ye get ma dr-rift? I think we might have found our team to lead us to victory,' he said, with a mysterious smile. He handed Fearless a bag of gold coins, just in case a bit of gentle persuasion was needed.

Mo slunk moodily behind the others as Brian led the way back. As far as he was concerned, the outlook was utterly bleak. No way were they going to win the race. They all walked on in silence, everyone lost in their own gloomy thoughts.

By the time they reached the stables, Circus Maximus was filled to capacity; thousands of spectators were already seated and waiting for the races to begin. They found Red and Jimmy who were waiting for Fearless to return with a cart.

The moment Jimmy clocked the donkeys, he turned to Red. 'Och, ye didnae drag me all the way here to race that moth-eaten crew?' he said, pointing to the donkeys.

'Crikey, the man speaks,' Miranda whispered to Mad-Mo.

'Yeah, well... I understand how he feels, there'd be no way that you'd get me in this arena with that lot; I'd rather get struck by lightning,' he grumbled.

Poor old Jimmy. Ever since stepping onto Sheba he'd let his imagination run wild. In his mind's eye, he could hear the roars of the crowd appreciating his skill in handling his mighty team of racehorses as he approached the winning post, beating contestants from all over the world. Instead, he was going to race four donkeys that looked as though they wouldn't last the first twenty metres.

The sound of a cart could be heard trundling along, and they all looked up to see Fearless, grinning from ear to ear and looking very pleased with himself.

'Your-r chariot awaits, Jimmy,' he announced.

Jimmy took one look at the cart and nearly fainted.

'I thought things just couldn't get any worse,' uttered Mad-Mo, spotting the ramshackle old cart.

Red walked over and inspected it. 'That's gr-reat, Fearless, except the rules state that only two wheels are allowed.'

'Nooo problem, we'll just saw it in half,' replied his younger brother.

Jimmy's legs gave way at that comment and he ended up on his knees.

'Perhaps he's praying for a miracle,' said Miranda, who felt like joining him.

'He needs one! A snail has more chance of winning,' groaned Mad-Mo.

Red took Miranda aside; he could see she had lost all hope and faith.

'Ye remember what it said in the poem, a creature of burden and a rickety old cart… well, what do ye think those are?' he said, pointing to Brian and the cart. 'And what else did it say… something aboot 'Faith', if I r-remember r-rightly?'

'Red, all the faith in the world isn't going to help Brian and his cronies. Have you seen Nasty's team of horses? They'll have won the race before our lot have even left the starting post. And as for that so-called chariot, it's a total joke. Mo's right; it's positively embarrassing.'

'As our good friend Frank Ness would say, 'Excuse em moi, have ye forgotten why we're here? We're no' on holiday ye know. Ye're here to be tried and tested. What do ye think this is – *Disney World?*'

'Okay, I'll try to have a bit of faith.'

'A BIT!' he roared, 'Mir-randa you'll have to have more than a bit. You'll need to have unquestioning faith if ye want tae pass the test. It's all in yer belief system; if ye believe it will happen, tr-rust me, it will.'

'Well all I can say is – *this* is certainly a very tough test. And why can't we use magic?'

'Och… for once there will be no cheating,' he said sternly.

She slowly dragged herself over to Brian and put her arms around his shaggy neck. 'Don't let us down, Brian; we're all depending on you,' she whispered in his ear.

'I know that you don't think we can do it,' said Brian, 'but if you have complete trust, courage and faith, I know in my heart we can win.' The donkey nodded his head vigorously, his eyes shining with hope. 'FAITH,' he brayed again.

Miranda looked into Brian's eyes, and saw his soul shining like a beacon on a dark night, beaming with love and optimism. She felt a stirring in her heart and a lovely warm glow began to spread throughout her body. With her faith coming back in leaps and bounds, she began to look at Brian with new eyes. She no longer saw an old donkey but a magnificent, four-legged, angelic beast that was going to win the race for them.

Red called the crew back; a lot had to be accomplished very quickly if they were going to transform the cart into something more durable.

Nasty's crew were taunting and jeering at Red and his crew as they laboured away, sawing and hammering in the hot sun. Nasty, feeling they presented no competition, decided to bet a considerable amount on the race. *Why not win all the money, as well as the trophy?* he thought, although he couldn't understand why Red appeared totally unconcerned. In fact, Red seemed to be thoroughly enjoying himself. Nasty stared at his twin, trying to read his thoughts and wondering what he might have hidden up his sleeve. It wasn't as if the donkeys had a chance in hell of winning, so it must be something else. Perhaps this was a plot to put him off the scent. He limped over to his second-in-command, Snarl saying: 'Keep an eye on ma twin, he's up tae something.'

Soaring Eagle and Chow Yen were inspecting the donkeys. Chow Yen took out his acupuncture needles and stuck them in various parts of their bodies. This was to help the flow of Chi. Soaring Eagle rubbed some lotion on their legs to help keep their muscles supple and pain-free.

Mad-Mo had silently slipped off and was about to do the unthinkable and bet all his savings on the opposition. Chow Yen, knowing that Mad-Mo couldn't resist a wager, followed him discreetly. Chow Yen was going to place bets for the whole crew, except they were obviously going to bet on Brian and his team. Even Red, who was dead against gambling – thinking it a fool's game – had a flutter and placed a substantial amount on the race. He had already decided that his winnings would be going to the home for elderly donkeys.

Chow Yen came back, having placed everyone's bets, and told Red about Mad-Mo.

'The wee tr-raitor, how much did he place?' he asked.

'All savings,' replied Chow Yen.

'Och... we'll see who has the last laugh then, shall we?' he said cheerfully.

Jimmy had changed from his tatty kilt and greying vest into full Scottish regalia. He wore a black velvet fitted jacket with two rows of shiny silver buttons, a brand spanking new kilt, a thoroughly majestic sporran, a pair of flying goggles to keep the dust out of his eyes and a tam-o'-shanter – a round, flat, brimless woollen cap with a bobble on top. He got into his makeshift chariot proudly, picked up the reins and guided the donkeys to the starting post. The rest of the crew had found their seats and were ready and waiting.

By the time Jimmy arrived, the rest of the contenders were there in all their glory. The turncoat Archibald was driving Nasty's chariot of gleaming black and gold, his horses pure thoroughbreds.

'So Jimmy, we meet again,' jeered the one-eyed gorilla, his diamond-studded eyepatch gleaming in the sunlight. 'And may the best team win,' he added, revealing his gold teeth.

'Fine,' said Jimmy, raising the reins and uttering a silent prayer .

The crowd was going berserk with laughter as they watched the donkeys ready themselves. Last-minute bets to see how many metres the donkeys would run before collapsing were now being placed.

The horn blew and the race was on.

Mad-Mo sat with his eyes shut, feeling very embarrassed by their team. Only Miranda and Red seemed to think that they had a chance of winning – until they realised that Brian and his team were still at the starting post and the other teams had already reached the first bend.

Miranda let out a groan and gave Red a questioning look.

'FAITH, Mir-randa, FAITH,' he roared above the din.

Miranda shut her eyes and concentrated with all her might. *Faith, I have all the faith in the world*, she kept repeating silently to herself. Suddenly she heard gasps and then roars of disbelief coming from the crowd. She opened one eye to see that the donkeys were miraculously gaining on the others. By now, the rest of the crew were out of their seats, jumping up and down with excitement, screaming: 'GO BRIAN – GO BRIAN!'

The first lap was over, only three more to go. Archibald was thrashing his team of horses; sweat was flying off their coats and their mouths were foaming. Jimmy, on the other hand, didn't believe in whipping animals, preferring to encourage them instead.

They were gaining on Archibald every second. Brian, his eyes shining, was shouting out to his team that they could do it. Well, for four old donkeys, they certainly ran like the clappers, their skinny knobbly legs running ten to the dozen. This team of courageous donkeys amazed the spectators and soon they were all cheering and rooting for them. 'COME ON BRIAN!' resounded throughout the stadium.

Even Sheba, who had forgotten her airs and graces, was up there with the rest, screaming, 'Finish the bleedin' oaf orf!' She let out an embarrassed titter. 'Ooh I say! Did that just come out of my mouth?' she said, feigning utter surprise. 'I don't know what came over me,' she added, madly fanning herself. 'I must have been temporarily possessed by a thoroughly *common* spirit.'

The teams were now neck and neck as they approached the third lap. Nasty was getting a little nervous. It had never occurred to him that Red's team would make it to the first bend, let alone catch up.

'HANG ABOOT… I DINNAE BELIEVE IT! They've nearly passed Archibald!' he screamed, beating his chest in fury. He walked up to Snarl and kicked him on the shin with his peg, causing Snarl's eyes to water.

'What d'ya do that for?' he yelped.

'IT'S-ALL-YOUR-FAULT!' he shouted, limping away in total frustration and disbelief.

They were halfway around the third lap, and Brian and his team were neck and neck with Archibald's team, having passed all the other chariots.

Mad-Mo sat with his head in his hands, groaning as he feared he would see his entire savings going down the drain. Red was finding it very difficult not to crack up every time he looked at Mad-Mo's face. News of his betrayal had spread amongst the crew but they decided not to let him know yet, and were greatly looking forward to teasing him.

Archibald was pushing his horses to their limits; their eyes were bulging from the strain of keeping up. Brian and his gang, however, appeared almost relaxed as they galloped along. Jimmy was doing a mighty job making sure they didn't crash into anything. He was so amazed by his team that he'd completely forgotten they were donkeys; to him they were now his team of magnificent racehorses.

'Ye're doing just fine, ma beauties,' he roared, above the racket of the galloping horses and the screeching wheels of the chariots.

But Archibald wasn't about to give in so easily. He drew his chariot nearer Jimmy's, hoping to drive him into the side. Jimmy could hear Archibald's chariot grinding into his. Splinters of wood were shattering and flying off everywhere. Then, adding insult to injury, Archibald started to beat Jimmy with his long whip.

Miranda looked on in horror as Archibald kept lashing relentlessly at the Scottish charioteer. The gorilla managed to wrap his whip around Jimmy's arm and yank him off the cart, dragging him along behind his chariot.

With fury in her heart at the injustice of what she'd just witnessed, Miranda – without thinking – got up and sped into the arena. Dodging oncoming chariots, she ran as fast as she could.

Upon seeing a child running onto the race track, the baying crowd suddenly became deathly silent. Now only the thunder of hooves and the screech of the wheels could be heard.

The rest of the crew stood by as Miranda, taking huge, leaping strides, caught up with Brian and his team. She jumped on and managed to grab the reins. 'KEEP RUNNING!' she bellowed at Brian. 'I'LL BE BACK IN A TICK.' To Archibald's complete surprise, Miranda leapt onto his chariot, quickly withdrew her magical knife, and cut Jimmy free, who managed to get up and hurl himself to safety. And before Archibald had time to react, she'd managed to jump back onto her makeshift chariot and grab the reins.

Archibald couldn't believe his eyes and for a split second he felt sheer admiration for her – but he couldn't let that deter him from winning. He edged his chariot nearer and raised his whip but Miranda sensed his approach and managed to dodge his blows. By now, her hair was practically on fire as it crackled and fizzed. The adrenalin was pumping through her veins; her muscles were screaming with pain as she strained to keep her body taut and balanced. Her arms felt as though they were being yanked out of her shoulders as she courageously gripped the reins for dear life.

Archibald was relentless in his pursuit and kept on ramming her cart. Planks of wood were flying off and crashing into the spectators.

The crew were all horrified that Red was standing back and not intervening. He looked at Fearless and, telepathically, he informed his younger brother that Miranda needed to harness her energy and learn how to use it. Fearless nodded back uneasily.

Miranda was now basically standing on a plank of wood which was connected to the wheels. *One more ram from Archibald and I'm finished*, she thought, managing to avoid another brutal lashing from his whip.

They were rounding the last bend before the final lap and Archibald realised he needed to act quickly. Miranda was now slightly out in front and could sense his energy charging towards her. She began to feel eerily calm and then, quite suddenly, a rush of extraordinary power surged through her body. She clutched the reins with one hand, and without thinking, she lifted her other hand and pointed at the gorilla.

For a split second, she saw fear in the gorilla's eyes. She had no idea what she looked like. Her hair was a blaze of sizzling colour and her eyes had turned a furious red. A gush of energy, so strong it actually levitated Miranda off the chariot, beamed with laser-like intensity and shot out from her fingers like lightning, striking Archibald in his chest. His body went rigid as the electricity bombarded him. His fur stood up on end, sending out tendrils of smoke as he fell over the side of his chariot into the path of the oncoming teams.

Miranda was utterly horrified, thinking that she'd murdered him. She looked back quickly and saw him lying on the dusty ground, not moving a muscle. She couldn't leave him there to be trampled on by the approaching chariots and horses, so she steered Brian and his team around whilst screaming her intentions. The crowd held their breath and looked on in stunned silence while Miranda raced back towards the lifeless gorilla. She somehow managed to summon the power she'd felt a few seconds earlier and, to the total disbelief of the crowd, she dragged the huge gorilla out of harm's way just in the nick of time. She bent over and quickly felt for a pulse. *He's still alive*, she thought, relieved.

Most of the other teams had now passed Miranda as she ran back to her plank of wood on wheels and got back on. 'Okay Brian, I hope you're in contact with Him up there, because right now we need a miracle.'

Brian let out a soulful bray and leapt into action, with the others eagerly following him. The crowd stood up and roared their approval as Miranda proceeded to rejoin the race. As they galloped along, she felt this extraordinary beam of light enter the top of her head and surge down to her fingers. The reins lit up as the energy travelled down to the donkeys. In no time at all, the donkeys were glowing with a luminous, golden sheen. They ran like the wind, their hooves hardly touching the ground. Miranda's hair flew out behind her, lit up like a banner of glorious iridescent colours. Soon, they had not only caught up but had also overtaken all but one chariot, and were racing neck and neck with all their might.

By now, none of the spectators was seated. Everyone was screaming and stamping their feet with encouragement. The noise and the vibration of the galloping horses was so intense, Miranda's head was swimming. The finishing post was within reach but still they couldn't quite get past the other chariot...

Finally, Brian spotted an opportunity and managed to squeeze his team past the other horses, reaching the winning post by only a few centimetres.

The crowd went berserk with excitement and threw garlands of flowers and coins into the arena. Like a true champion, Miranda happily did a lap of honour.

After soaking up all the attention, she dismounted and ran over to Red. 'We did it! We did it!' she cried, jumping up and down and punching the air with victory. Running over to Brian and his team, Miranda flung her arms around his neck. 'Thank you, Brian. Thank you!' She then hugged the rest of the amazing donkeys. The rest of the crew crowded around her, full of congratulations.

Soaring Eagle smiled. 'I do believe you just tapped into your energy when you blasted Archibald. That's what I was trying to get you to do. Now you need to do it on command and without anger. Just imagine you're the wind and the rain. If you can control that incredible energy of yours, you'll soon be conjuring up raging storms.'

Mad-Mo felt a mixture of emotions, ranging from fury that he'd been such an idiot, ashamed for not having faith, and highly embarrassed that he'd lost all of his savings. He was also seething with envy because, against all the odds, Miranda had won the race, and he desperately wanted it to have been him. He sidled up to her and hissed, 'That was stupid, what you just did. You could have killed yourself!'

'Well, I didn't, did I?'

'It was irresponsible and highly dangerous. It should have been me who took over from Jimmy. That sort of thing is a job for a man!'

'Well, that counts you out then,' she said, throwing her head back and laughing at her quick retort and his expression. 'Anyway, you had your eyes closed most of the time.'

Mad-Mo continued to scowl and looked as though he'd just eaten a sour lemon.

'You should be happy for me,' she cried, not really understanding his sullenness.

Red walked over to Mad-Mo and slapped him on his back. 'So laddie, what are ye going tae be spending yer winnings on? I thought ye might like tae tr-reat us to a celebratory dinner in one of the fancy Roman restaurants.'

Mad-Mo instantly knew Red had discovered his treachery and desperately wanted the ground to open up and swallow him.

The rest of the crew were now holding their sides with mirth. 'Sooo, how much did ye win, laddie?' asked Fearless, creasing up.

Ress-up was also beside himself with glee. 'No doubt you've won enough to pay me back all the money you've borrowed in the past,' he giggled. 'Humph!' he added, in disdain, 'next time you see me, make like an egg and beat it – traitor.'

'Traitor?' exclaimed Miranda. 'Why are you calling him that?'

She peered at Mo's ashen face and thought he looked like he had a case of acute food poisoning. 'What's going on?' she asked.

Mad-Mo's shoulders drooped even further and he stared at the ground, concentrating on an ant, which he suddenly found fascinating.

'Look at me,' Miranda demanded.

However hard he tried, he found it impossible to look her in the eye.

'Mo...' she said very slowly, 'what have you gone and done?'

By now he was squirming all over with humiliation and regret. Everyone was howling and roaring with laughter at his obvious discomfort.

Red couldn't contain himself any longer and told Miranda what Mad-Mo had done. Bending over and clutching his sides, he roared, 'Serves ye right, ye turncoat!'

Miranda stood rooted to the spot, unable to utter a word, her fury was so great. Suddenly, like an angry tornado, she sprang into action and pounced on Mad-Mo, pummelling his body with punches and karate chops, yelling, 'YOU TRAITOR!'

He knew he had no right to defend himself and let her continue until her anger was spent. Red eventually dragged her off. 'Calm doun, calm doun,' he hushed.

Miranda turned and glared at Mad-Mo. 'Don't you ever speak to me again,' she hissed menacingly and stomped off.

* * *

It had been the most exciting race anyone had ever seen and one that would be talked about for a very long time to come. The crowd stood up, saluting Miranda, Jimmy and the team of wonder donkeys as they went up to collect their prize trophy. And not only had Red's team won the race but, because the entire crowd had bet against them, they had also amassed an enormous amount of money!

Back at the stables, Red placed the trophy on a table and they all stood admiring it. Red kept picking it up and examining it, hoping to find the next poem.

Suddenly the squawks of Stavros could be heard up above as he searched for them. Finally spotting them, he did his customary crash-landing, stopping just in front of the trophy.

'G-day... when does the race start?'

'You've just missed it,' replied Miranda, eyeballing Mad-Mo. She was still seething and even more cross that he'd managed to ruin her happiness and glory.

'Ah... Flaming chariots! Don't ya just hate it when you're late for the races and miss all the excitement? I'd lost my way, so I landed on a galleon and this voice came out of nowhere and gave me directions. I thought it was God talking at the time, but now I'm not so sure, because I ended up in the Antarctic.'

'Did this voice have a Scottish accent by any chance?' asked Red, rolling his eyes in despair.

'Strangely enough, he did!'

Red now knew how Nasty had known where they were going. *I think it's time that that bird has his wings clipped*, he thought.

Stavros turned and laid his beady eye on the trophy. 'What's this?'

'It's our prize for sh-winning the race,' said Sly.

'And a gr-r-rand race eet woz,' added Monsieur Le Grand.

Stavros started to peck at the trophy.

'Don't do that, you'll scratch it!' said Miranda.

Suddenly, a little secret drawer popped out, revealing a rolled-up piece of parchment with the words of the next poem on it.

'Stavros, ye're a genius!' gasped Red. 'Hoow on earth did yooo knoow aboot that concealed door?' he asked in amazement.

'Ah, just doing what comes naturally,' replied Stavros, even more amazed.

Red picked up the poem and scanned it quickly.

Compassion and courage must be shown
For the skull you seek to be your own
Go to a time when a virgin Queen
In full regalia can be seen

Seek out the girl who has lost all hope
Standing alone with a necklace of rope
She is a witch, the crowd all cry
And scream and shout that she must die

Save this girl then you can go hither
Along the banks of a winding river
To courtly grounds where a puzzle may be found
Just let your senses guide you in and around.

Putting it carefully into his sporran, Red said, 'Mission complete. I'll have to study this riddle and see where it wants us to go next. In the meantime, I think the sooner we get back on board the *Wilderness* the better. I imagine Nasty is seething with fury and is already plotting his revenge. Mind yooo, he's absolutely broke at the moment, so he'll have to rob a few ships first.'

Nasty was limping around the stables, venting his fury on anyone who was unfortunate enough to be in his way. He hobbled over to Archibald, who was still unconscious, and stuck his peg in the gorilla's side.

'You don't want to wake up,' he snarled, bending over him. 'Tr-rust me, if ye do, you'll wish ye hadn't and that ye'd died instead!'

The pirate limped away and ordered the others to drag the gorilla back to the *Scavenger*.

* * *

Back on board his galleon, Nasty hobbled into his cabin, still cursing and roaring with anger. He limped over to his pet vulture, Scabies, and released him from his perch. The ugly bird immediately hopped onto the table and started to tear at putrid pieces of meat, gulping them down in great lumps, its scrawny throat bulging as it swallowed. Easing himself into his favourite battered leather chair, Nasty removed his peg and massaged his red, swollen stump.

'BLAST THE BR-RAT! I'll get yooo yet, Mir-randa Wyrd! Just you wait and see,' he bellowed with volcanic ferocity. Sweeping his hand across the table and sending plates and glasses crashing to the floor, he picked up a handbell and rang it violently. Getting out his chewing tobacco from his pocket, he rolled it between his grimy, nicotine-stained, stubby fingers and popped it into his mouth. Snarl was first in followed by his crew members Weasel, then Douglas, who was half-carrying his battered and bruised brother, Archibald.

'Sit doun,' ordered Nasty, spitting out brown saliva and removing bits of tobacco from his rotting black teeth. 'I've a lot of planning to do if we're to tr-rap the snivelling child,' he snarled. He squinted at the others, his small black eyes scanning their faces, looking for any signs of unrest.

'So, do you have a plan, then?' asked Snarl, attacking his nostril with his grubby little finger and removing a large green bogey. He then flicked it at Scabies, who caught it in his beak like a passing fly. The vulture swallowed, appreciating the titbit. Archibald winced in disgust and looked away.

'Thanks to our *illustrious* friend here…' sneered Nasty sarcastically, glaring at Archibald, 'who can't even win a chariot race against a pathetic team of donkeys, I now have to up the ante. I want all of yous to get in contact with every spy, super-gr-rass, mercenary, criminal and despot that has had the pleasure of working for me,' he growled. 'And tr-rust me, there are loads.'

Scrutinising each one of them, his eyes flickered with pure malevolence; his body sent out an energy that was so dark that even Snarl jerked with the ferociousness of it.

'And', he continued, 'no' just in this century but in all of them – and all the different dimensions too.'

The others just sat there, gobsmacked with the enormity of the task. 'W-what do you want them all for?' stuttered Snarl, desperate to please.

'I'm having wanted posters of Miranda printed up. I've placed a huge reward for her capture, which...,' he hissed, glaring at everyone, 'obviously, I have no intention of honouring. And I want them placed everywhere – and I mean *everywhere*.'

'But that's going to take forever,' piped up Douglas. 'Plus, we can't time-travel and dimension-hop without you.'

'Listen, the amount that I've offered is so *huge*, you'll have everyone looking fer her; the news will spread like wildfire. And dinnae worry aboot time-travelling – leave that to me. I've got plans...'

The others nodded grimly.

Nasty waved everyone away, with the exception of Archibald, and he sat silently, darkly eyeballing the gorilla, whilst tapping his fingers on the table.

'Ye've let me doun, BIG TIME! No' only has ma twin got the next poem, he still has the brat. Ye'd better watch yer step and come up with something extra special. I cannae believe ye let that skinny child beat ye.' Nasty spat on the floor and dismissed Archibald.

After everyone had gone, the pirate sat, daydreaming about the future he was going to weave once he had captured Miranda and the crystal skulls. He sat, imagining the desolation and the suffering he'd inflict upon the human race and felt a great deal better after the carnage he'd just imagined. He limped over to Scabies and put on a leather gauntlet; Scabies immediately hopped onto his arm. 'Time tae stretch yer wings, ma beauty, and see what's out there,' he growled as he hobbled up to the deck to set the vulture loose.

9

An Embarrassing Moment!

Miranda lay in her hammock trying to get to sleep, but her mind was still reeling from Mad-Mo's betrayal. *I HATE HIM! Hate, hate, hate, him! How could he do that? He's a TRAITOR!* She groaned miserably as she tried to get comfortable. 'AND I HATE THIS HAMMOCK AS WELL!' she yelled loudly.

'Will you please be quiet and stop fussing? Even angellings need to rest, you know,' said Orphia sleepily.

'Well, I'm so angry I can't sleep!' muttered Miranda, tossing and turning, the hammock now swinging dangerously.

'If you're not careful you'll fall out… and don't you think you've been a bit hard on Mo?'

'Hard? Hard?! I haven't even started yet,' she stated, her anger rising.

'What about Forgiveness? I thought that was one of the five virtues you were meant to display.'

'Stuff forgiveness!' she roared. 'He can rot in hell as far as I'm concerned,' she added, between clenched teeth.

'Miranda, that is not very saintly,' said the angel-ling.

'Listen, I'll leave the saintly stuff to you. After all, that's your department, isn't it?'

'Don't you think he's suffered enough?' added Orphia compassionately, because she had a soft spot for the young rogue.

'He doesn't know the meaning of suffering,' Miranda replied savagely.

'Oh, and I suppose you do?'

Refusing to answer, Miranda lay swinging in her hammock, thinking about Orphia's words. Deciding that she wasn't up to the task this evening, she stared up at the ceiling and said, 'OK, I promise to forgive him, but only after I've tormented him for one more day – deal?'

'Deal – now will you please get some rest? We've a busy day tomorrow.'

* * *

In the morning, Miranda could sense a change in the air. Gingerly sticking a leg out from under her covers, she drew it back rapidly.

'It's ruddy freezing,' she grumbled.

'Miranda, mind your language please,' said Orphia chirpily.

'Well, we've gone from boiling hot to absolutely freezing. Where are we, the North Pole?'

'Not quite; we're stuck in a parallel universe and it's a bit chilly so wrap up well.'

'Did you say a parallel universe?' Miranda asked in amazement.

An Embarrassing Moment

'I did, but not to worry, it happens sometimes. Red will steer us clear.' Orphia then broke into song.

'How come you're in such a good mood?' asked Miranda grumpily.

'Oh, I had the most delightful dream about an angel called Dorphia. You should have seen his wings. Breathtaking! Oh I say... Orphia and Dorphia... you don't think it's a sign, do you?'

'No, I don't! It was just a dream,' replied Miranda, even more grumpily. 'A sign indeed,' she added under her breath.

'Still in a bad mood I see.'

'Well, I've thought about forgiving Mo, but it's just not happening at the moment. I still hate him.'

'You know there's a fine line between love and hate,' said Orphia, swooping around Miranda's head and causing her hair to float up in the breeze.

'Right, that's it! I'm getting up... and don't think for one moment that love has anything to do with this,' Miranda snapped. Rolling out of the hammock, she promptly fell flat on her face. Staggering to her feet, her face the colour of over-ripe strawberries, she stomped around the cabin looking for something to wear.

'I think I'll leave you to it,' said the angel-ling, breezing through the wall.

Miranda got dressed and made her way up to the deck. Red was standing at the helm, looking like a humongous sheep. He had thrown a sheepskin rug with a hole in the middle of it over his head and had several more tied around his waist. He also had a Russian fur hat perched on his large head. 'Gooood moooorrrning,' he said, full of good cheer.

Oh, not another one, thought Miranda irritably.

'What was that you were thinking, hen?'

'Oh, it's just everyone seems to be in a good mood…'

'Everyone except you,' Red interjected. 'Sooo you've no' forgiven Mo yet?'

'No, and why should I?' she retorted, scanning the galleon for the offender.

'Because it's the only way forward,' he replied. 'Did it ever occur to you that this might be part of the test?'

Miranda, still not in the mood for forgiveness, pretended she hadn't heard that last comment. As there wasn't much to see from the bridge except a vast expanse of ocean, she decided to go and find Sly.

* * *

Halfway down the stairs, she bumped into Mad-Mo.

'Traitor!' she spat. She stuck her nose in the air and turned away, but not before a tendril of her hair sent out red sparks, catching Mad-Mo on his cheek and leaving a little burn mark.

'Oi, watch it!' he said, lashing out at her.

'NO, YOU WATCH IT!' she shouted, dodging his fist. 'And if you know what's good for you, you'll avoid me for *ever and a day*,' she snarled, managing to sneak in a quick karate chop to the ribs. She then darted up the stairs as fast as she could, with Mad-Mo staggering after her.

It was now his turn to be livid. He was utterly gobsmacked and totally humiliated that she'd managed to get him.

Cow! he thought, his rage bubbling over. 'I'll get you for this! NO GIRL IS GOING TO MAKE A FOOL OUT OF ME!' he yelled, furious that she'd been quicker than he. *How did she get so good in such a short space of time?* A terrible thought entered his head. *Blimey! She might get to be as good as me.* He paled considerably at the idea, deciding that that wasn't about to happen and that he'd have to train even harder. With a burst of adrenalin, he quickened his pace. Leaping onto the deck in a swashbuckling manner and flourishing his boomerang, he searched the galleon for Miranda but she was nowhere to be seen.

'Mo, do ye have tae always make such a loud and gr-rand entrance? I knoow that ye want to impress the wee lass, but...'

Mad-Mo stopped dead and spun around, scowling at Red. 'Impress her? I wanna strangle her!' he snarled.

Quickly sneaking around the galleon as quietly as he could, he tripped as a leg suddenly shot out from behind a barrel, sending him sprawling across the deck. Miranda then leapt out and quickly wrapped some rope around his ankles before shooting off.

He had a mouthful of blood where he'd split his lip and he hadn't yet noticed that his legs were tied. Seething with fury, he got up and charged at Miranda, who was taunting him in a very un-ladylike manner. A second later, he found himself spreadeagled across the deck for a second time.

Miranda threw back her head and howled with laughter. Jeering and jumping up and down in delight, she put out her hands, beckoning and daring him to catch her.

'Hey, Jet Li, you're not quick enough!' shouted out Chow Yen, who was rather enjoying Mad-Mo getting his comeuppance.

'That's enough, yous two!' barked Red.

Mad-Mo hadn't taken his burning eyes off Miranda while he was untying the rope. Turning, he nodded in Red's direction. He got up and nonchalantly meandered across to Miranda and put out his hand to shake hers.

'You got me there,' he smiled through gritted teeth. Miranda put out her hand and was promptly thrown over his back.

'I SAID,' shouted Red, icily glaring at them both. 'THAT'S ENOUGH!'

Miranda got to her feet, dusted herself down and went to walk away – but not before she'd slapped Mad-Mo hard on the head.

That was it. The chase was on.

Without thinking, Miranda shot up the rope ladders. Halfway up, she stopped and, realising how high up she was, she was instantly overcome by a wave of vertigo. Clinging to the ropes with all her strength, her face the colour of chalk, she found herself unable to move.

Mad-Mo started to climb up after her slowly, enjoying her look of panic.

'I'm coming to get you,' he kept repeating, with a menacing grin.

An Embarrassing Moment

Knowing that she'd pushed her luck with him by humiliating him in front of the crew, she was now getting increasingly worried as to what he might do to her. In her nervous state she was alternating between screaming with fear and hysterical laughter. *He won't do anything. He wouldn't dare... would he?* Knowing he was gaining on her by the second, her stomach lurched as she saw the black fury in his eyes. Her hair let out whispers and gasps and fizzled with fear.

Fighting her vertigo and the biting wind, she grabbed the next rope and, with a determination she didn't know she possessed, she pulled herself up. She could hear Red shouting for her to come down. Grappling on up and realising there was nowhere to go once she'd reached the top, she stopped for breath and prayed for inspiration.

'I'm getting closer,' Mad-Mo hissed.

'GET LOST!' she retorted, knowing he was right.

Out of nowhere, a huge gust of wind caught the sails, violently rocking the galleon. Losing her foothold, she found herself slipping down, the ropes burning the palms of her hands as she slid. Clutching on tightly, she managed to stop herself falling any further.

Looking down, she felt herself getting sick with dizziness. *Don't look down – don't look down*, she silently repeated, her knees turning to jelly. She could feel her body sag as her legs buckled underneath her. Another gust of wind shook the sails. Her hair was blowing about madly in the wind. She realised that Mad-Mo had no intention of stopping the chase. She pulled herself upright and tried to climb further up but her hair became caught in the ropes and yanked her to a stop. Another squall hit the sails and this time Miranda lost her balance completely and found herself hanging by her mane.

The whole crew let out a gasp as Miranda swayed precariously back and forth, screaming in pain. Mad-Mo's anger vanished instantly, replaced now by worry and guilt.

Stavros happened to be perched on the top sail. 'Mighty grand view, don't ya think?' he squawked.

'Oh, shut up, Stavros!' she screamed.

'Oh, charming! Only trying to make polite conversation,' said the albatross, ruffling his feathers.

'Hold on, Miranda, I'll save you,' Mad-Mo shouted out encouragingly.

'GET LOST! I don't need your help,' she lied, gulping and praying he'd get there as soon as possible.

'Suit yourself!' he said, pretending to turn and go.

'NO, STAY!' she wailed.

Secretly grinning, he eased himself up next to her and held her until she got her footing. When he tried to untangle her hair from where it bound her head to the rigging, Miranda slapped his hand away. Gritting her teeth and keeping her face turned so he wouldn't see the tears of pain watering her eyes, she slowly, gradually, strand by painful strand, released her multi-coloured mane.

'Get your filthy hands off me,' she hissed, as soon as she had freed herself. She grabbed the ropes, secretly very relieved that he was there.

'Do you know what you are? You're a stubborn old cow!' yelled Mad-Mo.

'Listen traitor, it's all your fault that this happened in the first place!' she said. Slowly, with his support, they inched their way down to where Red stood, fuming.

'Now yous two kiss and make up,' he ordered.

'I'd rather kiss a toad!' said Miranda.

'Yeah, and I'd rather sit on a hand grenade,' spat Mad-Mo.

'That's probably the first good idea you've ever had,' she retorted, rather enjoying the banter.

'R-right, yous two, in yer cabins... NOOW! And I dinnae want tae see either of you until you're fr-riends again. Oh, and don't for one minute think that you'll be getting anything tae eat.'

With their heads lowered, they sulkily went down below.

* * *

Miranda had been down in Red's cabin for three hours and was starting to feel a little stir-crazy. Not only that, she was starving. Deciding to cheat, she took out her magical lunchbox and ordered a huge slab of chocolate cake and a pineapple smoothie. She heard a knock at the door.

Opening it, she found Mad-Mo standing there, with a very sheepish grin spread across his face. Taking one look at his dimples, she felt her anger begin to dissolve. She nodded for him to enter, and his eyes lit up when he saw the cake. Without asking, he strode in and took a huge bite.

'Oi you – you could at least wait until you're offered some,' she snapped.

'Ah... you know you love me really,' he said cockily, his lips dripping with creamy chocolate icing.

'I certainly do not,' she growled, grabbing the cake out of his hands and ramming it into her mouth. After demolishing it, not leaving a single crumb, she gave him a sarcastic smile.

'Mmm,' she hummed, 'mmm, mmm, yummy, yummy. That was, without doubt, the most *delicious* cake I've ever had. Oh dear, did I eat it all? So sorry... next time,' she smiled devilishly.

'That's not very nice.'

'Neither is betting on the opposition,' she snarled, her anger returning. 'Why did you do it?'

'Well, it was insurance, wasn't it... and, of course, I planned on sharing it all.'

'OF COURSE!' she said mockingly. 'So that's your excuse, is it? Pathetic!'

'I'm not pathetic,' he cried, his indignation rising. 'On my life – I did it for us all.'

'Whatever!' she said, waving him away.

He was secretly hoping for some cake and decided he'd better get on her good side.

'Sorry,' he mumbled.

'What was that? I didn't quite hear you.'

'I said, I'm SORRY!'

'Apology accepted,' she said, not entirely meaning it, but she was bored with sitting on her own and was really enjoying winding him up.

'So, how about some more of that tasty cake then?' he said, fluttering his eyelashes wildly. Miranda decided he needed one last lesson. She silently asked for the same cake – but this time asking for it to be riddled with small black slugs.

'Cor,' he said, his mouth watering when a huge slice appeared before him. Biting off an enormous chunk, he chewed away merrily... until he bit into a writhing, rubbery blob. He inspected the cake and noticed it was moving! He leapt up, squirming in disgust, and spat it out all over Red's desk.

'I'll get you for this,' he hissed.

In that moment, Red walked in. 'Oh, so ye've made up. Splendid! splendid!' he roared, ruffling their hair, whilst they stood glowering menacingly at each other. Then Red noticed his desk, 'What the blazes…?'

'S-sorry, I've got an upset stomach,' said Mad-Mo, giving Miranda the evil eye.

'Well you'd better clean it up and go and see Chow Yen or Soaring Eagle. Oh, Miranda, go up tae the deck, I'll be up in a jiffy. Ye can inform the crew that I've solved Sarakuta's riddle and we're off to Elizabethan England. I want to see my old friend, Shakespeare and maybe even have an audience with Queen Elizabeth…'

* * *

Wandering up, Miranda found the crew all sitting about on the deck, reminiscing about past adventures.

'Guess what?' she interrupted excitedly, 'We're off to Elizabethan England!'

'Och, that's gr-rand!' said Fearless. 'Hopefully we'll catch one of Shakespeare's plays at the Globe Theatre.'

Monsieur Le Grand slid across the deck on his knees, stopping just in front of Miranda.

'Shall I compare zee to a soomerrr's day?
Zow art more lurvly and more temperate.
Rough winds do shake zee darling buds of May
And summer's lease hath all too short a date.'

Miranda, blushing furiously, clapped her hands.

Not to be outdone by the Frenchman, Mad-Mo – who'd also joined them – jumped on a barrel and, with hand on heart, cried, *Good night, good night! Parting is such sweet sorrow, that I shall say goodnight till it be morrow.*

Everyone except Miranda roared their approval.

'I see ye remembered yer lines,' said Red, arriving just as Mad-Mo was in full swing.

Nodding and swaggering about, Mad-Mo polished his fingernails on his T-shirt. Red informed Miranda that Shakespeare had allowed Mad-Mo to play Romeo in one of his performances and that he wasn't half bad.

Stavros was hopping about the deck, getting more and more excited about the upcoming visit. The prospect of going to see a Shakespearian play, not to mention the

An Embarrassing Moment

possibility of seeing Queen Elizabeth, was making him quite dizzy with delight.

Then Fearless began giggling, and soon he was getting quite hysterical with mirth. Miranda asked him what was so funny.

'N-n-nothing,' he replied, 'just had a flashback.' However hard he tried he couldn't stop laughing, and soon the whole crew wanted in on the joke.

'Och, I was just remembering and thinking about one of Red's most embarrassing moments,' he chuckled.

'Go on!' they all cried.

'Red and I had been invited to an important ceremony for Queen Elizabeth... '

'Watch it, Fearless! There'll be noone of that noow!' said Red, whose face had turned rather pink.

Noticing this, Miranda was even more curious to know what could have been so embarrassing. 'Go on, Fearless, tell us,' she implored.

'Well, as I said, Red and maself were attending the court of Elizabeth. It was a mighty grand affair and everybody who was anybody was there. Och, the pomp and ceremony was tr-remendous. Anyways, it came tae Red's turn tae meet the Queen, and lo and behold, just as he knelt down tae kiss her hand, he let rip... a MASTER-BLASTER FART!'

The others were now rolling around the deck, howling with laughter at the thought.

'Och, I did no'.'

'Ye did sooo.'

'I said, I didnae.'

'Aye, it was yooo, so stop telling porkies,' said Fearless, his face full of mischief.

'That wasn't me… it was that dandy, Sir Walter Raleigh!'

'Sir Walter Raleigh indeed, who are ye trying tae kid?' jibed Fearless.

'I swear on Neptune's beard. Sir Walter was standing right next tae me at the time.'

'Red, I've known ye all ma life and ye cannae get away with that one!'

Fearless turned to the others, 'And do ye knoow what? Good Queen Bess never even batted an eyelid! Hoow's that for self-control?' More howls of appreciation erupted. 'But I swear, I saw the corners of her mouth twitch just a fr-raction.'

Fearless fell about laughing hysterically, while Red, highly embarrassed, had turned a dark shade of crimson.

'So what happened then?' asked Miranda, shaking with merriment.

'Well, a few of the ladies fainted from the ar-roma and there was a deathly silence after that. Ye could've heard a pin drop.'

'Fearless, that's enough noow! Ye've said yer piece, sooo beat it. There's a deck that needs scrubbing.'

Fearless, still chuckling after his story, got up and set to cleaning the deck. The rest of the crew quickly busied themselves in case they were ordered to do some horrid task. Stavros decided to get an early start and meet them in Elizabethan England. He ran up the deck and took off in the direction of Greece.

That night, Red sat at the helm whilst everyone was asleep, knowing his twin was out there somewhere, silently stalking them. He also knew that Nasty wouldn't take this defeat lying down. Twice, they had foiled him.

An icy shiver ran up his spine as he pondered on what his twin would do next.

* * *

Stavros was happily singing to himself about the forthcoming adventure in England. 'I'm off to see the Queen – I'm off to see the Queen. Hey-ho daddy-o, I'm off to see the Queen.'

Stavros suddenly realised that he wasn't alone – he had company. Scabies had been quietly flying behind him, listening to the albatross's singing. 'That's a jolly song,' said the vulture.

'Strewth! That's not a song; I'm on my way to have an audience with the one and only Queen Elizabeth the First,' he stated with pride.

'Really?' said Scabies, 'How amazing. And who else are you going to meet?'

'Shakespeare, of course!' exclaimed Stavros. 'And my closest mate, Notorious Red MacNaughty.'

'Notorious Red MacNaughty? He's a legend! Wow, you must be one special albatross,' stated the vulture. *And extraordinarily stupid,* he thought to himself, saying farewell as he flew off towards the *Scavenger*.

10

Forgiving is so hard to do

The next morning, Miranda was desperately trying to wake up from a nightmare. She was dreaming that she was imprisoned in the Tower of London, waiting to be hanged. There was a loud knock at the door, and she tried to scream for help but nothing came out.

Before she knew it, she felt herself being shaken awake. Groggily opening one eye, she saw Sly bending over her, waving an incense stick right under her nose. Pushing his paw away, she sat up in her hammock and noticed he had two more incense sticks attached to his tail.

Lying back down again, she grumbled, 'I don't know which is worse, my terrible nightmare or waking up to find the place stinking. What are you trying to do? Choke me to death?'

Peeping over her sheet, she asked why he was burning incense.

'It's the stench, the Eli-sh-a-bethans, they're a sh-melly lot, they don't believe in washing or drinking water.'

'Water? How can they not drink water?' she asked incredulously.

'They think it's unhealthy, which it is true – due to the lack of sanitation – so they drink ale instead. Ale for breakfast, ale for lunch, ale for dinner and plenty of sh-lurps in between, of course. The wine is reserved for the rich.'

'I would have thought that was your idea of Heaven,' she teased.

'Me!' he said innocently, 'I've never touched a drop in my sh-life.'

With a look of total disbelief, she replied, 'Mmm, and I've never eaten ice-cream.'

A smell of singed fur began to mingle with the incense. Noticing his tail was now smoking, she informed him that it was on fire.

'Sh-wat?' he asked, looking slightly confused. 'Sh-amsters don't have tails…'

'Sly, how many times do I have to tell you? You're a rat!'

'Shush! Don't remind me,' he snapped.

'Umm… And your tail is still smoking,' she said, starting to giggle.

Peering at his singed tail, he let out a piercing scream, running over to Miranda's wash-bowl and plunging his tail in it. Grabbing the water jug, he thoroughly drenched his burnt appendage and, letting out an enormous sigh, he said, 'Phew! Shlat's better.'

Miranda was now hiding under her covers with her fist rammed into her mouth, shaking from head to toe with stifled laughter. 'Are you all right?' she asked.

'I'll sh-live,' he replied crossly. Sly hated being laughed at. 'Anyshway, you besht prepare yourshelf, Eli-sh-a-bethan England isn't all Shakespeare, ya know, it has a very grizzly sh-ide to it,' he said sulkily, nursing his burnt tail. 'Sh-well, don't say I didn't try to warn you.' With that, he waddled out, slamming the door behind him.

Deciding to find out for herself, she leapt out of her hammock, threw some clothes on and made her way up the stairs to find Red.

* * *

The minute she stepped out onto the deck, the vilest, most disgusting, sickening stench hit her nostrils. Heaving and retching, she ran to the side of the galleon and threw up violently. Wiping away the sick, she noticed the carcass of a maggot-infested dog float by. That wasn't the only thing she noticed; all manner of rotting, putrid things were bobbing along the river.

'Where are we?' she groaned, in between choking and gagging.

'The River Thames,' said Red, offering her a hanky. Then he took out a clothes peg from his sporran and stuck it on her nose.

'Thad's bedder,' she uttered, through her blocked nose.

'I suggest you remove the peg now and again so that ye can accustom yerself tae the stench because, tr-rust me, it gets worse once we hit the streets.'

'Why's it so pongy?' she asked, thinking it couldn't possibly smell any worse.

'They don't have the sewage system that ye have today. Everything gets thrown out into the streets and river, and they don't even have toilets!'

'What? No loos?' she said, now turning green.

'Nope, they relieve themselves in chamber pots and throw the contents out of the windows. So, I suggest that when ye're walking through the narrow streets ye keep close tae the walls of the houses.'

'Urgh!' she groaned, her face contorted with nausea. 'Thad's the most degusting thing I've ever 'eard. I'm off to find a pair of Wellington boots and an umbwella.'

'Actually, ye'll need tae be dressing like one of the locals. They're a suspicious lot. Go and find Sheba; she'll know what tae do.'

Miranda found the carpet lying prostrate on the floor with a bottle of smelling salts under her nose.

'Oh my Gaad!' she groaned dramatically. 'How I hate this period in history. The *smell*… haven't they heard of perfume?'

Removing the clothes peg from her nose, Miranda heartily agreed. 'According to Red, I've got to dress like a local and he said you'd know what to do.'

Raising herself off the floor, Sheba beckoned Miranda to follow her and, rifling through one of Red's chests, she found what she was looking for. Miranda was aghast at the amount of clothing she was supposed to wear.

'The problem is… the *sumptuary* laws,' said Sheba.

'What on earth are they?' Miranda asked, wondering what that had to do with the way she was to be dressed.

'You see, that wily old buzzard Queen Elizabeth enforces the law that dictates what people are allowed to wear.'

'Cor, that's a bit much!'

'It's all about social standing. The higher your ranking, the more expensive and brighter-coloured fabrics you're allowed to wear. Of course, the Queen has the best of everything and only she and her immediate family are allowed to wear silk and the colour purple, and only members of the royal family are entitled to wear ermine fur. So the Queen, of course, looks utterly glorious in her sumptuous dresses and outshines every lady in her court – all except me, of course! Nobody could possibly outshine me,' quivered Sheba, with a delicious self-appreciating sigh.

Miranda rolled her eyes and grinned at Sheba's vanity. Picking up an odd assortment of clothes, she asked, 'So what did the average person wear?'

'You mean the peasants and lowly classes?' said Sheba snobbishly. 'Oh, muddy colours and rough coarse fabrics, and if anyone – and I mean *anyone* – is caught wearing something above their station, it could be punishable by hanging! The Queen loves a good hanging, you know.'

Miranda was too horrified to speak and silently got dressed. *Wow, imagine being hanged for wearing the wrong type of clothes! I wonder what the Queen would have thought of twenty-first century Britain?*

The first item to put on was a linen chemise undergarment, then stockings, then a corset which Sheba pulled too tight, then a hooped skirt and a petticoat. Over that was a gown made of damask, with separate sleeves and a ruff around the neck, which felt most uncomfortable.

Miranda looked in the mirror at her attire and was glad that she didn't have to go through *that* every day.

'Don't you think I might be dressed above my station?' she asked, feeling the fur trim on her sleeves.

'Daaarling, you're the saviour of the world. If anything, you should be dressed far more lavishly, but we don't want to outdo Queenie now, do we?' Sheba tittered. She gave Miranda a pouch of lavender and tied it around her neck. 'It's to help with the ghastly stench,' she said, dabbing copious amounts of vetiver and orange blossom all over herself.

* * *

Back on deck, Miranda found Monsieur Le Grand. He was wearing tights and what looked like a peculiar pair of brightly coloured silk striped underpants. They looked as if they had been stuffed with loads of cotton wool, making him appear very fat around the hips. He also wore a doublet with separate sleeves and a ruff around his neck and, instead of his customary top-hat, he sported a floppy velvet cap with a feather sticking out.

'I juste luurve drezzing oop, eet's zuch fun,' he said, theatrically throwing a cape over his shoulders.

Red appeared, dressed in his kilt as usual.

'Aren't you going to dress up?' asked a disappointed Miranda.

'Och, if ye think I'm gonna dress like some foppish dandy, ye're wrong,' he roared, laughing. 'Noow I dinnae want tae fr-righten ye, but ye must cover yer ankles and arms up thoroughly.'

'Why?' she asked.

'Well, ye wouldn't want tae catch the plague noow, would ye?'

'THE PLAGUE?!' she squeaked, her face turning a deathly white.

'Aye, Elizabethan times were riddled with the plague. They caught it from fleas that lived on black rats and other rodents.'

'Are you telling me that fleas give you the plague? 'Cos our cats Rigor and Mortis constantly have fleas, and it doesn't matter how many times we de-flea them, there are always more.' Miranda immediately started itching all over. Frantically scratching, she told Red that she thought they should turn around and sail back out to sea.

'Och, you'll be fine. Like I said, just make sure that yer ankles are well covered, along with yer hands and head.'

Miranda tore down to Red's cabin, put on her Wellington boots, and then wrapped bandages around her wrists. Luckily, her sleeves hid them. After putting on a dainty pair of gloves, she wrapped a long cloak with a large hood around her, which more or less covered her head completely. *No fleas can bite me now*, she thought, searching through Red's drawers for some flea powder. Eventually finding some, she threw the contents over her. Grabbing an extra bottle, she made her way back up to the deck, sniffling and sneezing as the powder went up her nose.

By the time she'd returned, the rest of the crew were all standing to attention. Ress-up had dressed up as a Moor and had wrapped a blood-red turban around his head; this, with his flowing saffron-coloured robe, made him look most exotic.

Sly was wobbling back and forth in a highly agitated manner. 'I can't and I shan't' he kept muttering under his breath. 'The fleas-sh, they'll leap on me, they will.'

Miranda walked up to Sly and doused him with flea powder. 'There, that should keep them away,' she said.

* * *

As they approached Southwark, the magnificent Globe Theatre – perched on the banks of the River Thames – came into view.

Red was clearly excited at the prospect of catching up with his old friend William Shakespeare, and ordered the anchor to be dropped. Turning to Miranda and Mad-Mo, he told them that Sheba had decided to stay on board to avoid the appalling stench of the city. He then told them to get into the longboat, which was hanging over the side of the galleon, ready to be lowered to take them ashore.

'Sit there a moment, I'll be back in a jiffy,' he said and, under his breath, added, 'They can't get up tae much sitting there.'

Mad-Mo, with a devilish glint in his eyes, started to rock the boat back and forth. Considering that the boat was very high up, it caused Miranda great distress. Peering over the sides, Mo whispered menacingly: 'Imagine falling into that murky water... Cor, just one gulp of that could end ya days.'

Miranda was gripping the sides so tightly that her knuckles looked as if they might pop out. 'P-please Mo, stop it... I'm-I'm very sorry, I p-p-promise I'll never do anything mean to you again,' she pleaded, her eyes now filling with petrified tears.

The putrid smell of the river wafted under her nose, causing her stomach to heave. Peering over the side, she saw a headless corpse float by.

This was too much! Miranda covered her eyes and let out a piercing scream. The startled Mad-Mo jumped to his feet, sending the boat swaying wildly and dangerously. He tried to grab Miranda but... too late! She flew over the side and landed in the fetid river.

At first, Mad-Mo was too stunned to react. Then the knowledge of what he had done seeped in. Completely freaking out and knowing his days were numbered, he scrambled back on board and ran up and down the deck screeching, 'MIRANDA OVERBOARD!'

Without hesitation Ress-up dived in to rescue Miranda. The weight of her clothes was dragging her under, causing her to cough and splutter violently, her arms thrashing wildly as she tried to keep afloat. Finally, Ress-up managed to get his strong arms around her waist and, after dragging her back to the galleon, he carefully pulled her up the rope ladder.

Lying prostrate on the deck and coughing up slimy, dirty brown water, she burst into tears.

Red, knowing that Mad-Mo was behind this, grabbed him by the ear and lifted him high above his head, informing him that he'd better come up with a suitable punishment for himself.

Chow Yen immediately got to work and poured a vile-tasting liquid down Miranda's throat. Red tenderly lifted her up and took her down to his cabin and, laying her on his vast bed, he gently began to mop at her clothes.

Sheba shooed him out and undressed her. She washed away the slime and then dunked Miranda's limp hair into a bucket of clean water. After rinsing it thoroughly, she said, 'I think it's best that you lie here for a while.'

Sitting up, Miranda protested, saying that they had to get on with the search for the next poem. Marvelling at her determination, Sheba insisted she stay for a while longer.

There was a meek knock on the door and Mad-Mo cautiously popped his head around. With a quivering mouth and a crestfallen face, he slowly inched his way in and, with his enormous brown eyes full of remorse, he sat down on the bed and blubbered his apologies.

'I only meant to frighten you,' he snivelled wretchedly.

Patting his hand, she said, 'It's all right, Mo, I shouldn't have wished for a slice of chocolate slug cake.' And then, remembering the look of horror and disgust on his face as he realised what she'd done, she began giggling.

Wondering what could be so funny at a time like this, he found himself cheerfully joining in. Sheba was totally confused and quietly left the cabin. Red hurried in, saw that Mad-Mo was there with Miranda and nearly burst a blood vessel. He was just about to let loose with a tirade of insults when she spoke up and explained that it was entirely her fault.

'Is that sooo,' Red said, not believing a word.

'Yes, I was being an idiot and showing off.'

'Well, if that's the tr-ruth – which I highly doubt – then it serves ye r-right.' He gave Mad-Mo a scathing look and stamped out, slamming the cabin door behind him.

'Cor, thanks for that!' said Mad-Mo, utterly relieved. 'I thought you'd want me dead after what I did.'

'I hate to admit it... but I learnt a valuable lesson today.'

'You did?' he asked, wondering what on earth that could be.

'Red was right. Forgiveness *is* the only way forward and, if I had forgiven you sooner, I wouldn't have ended up at the top of the mast hanging by my hair or nearly being drowned.'

Deciding that Miranda was far more grown up than he was, Mad-Mo got up and left, with much food for thought.

11

Hangman's Noose

Luckily, the second attempt to disembark went without a hitch. Sitting in the longboat with the others, Miranda noticed three men chained to the embankment, up to their necks in the offal-ridden water, gasping for breath. Having experienced the river at first hand, her heart cried out with compassion.

'What on earth are they doing tied up in this filthy, germ-ridden river?' she asked, cringing from head to toe.

'They're being punished,' replied Fearless, in a matter-of-fact tone.

'Punished?!' she gasped, 'What could they have possibly gone and done to deserve that?'

'Och, they probably stole a loaf of bread or something.'

Miranda's eyes opened wide with surprise. 'Blimey! That's a bit extreme.'

By the time they'd reached the embankment, both Mad-Mo and Miranda were squirming all over as unspeakable things floated precariously near.

'Don't you think we should free them?' she asked, completely horrified.

'Are ye mad?' said Red. 'The last thing we need is tr-rouble before we've even set foot on land, and that goes for yooo especially, laddie,' he said, glaring at Mad-Mo. 'If they're still there when we've accomplished our mission, then we'll liberate them as we depart.'

'They'll be dead by then,' muttered Miranda through her lavender bag.

Red was right about the stench; once they'd hit the streets, it became unbearable, and everyone was slipping and sliding on the narrow cobbled streets. Kites flew here and there scavenging for food. Red informed her that the kites were birds of prey and would eat anything, which helped to keep the streets clean.

The City of London was hardly a sober place; people lurched about loudly, stinking of ale and shouting out their wares. The loud click of hooves and the clack of wheels resounded throughout. The sickly smell of tanneries, where they cured pig and cow hides, mingled with the terrible smell of the city. Occasionally a waft of fresh air from the surrounding countryside allowed a fleeting, welcome relief to all those who lived and worked there.

'You know, I'm not surprised that everyone only drinks beer! I think being drunk all the time would be the only way to survive this cesspit,' Miranda said in disgust.

* * *

Miranda grabbed Red's hand as they made their way through the pushing, jostling hordes towards the Globe Theatre for the afternoon performance. The playhouse looked pretty much the same as the reproduction that stands in Southwark today... except for the audience, of course, most of whom were a rowdy lot, reeking of stale body odour and ale.

Miranda and the others followed Red as he made his way over to the back of the stage, hailing acquaintances as he went. The lively crowd were getting themselves ready for the coming show. They were shouting, jeering and stamping their feet in anticipation.

Suddenly, a man sporting a moustache and a natty goatee beard jumped out of the crowd and slapped Red on his shoulder.

'Will! Och it's gr-rand tae see ye!' yelled Red, lifting the man up and giving him a bear hug. 'I've brought my great, great, etc., etc. gr-randchild tae see one of your marvellous plays. I dooo hope it's a comedy.'

Putting the playwright down, Red grabbed Miranda's hand and introduced them.

'Ah... you're one of the Wyrd sisters. I hope you don't mind that I used your surname in my play, *Macbeth*. Of course, I had to turn the sisters into cackling old hags to please the audience,' he said, with a twinkle in his eye. 'I based them on Varicose-Vera instead. After all, if they had been as beautiful as Karmela and her sisters, they wouldn't have frightened the spectators nearly so well. And, I must say, you're the spitting image of your mother.'

An image of Karmela dressed in her bohemian attire popped into Miranda's head... and she wasn't best pleased with the comparison.

'Your illustrious grandfather certainly gets about,' continued Shakespeare wistfully. 'Ah! How I wish I could time-travel; imagine the stories I could write!'

Putting out his elbow so that Miranda could link arms, Shakespeare asked her where she would like to sit.

Definitely not down by the stage, she thought, *I might get trampled to death.*

As if reading her mind, Shakespeare laughed. 'Don't worry yourself, I wouldn't dream of placing you in the Yard.' Pointing to seats up behind the stage, he said, 'You could sit in the Lords' rooms if you want.'

Miranda shook her head; she couldn't see the point in that as she wouldn't be able to see the play properly.

'That's where the nobility sit,' he said.

'Why would they want to sit there? It's not as if they could see much,' she asked.

'To be seen, to be seen, of course!' he replied theatrically. Then, pointing to the middle gallery in front of the stage, he said, 'Or there? Now that's got a very good view.'

Red decided that was the best place to sit and the crew climbed up to the middle gallery and got comfortable. Sitting in between Fearless and Mad-Mo, Miranda looked down at the heaving masses. She couldn't believe how so many people could be crammed together in the Yard.

Rubbing his hands together with excitement, Red asked somebody which of Shakespeare's plays was going to be performed. To his embarrassment, he was told that it was *The Taming of the Shrew*. Getting up to leave, he said, 'Och I dinnae want tae sit through this. After all – I *lived* it!'

Miranda persuaded him to stay, but the rest of the crew were beside themselves with hilarity, all nudging each other and cracking jokes. Fearless leant over and whispered in Miranda's ear that Shakespeare had based the play on one of Red's previous wives.

'I thought he was joking when he told me that,' she said.

'Och, she was a r-right old battleaxe. A dr-ragon, if there ever was. The term shrew didn't even begin tae describe the old bat,' he giggled.

'What happened?' asked Miranda, beginning to thoroughly enjoy herself.

'Well, ye know Red. He does love a challenge and, trust me, she must have been one of his biggest,' he confided mischievously. 'Och, the battle of words and the sparks that flew...! Of course, Shakespeare based it only loosely on the pair of them because, in the play, Kate's husband was a fortune-seeker... and we all knoow that Red only seeks fortunes to help the poor and needy.'

Suddenly there was a hushed silence, with everybody bowing their heads towards the Lords' room. Miranda whispered to Fearless, 'Who's the wrinkly old bag with white gunk all over her face?'

'Oh, goodness gr-racious, that's the Queen…,' he said, leaning over Monsieur Le Grand, poking Red, and nodding in her direction. 'Look, the Queen's arrived.'

Red leapt up from the bench and began waving frantically. 'Lizzie… over here!' he shouted. Spotting him, the Queen waved back enthusiastically.

'How are ye doin', lassie? It's grand tae see ye.'

The crowd looked on, gawping in shocked silence. The Queen's courtiers drew their swords and were just about to make their way over to arrest Red when the Queen waved them away.

Standing up, she bellowed back, 'Red, how marvellous to see you. I'm off to Hampton Court later so do drop by. I could do with your advice.'

By now, Sir Walter Raleigh had joined Her Majesty and was giving Red and the crew filthy looks. He whispered something in Elizabeth's ear, only for her to turn around and slap him around the face with a lace hanky.

'How dare you insult my noble friend Red. He's like a brother to me and, from what I've deduced, if it wasn't for him you would never have made it around the world and back!' she bellowed. Raleigh fell to his seat, seething with humiliation and vowing revenge.

The first act was a huge success and Red could be heard wheezing with laughter.

'Och, my Katherine wasn't *that* bad,' he said in the interval, wiping a tear from his eye.

'Oh, yes, she was,' said Fearless jovially.

Miranda took out the spyglass that Red had given her on the way and kept a keen eye on Sir Walter. She noticed him sneak off and reappear down in the Yard at the front of the stage.

To her utter horror, he was talking to Snarl. *How on earth did he know we would be coming here?* she wondered, frantically nudging Fearless in the ribs to tell him that

Snarl was there. But, as the play resumed, her words were drowned out and, by the time she'd got his attention, it was too late – they'd both gone.

When the play was finally over, Miranda tried to tell Red that she'd seen Snarl talking to Sir Walter Raleigh but still couldn't make herself heard over the voices of the departing crowd.

Shakespeare was waiting for them outside the Globe Theatre, beaming from ear to ear. 'What splendid timing!' he roared. 'How on earth did you know that *The Taming of the Shrew* was playing? So what did you think of it? Was it to your approval?' he winked.

'Aye, it was gr-rand. You're a genius, though I don't r-remember my Kate being that fearsome, and she was a damn sight better looking than Nicholas Tooley, the actor who played her on stage.'

* * *

Red hadn't seen Shakespeare for some time and wanted to take him to the local tavern for a catch up. He told Mad-Mo and Miranda to stay outside as it was far too rowdy for youngsters, but he warned them not to wander off.

Miranda had given up trying to tell Red that Snarl was at large and she was just bursting to go off and explore. But, after their experience in the underground passages at Red's castle and then the accident in the longboat, Mad-Mo was determined not to get into any more trouble.

The alley outside the tavern led into a small square, where people were starting to gather. They were booing, hissing, and shouting out, 'Hang the witch!'

Hang the witch? What do they mean? Miranda wondered, edging closer.

A voice was screaming inside her, telling her to go and look and she darted off into the throng of people, with Mad-Mo running behind, yelling at her to stop.

The square was now packed and Miranda couldn't see what was happening. Climbing onto an old cart, she saw – to her dismay and horror – a young girl, not much older than herself, standing on a platform with a noose wrapped around her neck.

'They can't do that, she's only a child!' she cried. She asked a toothless old hag why the girl was going to be hanged and was told that it was because she had used magic to cure her sick baby brother.

Miranda couldn't believe her ears. 'NO!' she roared, her lungs feeling as if they would burst from the strength of her cry. 'NO-NO-NO!' she continued to rant.

The crowd, in shocked silence, shuffled uneasily, trying to see where the shouting was coming from.

Standing straight, Miranda flung out her arms, pleading for them to stop.

'Silence,' said a gruff voice, 'I've been looking forward to this all week. We all have,' he grumbled.

Mad-Mo pulled at Miranda's cape worriedly. 'Get down or you'll be next,' he urged frantically, sensing that the crowd was getting dangerously impatient.

Ignoring him, Miranda continued her tirade: 'YOU'RE ALL EVIL, BLOODTHIRSTY BARBARIANS!' she cried, with tears of frustration streaming down her face.

Miranda looked into the young girl's terrified eyes and became overwhelmed with compassion for her. Then a powerful rage exploded inside her and she felt the blood surging through her veins. Before she had time to think rationally, she found herself running, jumping over people, pushing them out of the way, her hair crackling and hissing, flying around in the wind. She reached the platform and leapt onto it. She stood, glaring menacingly around, her hair now resembling a fireworks display.

The stunned onlookers edged back in fear; never in their lives had they witnessed such a spectacle. Whispers of 'Witch' started to spread, growing louder and louder.

Miranda suddenly realised that she was in big trouble. She quickly got out her knife and cut the rope from around the young girl's neck.

'Run! Run for your life,' Miranda urged.

By now the crowd was completely focussed on Miranda and the girl scrambled down from the platform, casting Miranda a look of gratitude as she fled.

Full of superstitious zeal and gaining courage from each other the horde now started inching towards Miranda like a pack of wolves going in for the kill.

'WITCH – WITCH – HANG THE WITCH!' they howled.

She was paralysed with fear as they began to encircle her. She stood rooted to the spot. 'Help', she whimpered.

Mad-Mo appeared, having managed to fight and claw his way onto the platform. He leapt gallantly in front of her, wielding his sword.

'Run!' he screamed, but Miranda was unable to move.

Then she felt the brush of Orphia's wings caress her cheek. 'Your magic flute,' whispered the angel-ling, 'Play your magic flute.'

Slowly Miranda took out her flute and began to play. The chanting stopped as they became hypnotised by the music. The crowd began to sway from side to side... all except for the hangman, who was profoundly deaf and couldn't hear the music.

Thinking that the devil was amongst them, the hangman charged at Mad-Mo, pushing him off the platform. Then he grabbed some sacking and threw it over Miranda's head. Once the flute had ceased to play, the mesmerised mob came to their senses and again began to force their way towards the platform, trampling over Mad-Mo in the process.

Suddenly Sir Walter Raleigh appeared and, pointing at a cart, he indicated to the hangman that he should throw Miranda into it. By the time a bruised and battered Mad-Mo had battled his way back onto the execution platform, Miranda had completely disappeared.

Just then the voice of Red could be heard, yelling 'Get yer filthy hands off ma lad!' He leapt onto the platform and Mad-Mo nearly fainted with relief. He'd sprained his right wrist badly and could hardly lift his sword, let alone fight with it.

'And where's ma great, great gr-randdaughter?!' Red snarled, towering over Raleigh.

'In the prison for heretics and witches,' Sir Walter hissed.

Red picked him up by the scruff of his neck and shook him violently.

'I've no' finished with yooo yet,' he growled, roughly throwing him to the floor.

'Wait till the Queen hears about this!' screeched Raleigh, seething with humiliation. 'She'll have you hanged, drawn and quartered.'

'I doubt that very much. Watch it, or I might just reveal the tr-ruth aboot your unsuccessful colonisation of Virginia. And that it was *me* who towed ye there in the first place, as ye were going in the wr-rong direction. Plus, it was *me* who suggested taking back the potato. So shut yer ruddy mouth before I disengage yer tongue.' With that, Red stormed off, with Mad-Mo meekly following.

The rest of the crew were still in the ale house with Shakespeare.

'Right, yous lot, Miranda has been imprisoned and we've got tae get her out,' stated Red.

Miraculously, they all sobered up instantaneously. All except Sly, that is, who was slouched in a chair, snoring. Red picked him up and shook him, then poured a flagon of ale over him. Waking up to find Red glaring at him, Sly immediately wiggled his tail and sobered up.

'I swear on the wrath of Zeus, if I ever find ye dr-runk again, you'll end up living in a stinking sewer!'

Sly shivered at the thought and wondered what could have possibly rocked Red's boat. Outside, Red ordered them all back to the galleon. They needed Sheba if they were going to get to the prison fast enough.

Back on board, Soaring Eagle healed Mad-Mo's wrist. Mad-Mo then gave Red a full account of what happened.

'I swear, Red, I told her to stay put but she was gone before I could blink an eye,' said Mo, trembling and handing Miranda's bag of magical gifts to Red. 'She dropped this,' he added, with downcast eyes.

'It's all right, laddie, I don't hold ye responsible. She was meant to save that young girl... after all, it was mentioned in Sarakuta's poem. R-right everyone, I know where she'll be. They'll have taken her to New Prison – that's where they stick heretics. Sooo, get yerselves ready!'

* * *

Miranda was thrown into a filthy, stinking cell, where she found a crowd of other unfortunate people. Her hair was still fizzing and sending out multi-coloured sparks.

Finding a corner, she slid down the wall and hid her face in her lavender bag. If it wasn't for her hair – which terrified the other inmates – they would have stolen her cape and anything else she had. She felt totally alone and sick to the stomach with fear and, as she'd lost her bag containing her magical gifts, she couldn't even put on her hat and talk to Red.

She was very relieved when she felt Orphia swoop in to inform her that Red was on his way. Glad that

Orphia was with her, she felt a little better and began to survey her surroundings. Most of the inmates were huddled together in a corner, glancing at her furtively. The rest lay lifeless on the filthy floor. She discovered that if she stared at them, they would all simultaneously gasp and look away. She didn't know whether to feel relieved or thoroughly rejected.

The smell of violets suddenly tickled her nose and, looking around, she nearly jumped out of her skin. There, crouched down beside her, was a very peculiar-looking elderly man. His head was covered in an old rag and his clothes were torn and in tatters. But under bushy, turquoise eyebrows, his lapis lazuli-blue eyes told her a different story. They were alive with intelligence and curiosity. His nose was regal and his smile was kind and compassionate. She inhaled deeply, relishing his scent, and felt herself relax. She saw hints of a vivid green beard under his dishevelled cloak and she was just about to ask who he was, when – in a rumbling, deep voice – he told her not to worry.

'Miranda, what you just did took enormous compassion and tremendous courage. You have done very well so far.'

Miranda looked around and then at him, as if he were mad. *Yeah! I've done so great that I might end up hanging for it,* she thought miserably.

'How do you know what I just did and how do you know my name?' she asked, her apprehension returning.

'I see all and know all,' he replied mysteriously. 'To find what you seek, go to the maze and feel your way.'

Miranda looked to the heavens. *Oh no! Not another cryptic clue*, she thought.

'What maze?' she asked, but the man had vanished. Jumping up and scanning the cell, she saw no sign of him.

Then, the door suddenly burst open and a guard approached her warily. He whipped out a sack, threw it over her head and dragged her out of the cell!

12

The Tower

Soaring Eagle had conjured up a summer storm, causing the skies to darken and the rain to fall, sending everyone to seek shelter. Sheba zipped in and out of the grey clouds at a tremendous speed. Mad-Mo, feeling utterly miserable, sat next to Red, mumbling, 'I should have protected her better.'

Patting him on the arm, Red said, 'Och dinnae fash, laddie, she's got a strong will that one, and an insatiable curiosity! Once she's made up her mind, there's no' much any of us can do.' Giving Mad-Mo one of his crinkly, knowing smiles, he added, 'It's probably all part of Sarakuta's divine plan.'

'There's nothing divine about being thrown in a stinking jail,' said Mad-Mo sourly.

Finally locating the New Prison, Red was furious to find she'd been removed. Puffing out his chest and towering over the petrified guard, he snarled, 'With r-respect, sir, where has she gone and on whose orders?'

'The Tower of London, on the orders of Sir Walter Raleigh's,' answered the guard, cowering.

'The Tower of London!' Red exclaimed, 'Why there, I wonder? That's used solely for political prisoners. I tell ye what, if I find out that Raleigh is in cahoots with Nasty, I swear it'll be him who's hanged, drawn and quartered.'

* * *

Miranda lay on the squalid floor, wondering why she had been removed and placed in yet another prison. She felt like a football which had been kicked around a playing field by a team of angry youths. Slowly, she eased her bruised and aching body up off the floor and inspected her surroundings. At least she was alone. One small window let in feeble rays, giving her barely enough light to see. Underneath it was a wobbly stool and a small, rickety table with an unlit candle stub placed on it.

She dragged her body over and hesitantly climbed onto the stool. Standing on tiptoes, she managed to get a glimpse of the outside world. The sun was setting and ominous grey clouds lay heavily, like a dark blanket swaddling the sky.

She looked to her right and saw several heads stuck on spikes, making her stomach lurch with fear and nausea. *I HATE this place, it's horrid-horrid-horrid and I hate the Queen as well for allowing such terrible things to happen, and... where's Red?*

She climbed down and sat on the chair. With deep despair overwhelming her, and wondering if she was ever going to see Red and her family again, she felt silent tears cascading down her grubby cheeks.

'Hush now, I promise you, Red is on his way and nothing is going to stop him,' whispered Orphia.

'Oh Orphia, I feel so alone,' she sobbed.

The weary walls of the Tower murmured and sighed, feeling Miranda's anguish; knowing that life was fragile and that her life might soon be over.

Agonising sharp pains suddenly stabbed Miranda's stomach, beads of perspiration began to run down her forehead and a rising fever began to wrack her body. She dragged herself over to the hard, flea-infested bed and lay down, thinking of the filthy River Thames and knowing that that was the cause of her illness. Clutching her stomach and praying her rescue wouldn't be long in coming, she fell into an uneasy sleep.

Orphia hovered above, absolutely terrified that they were going to lose Miranda. She was spent from trying to heal her charge; her energy was flagging dangerously. The angel-ling had to inform Red of Miranda's sickness. Although she didn't want to leave her, she reluctantly flew off to find him.

Dreaming that Nasty MacNoxious was standing over her, Miranda awoke with a start. The smell of stale tobacco and the sea poisoned the air. To her horror, the dreaded STEP… TAP… STEP… TAP echoed down the stone corridor, getting louder and louder. She tried desperately to sit up but her body was too weak to respond. Images of her family and past events ran through her delirious mind. *This is it! I've lost and Nasty has won*, was her last thought before she passed out.

The door flew open and a cold, biting wind rushed in. Nasty hobbled in and stood glaring at Miranda, savouring the moment. Archibald padded in after Nasty.

'Sooo, we meet again,' hissed the pirate, looming menacingly over her. Then, looking at her deathly pallor, Nasty instantly knew that she was seriously ill. He stood stock-still, fury engulfing him. Clenching and unclenching his fists, his whole body trembled as he tried to contain his rage. 'I don't believe it! After all this, she looks like she could very well die on us!'

Turning to Archibald, he growled 'Well? What are ye waiting fer?!'

Archibald leant over her and, for a split second, his heart melted with tenderness... after all, Miranda had risked her own life in order to save his in the chariot race. By now, he was beginning to regret bitterly his betrayal of Red. The riches that MacNoxious had promised hadn't materialised and he was now certain that they never would. Archibald was suddenly filled with a tremendous hatred for Nasty. While the ugly old pirate was outside checking the corridors to make sure no one was coming, the gorilla scribbled a quick note telling Red where she was being taken and that Sir Francis Drake was anchored behind the *Scavenger*. Perhaps Drake could assist Red in rescuing Miranda?

Archibald gently picked up Miranda and placing her over his powerful shoulder, he followed MacNoxious out, locking the door behind them.

* * *

The Tower

Red was beside himself with worry when Orphia told him of Miranda's failing health. He knew instinctively that Nasty was perilously close and that Miranda was in terrible danger. Urging Sheba to fly faster, they finally arrived at the Tower of London.

The guards didn't know what had hit them by the time the crew had pummelled them to the ground. Kicking down the heavy wooden door, Red marched into the cell and let out a roar that shook the walls to their foundations. 'She's gone!' he bellowed, punching the wall in frustration.

It was Monsieur Le Grand who noticed the note poking out under the thin mattress. 'Red, zer is a note from zat scoundrel, Archibald,' he said, handing it over. 'I don't trust zat rotten gorilla woon bit,' he added darkly.

Red scrutinised the note before crumpling it up and throwing it on the floor. Turning to Soaring Eagle, he told him to fly like the wind to find out exactly where the *Scavenger* was anchored, and then to inform Sir Francis Drake that his help would be needed.

The others shifted about uneasily, fearing the gorilla was up to something.

'Ye're no' going tae take Archibald's word for it, are ye?' asked Fearless, surprised.

'Aye, I am.'

The crew mumbled their dissent, but Red cut them short and ordered them back to the *Wilderness*. They left in silence.

* * *

Back on board the galleon, Red was in his cabin working out a strategy for rescuing Miranda, when Drake walked in. After they had warmly embraced each other, Red told him what had happened.

'And you say that Raleigh is involved? The sneaky, slimy toe-rag! I'm amazed he found the time, since he's usually so busy sucking up to the Queen,' spat Drake disgustedly.

'Aye… now listen here, obviously I'd like tae blast ma twin out of the water but, as Miranda is on board, I cannae be doin' that… so, I thought we'd bait him like we did the Spanish Armada.'

Drake looked up wistfully. 'That was a grand battle if ever there was…'

Red interrupted him; he didn't have time to reminisce about past battles. 'I'll sneak up behind and while you're taunting him, I'll make ma move.'

'How are you going to do that without being seen?' asked Drake.

'Och, dinnae fash yerself aboot that. I've a few tricks up ma sleeve. Once I've rescued Miranda then, by God, blast him with every cannonball ye've got – but no' before I turn the *Scavenger* into a funeral pyre; *his*, with any luck!'

Sheba flew Drake back to his ship and speedily returned as the *Scavenger* was making its way down the Thames to the sea. Red ordered 'Operation Invisible' and the crew got busy throwing magical fabric over the sides of the *Wilderness* which turned her invisible to the naked eye. The sails were adjusted, making them invisible too and the galleon sailed silently towards Red's unsuspecting twin.

MacNoxious was beside himself with fury when he spotted Drake's ship, the *Revenge*. He knew that in the past Drake and Red had been pirates together, plundering Spanish bullion for the Queen. Nasty also knew that he'd been set up. The *Revenge* was too far away for him to order a cannonade, and it was bigger and better equipped than the *Scavenger*, being five hundred tons with a crew of two hundred and fifty.

Miranda was perilously near death. Nasty knew he couldn't afford to let her die; he needed her so that he could carry out his evil plan to control and plunder the world.

'BLAST it!' he bawled. 'BLAST my ruddy twin!'

Limping down to his filthy cabin to check on her, his heart sank when he saw Miranda. Archibald was sitting next to her, wiping her forehead with a cool, damp cloth, trying to bring her temperature down.

Miranda was muttering, 'Maze, got to get to the maze.'

'What's she yabbering on aboot?' snarled Nasty.

'Oh, she is just delirious. Take no notice,' answered the gorilla, secretly reading her thoughts.

'Is she no' getting better?' asked MacNoxious.

Archibald silently shook his head.

'If she dies, you die!' Nasty snarled, eyeballing the gorilla as he left.

'Ignore him,' said Archibald to Miranda. 'Listen, Miranda, you have to get better, you must fight this illness. I've let Red know where you are – his ship is on the way.'

Miranda opened one eye drowsily and saw the hazy shape of Archibald. Wondering if she was dreaming, or if he was actually sitting next to her, she tried to sit up, but she was too weak to even lift her head.

'It's all right, I won't hurt you,' soothed Archibald.

Miranda tried to answer but her mouth felt dry and full of sand. Archibald got a glass of water and, gently lifting her head, trickled some into her gasping mouth.

The gorilla sensed the *Wilderness* closing in on them. Wrapping a blanket around Miranda, he cautiously lifted her up and padded silently out of the cabin. Looking left and right, he made his way up to the deck. Luckily, everyone was at the front of the ship keeping an eye on the *Revenge*. Hiding behind one of the longboats, Archibald waited patiently.

Like thieves in the night, Red and his crew climbed silently on board. Ress-up and Mad-Mo immediately got to work. Ress-up, dressed entirely in black, sneaked down the side of the galleon and quietly picked up a barrel of gunpowder, leaving a trail of it in his wake ready to be lit later. Mad-Mo strategically placed different types of fireworks all over the back of the ship.

Archibald bravely stepped out from his hiding place with Miranda in his arms and, within a split second, he was surrounded. Red raised his hand to stop any further action and stepped forward. As they stared at each other, Red saw the remorse in the gorilla's eyes. Red nodded his head in gratitude and reached out to take Miranda – just as Weasel appeared.

Staring in disbelief at Archibald's betrayal, Weasel opened his mouth to raise the alarm but Fearless speedily rammed a tennis ball in his mouth and touched a spot on his neck, causing the pirate to crumple down like a leaf. Red quickly handed Miranda over to Soaring Eagle and told him to get Sheba to transport them both back to the *Wilderness* to begin her healing process. The rest of the crew scattered to find places to hide.

Nasty could be heard shouting for Weasel. 'Where in the blazes is he?'

Turning to Snarl, he ordered him to go and find him. When Snarl didn't come back, he sent another crew member and then and another until there was no one left to send. Nasty had been so preoccupied with the *Revenge*, which was now slowly heading straight towards them, that he hadn't noticed all of his crew had disappeared.

Suddenly, firecrackers were bouncing along the deck and Catherine wheels were spinning, lighting up the sails.

'What in Hades is goin' on?' screamed Nasty. Twisting around on his peg, he speedily hopped out of the way of a sizzling rocket, which was heading straight towards him.

'I'll tell ye what's going on,' snarled Red, stepping out of a cloud of green smoke, 'ye've been had and now ye're goin' down.'

He laughed and gave a shrill whistle.

Sheba swept back in. 'Foiled again, Nasty,' she tittered happily. With that, she lowered herself to the deck and Red eased himself on.

Nasty scuttled forward in fury, hoping to wrestle his twin off the carpet but Sheba tauntingly moved out of reach and infuriated him even more by blowing him a kiss. Nasty screamed with venom and lunged again but a cannonball from Drake's ship tore into the side of the *Scavenger*, throwing him to the deck. As Red and Sheba flew off, more gunpowder exploded, turning the *Scavenger* into an enormous floating bonfire. The rest of Red's crew made a quick exit and climbed back onto the *Wilderness*.

* * *

Red was in his cabin sitting next to Miranda, hoping and praying for her speedy recovery. Archibald stood in the shadows, nervously wondering what his fate held in store.

Soaring Eagle was deep in concentration as he laid his hands over Miranda. She felt as though a hundred angels were stroking her with their wings. A warm, tingling, golden glow enveloped her, healing every cell in her body.

Slowly, she could feel herself rising through layers of rainbow-coloured mist until she regained consciousness. She sat up groggily, smiled weakly and then lay back down again. 'I just had the most terrifying dream. I dreamt I nearly got hanged and I ended up in the Tower of London! I don't remember much after that, except I'm sure I could smell Archibald's expensive aftershave.'

Miranda sniffed the air and sat bolt upright. 'I can still smell it,' she gasped fearfully.

Archibald stepped forward and gave her a nod. Miranda stared, open-mouthed with shock.

'It's all right, lass, if it wasn't for Archibald here, goodness knows where ye could be r-right noow,' explained Red. Miranda was totally confused by now. 'That wasn't a dream, lassie – ye were indeed locked up!'

Miranda closed her eyes, trying to recall what she'd been through. Slowly but surely, her memory returned. 'Maze!' she suddenly yelled. 'I've got to find a maze, if I'm to find what I seek. I think that's what the strange old man said,' she mumbled, rubbing her head as different recollections tumbled in and out of her mind.

'What man?' asked Red, instantly alert.

'Some peculiar old man with turquoise eyebrows. He seemed to know who I was... One minute he was there and the next – gone, just like that!' she said, snapping her fingers.

Red's eyes lit up. 'The crafty old devil... Well, the only maze I knoow aboot is at Hampton Court.'

Suddenly, the door flew open and the rest of the crew burst in, overjoyed to see Miranda sitting up.

Mad-Mo was first on the bed. 'We thought you were a gonner,' he said, fighting back tears of relief.

Soon they were all crowding around, hugging her and cheering.

'R-right, this calls for a celebr-ration,' said Red, jumping up. 'Soaring Eagle, go and inform Dr-rake and Shakespeare that they are formally invited to get down and boooogie!'

* * *

It was a night to remember. Sly conjured up a magnificent feast of Elizabethan fare and Ress-up blasted the River Thames with everything from calypso to hip-hop. Shakespeare and Sir Francis Drake had never heard anything quite like it. Once he'd got used to it, Shakespeare was very taken with the rapping. Drake, on the other hand, thought it all appalling and stuffed bits of cotton wool in his ears.

Miranda thought this an opportune moment to ask Red his exact age. Getting up and strutting back and forth, rapper style, this was his reply:

I'm as auld as the sea
And forever I'll be
Sailing the mighty ocean

I'm as auld as the wind
And I've been everything
And seen every sight to be seen

I'm as auld as the earth
And I've travelled her girth
Questing for truth and justice

And I've come to the conclusion
That it's all an illusion
So it's best not to take it too SERIOUSLY!'

Roaring with laughter, he sat back down.

Miranda nudged him in the ribs again, 'No, I'm serious; I know you're very old, but how old exactly?'

'I told ye, I've been around since time began.'

Mad-Mo, brimming over with excitement and relief, leapt up in the air and shouted: 'All's well that ends well!'

Shakespeare stood up and raised his glass. 'Yes my boy, you are right! All is well that ends well!' After that, he set about writing down Mad-Mo's words.

'Why, boy, I can feel a play coming on.' He sat down, stroking his beard, 'Mmm, all's well that ends well… by God, that's going to be the title!'

Looking as though puffs of smoke were coming out of the sides of his head, Drake sat with a pained expression, begrudgingly tapping his foot to the beat. Miranda wandered over and sat next to him, asking him how he knew Red.

Screwing up his eyes, Drake leant forward and took out the cotton wool.

'Pardon?' he asked.

'How do you know Red?' she yelled.

'We used to plunder the Spanish galleons carrying silver and gold from the South Americas.'

'You didn't!'

'Of course we did. After all, they stole it in the first place! Red, of course, returned his share to its rightful owners. I, on the other hand, am not nearly so generous.'

By now, other old friends and a few rowdy gatecrashers had arrived via the numerous water-taxis that ran back and forth across the Thames, and Monsieur Le Grand was teaching them how to line dance up and down the deck.

'Of course, defeating the Spanish Armada was one of our finer moments,' Drake declared wistfully.

'The Spanish Armada – do you mean to say that Red was involved in that? So, how come he's never mentioned in the history books? He seems to have known everyone of importance throughout history.'

'Heads of state, royalty and anyone else of importance can't be seen cavorting with time-travelling rogues. And this, of course, suits them well as they can then reap all the praise and glory for themselves,' said Drake.

'That doesn't seem fair,' said Miranda.

Drake nodded in agreement and wandered off in search of Red.

Out of the corner of her eye she noticed Archibald, sitting on his own. She had also noticed that nobody had spoken to him since his return. In fact, all of them, except for Red, were going out of their way to avoid him. Miranda got up, dodging her way through the over-zealous dancers and sat down quietly next to him. After a while, she put her fingers round his simian hand and gave it a squeeze. Archibald nodded solemnly as he looked down at her, and gently squeezed her hand in return.

'Thanks for saving my life,' she said, smiling up at him.

The gorilla grunted.

'What made you do it?'

He shrugged his broad shoulders. 'I don't know… I looked into your frightened, sick eyes and then I looked at Nasty – and suddenly I *hated* him. I thought of Red and how just and fair he is and I realised I'd made a massive mistake. Not only that, I owed you one for saving my life. There's something about you, Miranda, that reaches into the heart and I felt mine begin to melt,' he said softly.

They both sat there in quiet contemplation amongst the razzmatazz of party-goers, both lost in their thoughts. Archibald's mind was filling up with long-forgotten, loving memories of his childhood and family. A light flickered in his soul, growing brighter by the second. One solitary joyous tear trickled down his worn, leathery face, whilst Miranda, swinging her legs back and forth, pondered on the human heart and its capacity to both love and hate.

13

Maze on Fire

The following morning, the only people feeling bright and full of good cheer were Red and Miranda. The rest of the revellers were skulking around, moaning and groaning, clutching ice packs to their throbbing temples.

The night before, Sly had dreamt that he was a hamster; the dream felt so real that he was having great difficulty in coming to terms with his tail, wondering how it got there. He was waddling up and down the deck proclaiming, 'To be or sh-not to be, that is the question.'

'W-w-what did you just say?' asked Shakespeare, who was sprawled across a barrel.

'To be or sh-not to be…' repeated Sly.

'To be or not to be… what?' asked the playwright.

'In my case, a shl-hamster… or is it a rat?' he mumbled to himself, getting more and more confused by the second.

Shakespeare leapt up. 'Yes, that's it!' he yelled, 'I have found the opening line for Act III, Scene I, of my new play, *Hamlet!*'

Turning to Sly, he slapped him on the back. 'I can't thank you enough, my good rat.' He trotted off, uttering,

'To be or not to be? That is the question. Whether 'tis nobler in the mind to suffer the slings and arrows of outrageous fortune, or to take arms against a sea of troubles, and by opposing end them?' He was absolutely delighted because the opening scene had been bothering him greatly.

Red was reproaching everyone for drinking too much the night before. He, of course, rarely touched a drop. For the life of him, he couldn't understand why people would do such a thing to themselves. Why anyone would want to make themselves sick, behave like a blithering idiot, and then wake up feeling thoroughly wretched the next day was totally beyond his comprehension. 'Looks like I'll have to sail up the Thames to Hampton Court by maself,' he laughed, as more moans and groans were heard.

However, by the time they'd arrived, everyone was feeling much better. Shakespeare had stayed on board, frantically penning his new play and Drake was boring the pants off Mad-Mo with his tales of past adventures which he'd heard many times before. Red chuckled at Mad-Mo's jaded expression and saved him by telling him to drop the anchor because they'd arrived.

Miranda sidled up to Mad-Mo. 'I have no intention of meeting that pasty-faced old bag,' she declared, referring to Queen Elizabeth. 'Anyone who'd let a young girl be hanged because she couldn't afford to pay for a doctor ought to be hanged themselves.'

'Innit,' agreed Mad-Mo.

'That's no way to refer to your Queen,' said Drake, highly affronted.

'She may be your queen, but she certainly isn't mine. My Queen – Elizabeth II – is lovely, and she'd never allow something like that to happen,' said Miranda defiantly.

Drake walked away, muttering that children should *not* be seen and *definitely* not heard.

The crew were all dressed up in their finery. Even Sly had managed to put on a pair of tights, exposing his skinny legs and knobbly knees. He resembled an enormous Easter egg fit to crack. Miranda had rebelliously dressed as a pirate. No way was she going to put on all that clobber just to impress *that* old tyrant.

'Miranda, I thought ye might have made more of an effort tae meet the Queen,' said Red, eyeing her tatty, dishevelled state. He, of course, was in full Scottish regalia.

'I don't want to meet *her*, I'd rather meet Genghis Khan,' she growled.

'That can quite easily be arr-ranged,' he said, with a twinkle in his eye. 'Noow, we're no' going anywhere until ye've put on some decent clothing.'

'Come on, daaarling, I'll help you,' said Sheba.

Miranda finally appeared looking every inch an Elizabethan young lady, with only her face betraying her true feelings; her mouth was turned down and her nose was puckered up. Snorting and snuffling with righteous anger, she stomped behind Red.

Having flown in on Sheba, they all disembarked and headed towards the Castle. Miranda's bad mood hadn't lessened in the slightest. In fact, she now had a raging storm in her heart as the injustices of Elizabethan life swirled around her head.

'What is your pr-roblem?' asked Red, slightly bemused by her bad mood.

'It's her and this place… this time in history,' she replied heatedly.

'Who's HER?'

'HER! – that lives in THERE!' she said, pointing to Hampton Court.

'Ye mean Good Queen Bess?'

'Good! What's good about her? Did you see those women wearing those metal-type helmets with a bit that goes in their mouths which stabs their tongue if they try to speak? Only a man could invent that! And what is so fantastic about hanging a young girl for trying to save her baby brother?' Miranda was really on a roll now, and Red patiently let her finish.

'And… and… and the fact you can't wear what you want… and the place stinks. Any Queen who allows all that cannot possibly be called GOOD!'

'I quite agree,' said a shrill voice.

Looking around, Miranda came face to face with Her Majesty. *I'm dead – I'm dead – dead – dead*, she thought, imagining the rough rope around her neck. She felt her throat constricting, and Red's rough hands pushing her down into a curtsey. She prayed for an earthquake so she could disappear into a hole and after a few seconds, Red finally let her rise.

'Lizzie,' he said, 'I'm ashamed tae introduce ye tae ma wee gr-randdaughter here.'

The queen's courtiers gasped in horror; nobody had ever addressed the Queen like that!

With a hint of a smile, she waved them all away and linked arms with the mighty Notorious Red MacNaughty. 'I'll be quite safe with Red here to protect me.'

'But Your Majesty, this is most irregular,' protested a burly-looking man with a ruddy complexion.

'Did you not hear me the first time?' she replied, steely-voiced.

'B-but…'

'BUT NOTHING!' she snapped, glaring icily at them all.

Thee courtiers walked away hesitantly, terrified that Red might poison the Queen's mind with new and unsettling ideas.

Looking at Miranda, she said, 'You're right; some of our practices are barbaric but, alas, I'm surrounded by a bunch of buffoons who are forever opposing me. It's a man's world, my child, and I am but a lone woman, trying my best to educate them.' Smiling up at Red, she added: 'And if you don't mind, I'd like to speak to your grandfather alone while we have the chance and are free of prying eyes. Feel free to roam the grounds.' And with that, she waved them away and led Red off.

'COR,' exclaimed Mad-Mo, 'I thought you were definitely a gonner then,' he said, bursting into peals of giggles.

'Me too,' squeaked Miranda in relief, 'I swear I could actually feel the noose around my neck.'

'You should have seen the look on your face when you realised it was the Queen, and that she'd heard what you'd said!'

Laughing hysterically with relief, they both collapsed on the ground, Finally, jumping to her feet, she said, 'C'mon on, we've a maze to explore.'

'I'm tired,' moaned Mad-Mo, who hadn't been to bed yet.

'Serves you right for showing off all night,' replied Miranda, marching off.

He didn't dare let her out of his sight and reluctantly followed her.

'What's the matter with you? I'd have thought you'd jump at the idea,' she said with surprise.

'Listen, everywhere you go, trouble follows, and I'm fed up and would like at least one day off.'

'I quite agree,' piped in Orphia, wanting to eavesdrop on the Queen and have a good snoop around the castle.

'Well, buzz off then,' said Miranda, storming off.

Mo knew that Red would have his guts for garters if he left her, and dragged himself behind. Orphia, on the other hand, thought she'd whizz through the castle in no time at all and promptly disappeared.

* * *

The grounds were huge; peacocks strutted around here and there, fanning their magnificent plumage, shrieking their mournful cries. Gardeners were busily tending the borders whilst young boys scurried around, pushing wooden wheelbarrows filled with manure from the stables.

'Cor, fancy owning all this; it would take you six months to get round it all,' said Mad-Mo, trying to take it all in. 'You could wake up in a different bed every day of the year, I bet,' he added, now straggling behind Miranda, who was marching ahead like a sergeant major.

'Can't stop to look or talk,' she barked, 'I'm on a mission.'

The revelries from the night before were starting to catch up with Mad-Mo. His pace became slower and slower, until he finally staggered to a halt. Spotting a particularly inviting tree with the perfect indent for his body at the base of the trunk, he sat down and made himself comfortable, thinking it would only be for a second or two. With his eyes drooping, he thought, 'What's the harm? Nasty's been foiled… ZZZzzzzzz… '

Miranda, realising she was alone, felt relieved to be on her own for once. She skipped happily to the maze, enjoying the warm sun and fresh air. The scenery was lovely and she was delighted to be out of London. *Life would be even better if I didn't have to wear all this clobber*, she thought, and stepped out of her hooped skirt, leaving it in a heap.

The maze was smaller than she imagined. Peering around to make sure she was alone, she slipped through the entrance. *Now what did that man say… feel your way… what does he mean by that, I wonder?* Getting increasingly annoyed with all the dead ends, she wondered when she was finally going to reach the middle. *And what if the poem is not there when I arrive?*

Miranda was so busy scurrying around, she failed to notice that the sun was fading and that there was a chill to the air. She found herself back at the entrance and let out a scream of frustration. The peacocks responded with their cries.

The scream woke up Mad-Mo. Sitting up and rubbing his eyes groggily, he wondered where he was. With the realisation that he was in the grounds of Hampton Court and that the scream was probably Miranda's, he leapt to his feet, almost sobbing in panic. 'Oh my days! Oh my days!' he whimpered, running around in circles, terrified of Red's wrath when he discovered that he'd fallen asleep. Flying towards where he thought the scream had come from, he found the maze – and Miranda's abandoned clothes. Crumpling down to the ground with his head in his hands, he wailed, 'I'M DEAD!'

'Who's dead?' asked Miranda, stepping out of the entrance.

Nearly jumping out of his skin, Mad-Mo leapt up and spun around to find that Miranda had only her undergarments on. He covered his eyes with embarrassment and growled, 'Get ya clothes on.'

'I'm hardly naked,' she said, pointing to her long cotton pantaloons and chemise.

Staggering about with relief that she was safe, he felt like thumping her.

'Oh, so you weren't worried that *I* might be dead, just yourself,' she said teasingly.

Both their stomachs grumbled at the same time.

'I'm starving,' groaned Mad-Mo.

'So am I,' said Miranda, fishing out her lunchbox. 'So what's it to be?'

'Ooooh, I've had a right craving for a chicken tagine recently,' he said, licking his lips.

'What's that?'

'It's done in this special Moroccan clay pot with a pointy lid, which you bake in the oven. The chicken is cooked with apricots or dates and vegetables, all simmering in delicious juices. My mum used to make it before she died; we'd have it with couscous… it was wonderful.'

Miranda was shocked to find his mother had passed away: he'd never mentioned it before. 'I'm sorry to hear about your mother… '

'S'all right, I don't remember her much; I was four at the time... though I'll never forget her cooking a tagine.'

'I thought you said you ran away from home.'

'Oh, I meant the children's home I was in.'

Miranda sat quietly, imagining what he'd been through. A wave of homesickness bubbled up inside her as she thought of her warm, loving, eccentric family. *Perhaps Karmela could foster him*, she thought, realising just how lucky she was. Looking at his cheeky face, she felt her heart welling up with tenderness for her new friend.

Snapping out of her thoughts, she got back to the problem of what to eat. Fervently wishing for a delicious chicken tagine with couscous and bread, she was amazed when a beautifully painted pot appeared, steaming and bubbling. Mad-Mo took a deep breath, savouring all the delicious, different-smelling herbs and spices. 'Aaawww!' he smiled, his eyes filled with tears as he was overcome with emotion. 'Cor, thanks!'

Miranda, secretly delighted that she'd made him happy, went and fetched her skirt and laid it on the ground for them to sit on. They both tucked in, eating ravenously, happily mopping up the juices with the bread and gleefully licking their fingers and smacking their lips. After they had finished, Mad-Mo lay down and, feeling thoroughly satisfied, he closed his eyes.

'What do you think you're doing?' snapped a sharp voice.

'Digesting my food, of course,' he replied drowsily.

'Oh no you're not, get up – now!' ordered Miranda.

Thinking that she was like a dog with a bone, he stood up reluctantly and followed her into the maze.

The bushes were casting dark shadows as they tried to find the right turns. Mad-Mo began to make ghostly noises and kept leaping out from behind the bushes, trying to frighten her.

'You just can't help yourself, can you?' she grumbled, wishing he'd grow up and disappear.

'Shush, I think I heard something,' he whispered, wide-eyed, listening intently.

'Very funny!' she said sarcastically.

'No, I mean it... listen... '

An uneasy feeling crept into Miranda's stomach.

By her expression, he knew he was getting to her and he burst out laughing. 'Gotcha…' he grinned mischievously.

Miranda felt like giving him a dead leg. 'OOH, BOYS!' she exploded, 'You are *so* annoying… just for once, can't you be serious?'

'All right, all right,' he said, putting up his palms. 'What are we looking for exactly?'

'The next poem, you twit,' she said, getting more and more exasperated.

'So where is it then?'

'Well if I knew that, I'd already have it… Plonker!'

'There's no need to be insulting,' he said, feeling a little hurt.

'Mo… JUST GET LOST, before I burst a blood vessel. I can't concentrate with you around.'

'Tell you what, why don't I go and stand guard at the entrance.'

'Good idea.'

Mad-Mo bounded away like a puppy chasing a ball.

* * *

Now that she was alone, Miranda sat cross-legged on the ground and got out her meditation balls. Rolling them around in her hands, she felt a quietness envelop her. The sky had turned a glorious pink, with ribbons of orange floating across the horizon. Larks swooped overhead and cows could be heard mooing in the distance as they made their way back to the fields from the evening milking.

She stood up as if in a dream and began to walk slowly, letting her intuition lead the way. Before she knew it, she had reached the centre of the maze without once coming to a dead end. She stopped and, with her hands tingling, she moved towards the hedge, her fingers beginning to tremble. Instinctively, she got out her knife and started digging. A smell of burning wafted through the air. Thinking it was just the gardeners having a small bonfire, she carried on. She was so busy digging that she didn't notice the smell of the sea and stale tobacco, mingling with smoke. And, because she was bending down, her pendant had swung forward so she didn't feel it heating up... nor did she notice the serpent's tongue flickering in and out.

Suddenly she found something! A small box! But, just then, she found herself shrouded in darkness, making it hard for her to see. 'Oh blast, it must be a rain cloud,' she said, looking up to see that the rain cloud was in the form of a rectangle and had a beautiful pattern on it... Then she realised that the air around her was becoming thick with smoke and she could now hear the sound of crackling branches. As she started coughing and spluttering, it all suddenly fell into place. It wasn't a rain cloud – it was Salome! And the crackling and smoke was coming from the maze – it was on fire!

At the entrance to the maze Mad-Mo could smell the smoke and was running around, totally panic-stricken. However hard he tried to get into the maze, the flames held him back. He didn't want to leave Miranda, but at the same time he knew he had to run for help. Beginning to cough up black smoke, he tried to call out to her, but the roaring fire drowned out his voice.

* * *

Red and the crew were in the Queen's parlour, discussing politics and the state of the nation. Red, Chow Yen and Archibald simultaneously tuned in to Nasty's presence and when they looked out of the window they could see that the maze was ablaze! Archibald was the first out of the room. Red leapt up and opened a window, allowing Soaring Eagle to fly out, with Chow Yen quickly following Archibald.

Soaring Eagle was the first there. He changed back into his human form and immediately wove his magic, creating a small tropical rain cloud that burst with huge drops of water. But it had been a dry summer and the maze was now a roaring furnace; the rain hardly made a difference. Workers were running with pails of water, trying to douse the flames.

Nasty – perched on Salome – looked on menacingly. 'It's Uncle Nasty to the rescue,' he sang.

Miranda had the box she'd discovered in her hand and, clutching it tightly, she spun around looking for an escape route. The heat of the fire was getting closer and closer; she could feel beads of perspiration forming on her forehead.

'Grab ma hand and I'll save ye,' cajoled Nasty.

'I'd rather burn than let you get hold of me!' she yelled.

'Be ma guest!' he roared furiously, at the same time a little worried that she might actually mean it; he most certainly didn't want that to happen.

Archibald had thrown a sodden blanket over himself and with a large machete he charged the hedge of the maze, slashing his way through the burning branches until he reached Miranda. Sweeping her up in his powerful arms, he selflessly covered her from head to toe in the wet blanket, not caring that his scratched hands, face and already burnt fur were left totally exposed. Crouching down and protecting her with his body he carefully made his way back, ignoring the sparks of fire and burning branches which were falling on him and setting his clothes on fire.

Nasty hadn't reckoned on the maze burning so fiercely and he couldn't get close enough to Archibald to stop him. Roaring with fury, he cursed, vowing revenge against the gorilla, screaming that his days were numbered and that he was going to experience the worst type of death imaginable.

Ignoring him, Archibald broke free from the maze and ran, panting, trying desperately to ignore the pain he was suffering. Gently placing Miranda on the ground, he threw himself down next to her and rolled on his back to douse the flames.

Mad-Mo quickly drew his boomerang and threw it at Nasty, catching a corner of Salome's weave as she made her way towards Archibald. Salome spun out of control, rapidly wheeling down towards the burning maze.

Hanging on with all his might, Nasty looked horrified, as they fell. This time he had no back-up and nowhere to run. Just before she hit the ground Salome, with a high-pitched screech, managed to regain her balance and she shot straight up... causing the evil pirate to lose his grip and slide off. He tumbled to the ground, his roars filling the air. By now, the Queen's guards had encircled the maze and there, in the middle, lay Nasty, grunting and groaning, savagely beating at the leaping flames.

Both Archibald and Miranda were lying on the ground, surrounded by the crew. Archibald was covered in burns; his skin was blistered and most of his fur had been burnt away. Although he didn't utter one complaint, his eyes revealed the pain he was in. Soaring Eagle quickly got out his magical salve and gently covered the gorilla's body. Soon, the blisters were drying up and falling off. His fur was going to take some time to grow back but he felt much better already.

Miranda unravelled the blanket and threw herself at him. 'I'd be burnt to a cinder if it wasn't for you,' she sobbed, in between spluttering and coughing up smoke.

Stroking her hair, he whispered, 'It's the least I could do. I needed to put right my wrongs.'

'But your fancy clothes are now burnt rags,' she cried.

'Unlike you, they can be replaced,' he smiled. 'Anyway, in the greater scheme of things they now seem rather immaterial.'

The Queen arrived and gasped when she saw the maze, which was now just burnt stumps. Spotting Nasty in the middle, rolling around in agony, she ordered: 'Lock him in the tower and throw away the key!'

Red knelt down by Miranda, his eyes alive with questions. Slowly, she withdrew the box. Putting his index fingers to his lips, he slipped the box into his sporran. He didn't have to say anything; his expression told her how proud he was of her and how magnificent he thought she was.

She leant over and whispered in his ear, 'Red, let's just get the hell out of here, I don't like this place one bit.'

'Your wish is my command,' he whispered back. Getting up, his weary, timeless body ached. Taking one last look at Nasty, who was being dragged away, his head now encased in an iron mask, Red knew in his heart that he hadn't seen the last of him. He took Queen Elizabeth aside and explained it was time to leave and that on no account was his twin to be released, if that was possible. But deep down, Red knew his twin would not stay locked up for long.

Sailing back down the River Thames towards the *Wilderness*, Miranda saw that the prisoners she'd seen when they'd first arrived were still there... and still alive. Then, as he had promised, Red managed to release them and gave them money so that they could flee the city.

* * *

Back on board the galleon Red took out the box Miranda had found, opened it and saw that it contained Sarakuta's next poem. He looked at it quickly and then told the crew to set sail. Soon they were passing through an opening into yet another dimension... just in time to see Stavros flying out of it. Spotting the *Wilderness*, he flew down and crashed into a crate of cannonballs. Lurching to his feet, he staggered around dizzily.

'Flaming, exploding-cannon-balls!' he gasped. 'It's my bifocals,' he said, removing his glasses. 'So what time does the play start and at which of her residences are we to meet the Queen?'

'You're too late... again,' said Miranda, giggling at the look of confusion on the albatross's face.

'Well, if it hadn't been for that ugly, scrawny vulture who sent me flying in the opposite direction, I might have got here sooner. I guess he suffers from the same navigational problems as I do.'

Red immediately realised that Stavros had met Scabies, and that *that* was how Nasty had found out that they were going to Elizabethan London. He was beginning to think that Stavros should be put to sleep – for eternity.

14

Mer Island

The dimension they'd just entered was shrouded in fog. Miranda popped down to Red's cabin and grabbed a warm jumper as the temperature had dropped considerably. By the time she'd returned, the fog had thickened so much she could hardly see her hands in front of her.

'Hello… is there anybody there?' she called out.

'I'm over by the wheel,' shouted Red.

Miranda edged her way forward until she was practically on top of him. She could hear Lucille singing in the distance; it sounded as though she was singing to the dolphins, Dolphus and Delilah, who had joined them.

The place had an eerie, disturbing quality to it, made more so by Lucille's mournful voice. Miranda shivered, the unnatural stillness and silence scaring her. The *Wilderness*, groaning and creaking, slowly made her way, the waves gently lapping her sides. Miranda felt as though she was sailing on a haunted ocean, shivering again at the thought.

'Where are we?' she asked.

'We're tr-rapped in another dimension.'

'Ooh… it's a bit spooky.'

'Aye, it is indeed… but dinnae fash, as soon as the fog clears I'll be able to find a suitable exit point.'

'This place gives me the creeps; it feels like a burial ground,' she said, hunching her shoulders and crossing her arms.

'Aye… that's because it is, hen! This is where all the sunken boats and dead sailors come to rest before they go on to their next journey. It's called the Sea of Lost Souls.'

Suddenly, Miranda felt an icy breeze whip past her face and she saw a ghoulish apparition fly by. The more she looked, the more spectres she saw. The place was awash with ghosts flying in and out of the fog.

'Red,' whispered Miranda, wanting to scream but terrified they'd hear, 'the place is full of ghouls.'

'Dinnae fash, they cannae see ye. They're searching for their families.' Red pulled her close, wrapping a big blanket around her.

Miranda looked out into the fog. 'How can you see where you're going?' she asked.

'Oh, the dolphins are navigating the way by using their sonar; that strange noise ye can hear is them communicating with Lucille, who then sings to the *Wilderness*, telling her where to sail. Aye, they have a real special relationship, those four.'

'You mean, this galleon can communicate with Lucille?'

'Of course,' he replied.

'But ships can't talk, Red. They are inanimate objects that don't possess a mind or a soul.'

'Who told yooo that? I can assure yooo that this here mighty ship has a mind *and* a soul of her own! Ye can tr-rust me on that one. And she dinnae take too kindly to people thinking otherwise.'

Miranda sat down and thought about what Red had just told her. She felt Orphia waft by. 'This place gives me the creeps! It reminds me of the Haunted Ocean,' complained Orphia.

'It's the Sea of Lost Souls!' said Miranda.

'Well, in that case I'm outta here!' Miranda felt her brush past and disappear.

Strange, haunting noises drifted through the fog. The ghouls were howling, desperately crying out for their loved ones; screeching their anguished pleas to be released from this shadowy graveyard.

Lucille began to sing a gentle lullaby, hoping to ease their suffering, and the murmurings soon subsided.

A bell could be heard ringing in the distance.

'Why is the bell ringing?' Miranda asked.

'Ah! The bell rings when another sailor has died, or a ship has sunk… God rest their souls,' Red replied.

Miranda couldn't wait to get away from the Sea of Lost Souls; it was starting to chill her blood as more anguished cries howled forth. Another sound could be heard drifting over the sea, but this was a voice as beautiful as Lucille's, and was singing the same lullaby.

'Red, who's that singing? It's not Lucille.'

'It soonds like another mermaid has lost her way.'

Patches of fog slowly began to clear revealing ancient, weary, war-torn shipwrecks with tattered sails, broken masts and gaping holes where cannonballs had blasted through the sides. A huge sadness invaded Miranda's heart; she felt the loss and grief for these sailors and their families and friends.

Red and Miranda made their way over to Lucille, whose excitement was mounting as they approached the source of the singing.

'I swear that's my granddaughter, Olivia. I'd know her singing anywhere!' cried Lucille. 'Oh, look! There she is!'

Sitting on a rock up ahead was the most dazzling, honey-brown young mermaid. She had a mass of black curly hair, entwined with fresh water pearls and bright coral. Her large eyes were dark brown, her lips were pale pink and luscious. It was her tail, however, that created the biggest impact. The Mer-people could change the colour and patterns of their tails at will and were highly competitive when it came to showing off their creations – and Olivia's was the swankiest multi-coloured tail imaginable!

'WOW!' was all Miranda could say.

'Bling-a-ding-ding, she's beautiful,' said Mad-Mo, his eyes out on stalks.

'Olivia, what on earth are you doing here?!' asked Lucille.

'Well, I was on my way to the annual Mer-ball at Mer Island. Of course, I was late as usual, when I got caught in a giant bubble. It eventually popped and I found myself here and, let me tell you, it's not very nice.'

Olivia spotted Red and waved. 'Why, if it isn't Uncle Red! I hope you're well?' she called.

'Why, if it isn't ma favourite mermaid. Ye're looking mighty bonnie! That's a right cr-racking tail ye have there – most imaginative.'

'I know, I hope to win the Best Tail Competition.'

'Did I hear ye mention the wor-rd Mer-ball? Because that's where we're off tae, as soon as I can find a suitable exit point. So ye can swim along with us and we'll escort you to the ball in style.'

Lucille, Olivia and the dolphins carried on swimming until Red spotted a suitable place to make their departure. He stood up and lifted his arms and, when a gap suddenly appeared, steered them through into a magnificent sunset on the other side.

'How do you know we're off to the Mer-ball?' asked Miranda.

'Look at this,' Red replied, taking out the piece of parchment from the box Miranda had found in the maze and handing it to her.

The Isle of Mer, the mermaids agreed,
Is where you need to be.
A poem awaits so make sure you're not late
For instructions on how to proceed.

The Weird Fate of Miranda Wyrd

* * *

By now, the *Wilderness* was surrounded by Mer-people gracefully leaping and diving through the turquoise water. They were all heading in the same direction, joined by small bands of dolphins, frolicking in the water and joining in the fun.

Miranda and Mad-Mo were leaning over the sides, trying to get a better look at the fabulous Mer-people. Each tail was unique in colour and pattern; glorious iridescent colours that Miranda had never seen before flashed before them.

Red came and stood next to them. 'It's a mighty gr-rand sight, is it no'?'

'Red, they're beautiful but where are they going?' she asked. 'There's nothing out there except the deep blue sea,' she added, hoping the island would soon appear.

Then something very strange happened: the Mer-people were disappearing. One minute they were there, and the next they were gone. It was as if they'd slipped through an invisible wall.

'Where have they gone?' shouted Mad-Mo, feeling a bit let down by their disappearance.

Laughing, Red replied, 'Wait and see.'

Soon, the front of the ship began to vanish as well. Slowly, the rest of the galleon followed. Mad-Mo was standing a couple of metres in front of Miranda with his mouth agape and then, suddenly, he too was gone from view.

Mer Island

Miranda gasped but, before she could cry out, she felt a very odd rippling sensation cascade down through her body. It was as if her whole being had turned inside out. Once the feeling had passed, she shook her body and found Mad-Mo standing in front of her, doing the same thing.

'That was totally weird…' he said, grinning from the experience.

'Yeah, but I quite liked it,' said Miranda, feeling the last of the ripples gently fade.

Looking around at their new surroundings, they spotted a rock jutting out of the sea.

'That doesn't look much like an island to me,' said Mo, thoroughly disappointed. He was hoping for some tropical jungle where he could fight and slash his way through, blazing a trail for the rest of the expedition, and lead them to safety to their final destination.

'Aye, it looks plain enough, but don't let that deceive ye,' said Red, who'd joined them. 'The Isle is a bit like an iceberg – most of it being under water – and that's where the Mer-people meet to have their annual ball.

A short time later, after having changed into a pretty summer dress for once, Miranda raced up to the deck to find everyone dressed up in all their finery. Red was wearing his best kilt, with a pair of purple velvet breeches underneath. He also wore a crisp white frilly shirt with a tartan bow-tie and to top it off, a Viking helmet with horns sticking out on either side. Monsieur Le Grand wore his best waistcoat, a feather boa, a pair of cowboy boots with Cuban heels and his crumpled top hat. Mad-Mo appeared looking like Al Capone in a black and white pinstriped suit and black suede trilby.

The *Wilderness* had dropped anchor and everyone was ready to disembark. They could see that scores of Mer-people were swimming towards the mouth of a large cave. Sheba prepared herself to take the crew ashore and called Red, Ress-up and Miranda to climb on first. Ress-up had brought a selection of his instruments with him, including a big double bass. Sheba stretched herself and then off they flew to the Mer-ball.

Miranda was totally awestruck as they entered. Millions of fairy lights lit up the enormous cave, revealing hundreds of pools and colourful lanterns hanging from the roof. Flickering shadows caused by the candles placed in every nook and cranny danced across the walls. Mosaics made from different shells patterned the walls of the cave. Open giant clams were used for seating and large flat shells were used as plates. Beautiful gold goblets were filled with a strange green liquid which the Mer-people drank with great enthusiasm.

In the middle of a large ledge sat Neptune, his trident at his side, his huge, shimmering, multi-coloured tail flapping to the beat of the music.

Everywhere Miranda looked Mer-people were hidden behind exotic masks, laughing and playing with the dolphins. In one particular pool, ten mermaids were doing synchronised swimming, creating patterns that reminded Miranda of lotus flowers.

Sheba flew over to Neptune and dropped the three of them off and then flew back to pick up the others. Neptune's weather-beaten face lit up when he spotted Red, large crevices appearing as his smile formed.

'NOTORIOUS RED MACNAUGHTY,' his voice boomed throughout the cave. 'Gatecrashing as usual, I see. You never could resist a party.'

'Aye, true enough… and you always did throw the very best,' Red replied.

Neptune then turned to Miranda. 'Well, it doesn't take a rocket scientist to work out who you are!' he said, pointing a webbed finger at her. 'I see you take after your mother and grandmother Mimi. I hope you've inherited her sense of humour?'

Miranda nodded her head absently, totally mesmerised by the sight of the small sea snakes and tiny crabs scuttling amongst his long, curling beard.

'You are all most welcome to the Annual Mer-ball,' he boomed. He clapped his hands and an octopus arrived, carrying eight trays laden with food and drink, which were offered to the guests.

Sheba arrived, carrying the rest of the crew and, after she had dropped them off, she presented herself to Neptune and fluttered her eyelashes at him. Sheba just couldn't resist a powerful merman, especially one that ruled the sea.

Red rolled his eyes. *Och, she's a real dollop of tr-rollop*, he thought, watching her cooing and gurgling with pleasure.

Neptune, like Red and Ress-up, was a real music lover and enjoyed a wide range of genres. He was a huge fan of Ress-up and was always delighted to see and hear him play. Before Neptune had even asked, Ress-up was setting up and getting ready to delight the Mer-people.

He magically produced an odd assortment of percussion instruments, which he passed around in case anyone wanted to join in. There were large conch shells, which sounded like horns, and tiny seashells that tinkled when gently tapped. One mermaid sat behind a large harp and was happily plucking away, creating a beautiful melody.

Monsieur Le Grand got out his fold-up chair, climbed onto it and started to play the double bass. Attacking it with great zeal, he imagined he was playing in twentieth-century Paris for his beloved Edith Piaf. Ress-up set up his steel pans, adding a Caribbean flavour to the ball.

The Mer-people danced in the water, leaping up and flashing their glorious tails, their arms gracefully swaying in time to the rhythm.

An octopus approached Miranda and handed her a fortune cookie. Absentmindedly, she broke it open and nibbled a bit of it. As she was wishing that she had brought her swimsuit, she noticed an old piece of parchment poking out of the cookie which looked similar to the other poems.

Her pulse quickened as she eased it out and, unrolling it, she gasped. It was the final poem! *But I haven't done anything yet! How come I've got it now?* she asked herself.

Mer Island

Behind a boulder you must travel
For this last riddle to unravel!
The sight you'll see will make you shiver,
Alone, you'll cross the deadly river.

But when you reach the other side
A bird will come, to be your guide.
It will lead you to a meeting
A special person you'll soon be greeting.

Miranda sat in shocked silence but, at the same time, she was filled with both excitement and dread. This was obviously something she was going to have to do alone. She wondered how she was going to disappear without anyone, including Orphia, noticing.

Red appeared and offered her a bathing suit to change into. 'I thought ye might need this…' he said.

Noticing she looked very distressed, he asked, 'Is anything the matter, hen? You're looking a bit peelie-wally.'

'No, I'm fine,' Miranda lied, 'and I'll be even better when I've found somewhere to change.'

Red pointed to a large boulder. 'Why don't ye pop behind there; that should do it.'

Miranda scrunched up the parchment in order to conceal it from Red. 'I'll be back soon,' she said, slipping behind the boulder.

Sure enough, just as the poem had said, there was the small opening in the cave wall behind the boulder. She stood for a while trying to calm her anxiety. Checking to make sure she still had all her gifts in her rucksack, she grabbed a burning candle and began to ease through the gap.

'Excuse me! Where do you think you're going?' chided Orphia, causing Miranda to nearly jump out of her skin.

'Orphia!' she hissed. 'I wish you wouldn't sneak up on me like that.'

'You haven't answered my question.'

'Well, I'm not allowed to discuss it with anybody.'

'Discuss what, exactly?'

'The fact that I've found the last poem…' As soon as Miranda had uttered those words, she gasped and covered her mouth. 'Now look what you've made me do,' she mumbled crossly.

She could hear Orphia flapping her wings with excitement. 'What does it say?' she asked, her curiosity bubbling up.

'It says I'm not to discuss it with anybody. And I mean *anybody*.'

'But I haven't got a body. I'm your angel-ling, so I don't count,' Orphia breezed.

Miranda was now in a quandary. *Does Orphia count as a person? Since I can't actually see her, I guess not.* Feeling relieved by her decision, Miranda told her angel-ling what was written on the parchment.

'Don't you think we'd better let Red know?'

'No, I don't,' said Miranda, instantly regretting telling her angel-ling. 'I'm meant to do this alone! And alone I shall do it,' she added bravely, continuing to squeeze through the gap in the wall.

'Well, at least I can accompany you and make sure you don't get into too much trouble,' Orphia said, trying to follow Miranda... but the angel-ling couldn't get through. It was as if an invisible barrier was there. Every time she tried, she just bounced off the gap.

However, Miranda hadn't realised that Orphia wasn't with her when she slipped through.

15

The Lost City

Once through the slit in the wall, Miranda entered a tunnel and, crouching down, she kept going. Soon the tunnel opened up, allowing her room to stand. It was dark, musty and cold. She shivered and considered going back to get some warmer clothing but decided against it, thinking she might not be able to return quite so easily.

Holding up the candle and, with every step she took, she wondered if she'd made the right decision. Strange inscriptions and terrifying macabre faces were carved into the walls, made even more sinister by her flickering candle. She could feel their hollow eyes following her every move.

Her hair was starting to rise as menacing whispers and murmurings echoed along the tunnel. *This place gives me the willies!* The passageway echoed her thoughts.

'Orphia, are you there?' Miranda looked around. 'Orphia, where are you?'

Again, only her own words echoed back. Shaking with fear, she kept on going until she reached a door which creaked open before she'd even lifted her hand. Miranda stepped through the door and found herself high up on a ledge, looking down into a vast cave. She gasped in awe at the magnificent sight before her. She could see a city, sculpted out of gigantic stalagmites and stalactites. Thousands of tiny windows sparkled, reflecting light from the glittering crystals that were placed around the immense cave. Layers of multi-coloured crystals covered parts of the buildings and exotic flora bloomed amongst the stalagmites.

The air seemed to shimmer with hints of green and silver. Far below her, she could see a river of what looked like liquid mercury. She realised that this must be the deadly river mentioned in the poem. She knew she had to cross it but there was one enormous problem – the only way across was by stepping on crystal poles that spanned the river. The top of the first pole was about a metre and a half beneath the ledge where she was standing and it was barely wide enough for her foot! The other poles stretched ahead, gradually decreasing in height until they levelled out at the far side of the river.

She peered down over the ledge and instantly felt sick. 'I don't believe it!' she sobbed. 'After everything I've been through... now this!' She crumpled to the ground in utter despair, wondering what to do next.

A breeze whipped up around her, whispering, 'You can do it... feel your way... trust your body... trust your instincts... surrender... surrender...' And then it was gone.

'I can't do it!' she shouted, her voice echoing back and forth throughout the vast cave.

'You can...,' murmured the cave walls.

'I can't…' she wailed.

'You can…,' tinkled the crystals.

'I can't… I can't,' she shouted.

Her echo resounded back, 'You can… you can…'

Fishing for her stone of courage, she sat down, feeling as small as an ant. Overwhelmed by the vast surroundings and the ordeal that lay ahead, she wondered whether or not she should go back. She turned around but, to her surprise and horror, the door had vanished leaving her with no choice but to go forward.

Still gripping her stone of courage, she made sure her bag was secure and made ready for the dangerous crossing. She stood, staring ahead, for what seemed like an eternity. Breathing deeply and rhythmically, she concentrated on the silence that now engulfed her, allowing her mind to expand into infinity. She could feel the energy of the crystals pulsating through her body, causing her cells to glow. She had no thoughts, no internal dialogue, just a serene sense of being in the here and now.

She felt her aura stretching out, feeling its way across the river, gently caressing each pole until it got to the last one. She began to feel a soft pulling sensation in her stomach, as if she was being reeled in by an invisible fishing line.

Her eyes closed and, in a dream-like state, she lowered herself over the ledge and stepped onto the first pole. The pole swayed from side to side, like bamboo in a soothing breeze. Breathing in more and more deeply and balancing on one leg, she waited until the movement stopped.

Stepping onto the next pole, the same thing happened and soon she had developed a rhythm, swaying and stepping, swaying and stepping, each pole slightly lower than the last.

She didn't have to open her eyes to know that she was almost across. It was as if she could see with her entire body instead. Everything was made up of colourful, pulsating energy that she could see in her mind's eye. She now understood how Chow Yen viewed the world, and envied him because it was all so beautiful.

Her foot suddenly hit hard ground. Opening her eyes, and with the realisation that she'd made it across the deadly river, she fell to her knees in gratitude. Looking up, she saw a cloud of dazzling butterflies which scattered like blossoms. A tiny hummingbird appeared, hovering in front of her, beckoning her to follow it.

Feeling as if she was in the twilight zone, Miranda got up and danced behind the bird, twirling like a dervish. The hummingbird flew just fast enough for her to keep up. Peering through windows, she saw evidence of everyday life but no people; the city was empty except for the wildlife. Only the squawk of exotic parrots, the hum of insects and birdsong could be heard. The place had an eerie, haunting quality to it which made her senses swirl.

The hummingbird paused and hovered at a stalagmite, higher than the others, in which there was an ornate, copper door. It guided her through the door into a series of tunnels before finally arriving at a large, square, marble room.

In the centre of the room, sitting on a stone bench, was an elderly man dressed in a long, white robe covered with gold embroidery, clutching a solid crystal staff. He was most peculiar to look at: he had a violet Mohican hairstyle, a vivid green beard and turquoise eyebrows.

He got up and beckoned her over and, looking into his eyes, she had the distinct feeling that they'd met before.

'So Miranda, I'm delighted to be meeting you under more pleasant circumstances,' he said, smiling, his lapis-lazuli blue eyes twinkling. 'Elizabethan prison is far from ideal, don't you think?'

'It *is* you!' she exclaimed. 'You're the one who told me about the maze!'

'Yes, and by the looks of it you have succeeded in your task. Congratulations, my dear, you have shown all of the virtues which were asked of you, except for one – which is yet to come. I am extremely proud of you.'

A sense of pride bubbled up inside Miranda; she hadn't given her trials and tribulations much thought as she was so busy surviving or having fun.

Suddenly, everything fell into place.

'You're my grandfather, Sarakuta!' she said, pointing a finger at him.

'Yes, I am indeed,' he answered, his face breaking into a large creased smile.

Miranda was shocked; she'd thought all sorcerers had long white hair with flowing white beards but he looked more like an ancient, theatrical punk-rocker. *Not another weirdo*, she thought, studying him.

Sarakuta let out a rumbling laugh and said, 'I may appear to be a weirdo, but I'm quite safe really.'

Oh no! Not another mind-reader. I'll have to watch what I think.

'You will indeed,' he chuckled.

'But Red told me you were on a spaceship!'

'I was, but now I'm here and I'm so very delighted to finally catch up with my great, great etc., etc. granddaughter.'

'Does this mean I'm at the end of my journey?' she asked, hoping and praying.

'Not quite,' he replied.

'NOT QUITE?' she cried, dismayed. She felt an overwhelming lethargy invade her being. *I want to go home*, she wailed silently.

'Well,' said Sarakuta, 'you didn't think it was going to be easy, did you?'

Miranda's weariness was rapidly replaced by fury. 'EASY?' she stormed. 'EASY?!' she raged. 'EASY?!' she roared. 'Do you have *any* idea what I've been through?' she bellowed, marching back and forth, wagging a finger at him.

'Absolutely,' he replied calmly, thinking *She's plucky... Good, she needs to be.*

Miranda began to feel numb and stumbled around looking for a place to sit. A comfortable chair magically appeared and she plopped down into the soft, inviting cushions. The lethargy was back and worse. *I haven't got the energy to continue anymore*, she thought, filled with self-pity.

'Miranda, there were five virtues that you had to display and you've shown four. Only one more to go and then you'll nearly be able to go home.'

'What do you mean, *nearly* go home? What else do I have to do?'

'You will have to pick your own special crystal skull. If you pick the wrong one, your journey will be in vain and you won't be able to continue with your quest,' he said gravely.

'Is it going to be difficult? Because I'm on my own now,' she whimpered.

'Miranda, look at what you've accomplished so far. Do you know that you are the *only* person to have crossed the river of mercury and lived to tell the tale?' he stated proudly.

'I AM?' she exclaimed, deciding that if she could survive that, then she was pretty much capable of anything. But then the thought struck her, *I only managed to survive with the help of my gifts and Monsieur Le Grand's remedies.*

'As for the homeopathic pills… they were placebos,' said the sorcerer, reading her mind.

'Placebos, what do you mean?'

'They weren't real, they were sugar pills. And your stone of courage is just an ordinary stone. Your courage was always there – even if you weren't aware of it.'

Miranda felt completely hoodwinked and was very annoyed that she'd been fooled.

'So what's this last trial then?' she asked. 'As you've said, I've shown nearly all the virtues that were necessary.

What else is there?'

'You are required to give up something of great value; something that you feel you couldn't live without.'

'Is that all?' she said, feeling slightly relieved, but also wondering what on earth it could be. She thought about her few possessions – mainly her gifts from the crew – and realised that it wasn't going to be so easy.

Getting up, he said, 'Follow me, there are some people whom you need to meet.'

16

The People of the Crystals

Miranda was terrified at the thought of her last trial. *What if I pick the wrong skull?* Feeling more and more despondent by the second, she dragged her leaden body after the sorcerer and followed him back out to the city.

Sarakuta stepped through the copper doors and the butterflies gathered around him, completely covering his long, white robe and even perching on his hair.

He was amazing in his multi-coloured coat, and looked every inch the powerful Sorcerer. The hummingbird was perched on his little finger and the parakeets and birds of prey circled above his head.

Blimey! And to think we're related, she thought with awe, wondering if she'd grow to love him as much as she loved Red.

As they continued to walk through the Lost City, Sarakuta explained that the People of the Crystals had once lived there, after they were driven underground by humans. They used crystalline technology to power the city and were very advanced compared with humans. He then went on to explain that the People of the Crystals were the ones looking after her skull, and that they were now going to travel to their spaceship.

'SPACESHIP!' she cried. 'Whoa... wicked! How are we supposed to get there?'

'They don't call me the greatest sorcerer for nothing,' he said, with a twinkle in his eye as he strode off.

With the thought of visiting a spaceship on her mind, her worries temporarily disappeared.

Sarakuta led her to the outskirts of the city, until they reached a solid cave wall. Lifting his staff and uttering mysterious words, a gap appeared in the wall. Peeping through, Miranda saw a mountain made of crystals in all shapes and sizes. Some were jutting up as far as a hundred metres high; others were tiny and covered the mountainside like the sparkling crystal moss that covered parts of the city. Sarakuta then informed her that she must climb to the very top of this crystal mountain and that he would meet her afterwards.

'Why?' asked Miranda, her heart sinking.

'You will find out for yourself,' he replied, mysteriously.

As she stepped through the gap, a perfectly carved staircase appeared in the bed of crystals, winding its way around until it reached the top of the mountain. At that moment Miranda would have liked to have been anywhere else but there. However, letting out a heavy sigh, she slowly dragged herself over to the stairs.

But, as her foot touched the first crystal step, she could feel a gentle pulse of energy flowing through her body. It wasn't an unpleasant sensation; it felt as though all the cells in her body were being softly tickled. By the time she'd reached the top, her body felt recharged and she was brimming with energy; all the tiredness that she'd felt earlier had disappeared.

Sarakuta suddenly reappeared in a cloud of smoke, causing Miranda to cough and splutter.

'Do you have to do that?' she asked.

'Do what?' he replied.

'Create all that smoke when you appear.'

'Don't you like my grand entrances?' he asked, in surprise.

'No, it makes me cough and my eyes sting,' she said irritably. 'And what was the point of climbing up *all* those stairs?'

'Isn't it obvious?'

'No,' Miranda grumbled.

'Your energy was flagging and you're going to need all your strength for the next part of your assignment. Climbing the mountain has helped you...'

Miranda suddenly realised that was true: minutes ago she had felt utterly exhausted but now she was positively bubbling with energy.

Sarakuta raised his staff and tapped it on the floor three times and a crystal cylinder rose up before them. Sarakuta stepped into it and waited for Miranda to follow.

'Why are we going in there?' she asked nervously.

'It's a transportation device...'

Miranda looked at him questioningly.

'How else are we supposed to get there? It's quite safe. Trust me,' Sarakuta responded.

Miranda stepped cautiously through the door and joined him. Sarakuta raised his crystal staff and flashes of brilliantly-coloured lights shot forth. Miranda squeezed her eyes shut as her head began to spin; she felt as though her body was liquefying into bubbling champagne. It was the most peculiar feeling.

* * *

Moments later, the sensation stopped. Opening her eyes, she found herself in another crystal cylinder – in an entirely different location.

'I always find dimension-hopping the most pleasurable of experiences,' said Sarakuta, joyfully shaking his body.

The cylinder swung open and the wizard stepped out grandly, with Miranda following him. She was totally amazed by what she saw. She was standing in a large, round glass dome which seemed to be floating in the middle of an oval-shaped spaceship! She looked up and realised that the trillions of sparkling lights above her were the stars and planets of the universe, stretching out into infinity, staggeringly beautiful. She could hardly bear to tear herself away from such a sight but finally turned to look around to where Sarakuta was standing, patiently waiting for her.

The glass dome appeared to go on forever and it was possible to see the entire spaceship from all angles. In the centre of the dome was a huge quartz crystal that pulsed and glowed and, next to it, stood two of the most unusual, most exquisite people she'd ever seen! The taller of the two was obviously male, his skin a pale purple. His robe was the colour of iridescent mauve and the fabric looked like extremely fine chainmail, made up of tiny crystals which shimmered when he moved. His companion was female and she was the colour of orange sorbet. Her dress was the same fabric as the man's but in saffron yellow. They both had long, pointed ears and sharp chins. Their hair was all the colours of the rainbow and their pale amber eyes were filled with kindness.

The male stepped forward and bowed. 'Namaste, it is a pleasure to meet you, Miranda. You are most welcome. We have been waiting a long, long time for this occasion. My name is Niger. I am the leader of the People of the Crystals and this is Saraya, my partner.'

His voice sounded strange and rusty and, when he spoke, a clicking sound could be heard coming from the back of his throat.

Miranda bowed her head hesitantly and stammered a greeting.

'Please excuse my voice, but I am a little out of practice; we don't communicate through speech, only telepathically,' explained Niger.

Oh No! Here we go again, not more mind-readers! she thought, hating the idea that someone could see inside her head and know exactly was she was thinking.

Niger swished over to Miranda and placed his hands upon her shoulders, saying 'It is time for you to meet my people and choose your skull. They have gathered in the meeting hall and are waiting to greet you.'

'Why are they waiting for me?' asked Miranda, looking highly puzzled.

'Miranda, if you accomplish your task of picking your own skull and – when you manage to collect Nasty's skull – we will finally be able to return to Earth. So, as you can see, we are very much reliant upon your success.'

Miranda felt her throat constrict under the weight of such a huge responsibility.

Niger and Saraya led the way to the meeting hall and Miranda noticed that their feet didn't touch the ground as they moved; they glided gracefully instead of walking.

Cor! I wish I could do that, thought Miranda. The moment she had that thought, she felt her body rise about ten centimetres off the ground. Sarakuta followed suit and hovered next to Miranda.

'These people are much more evolved than Earthlings but, one day, the population of planet Earth will ascend to a higher dimension and speech will become a tool of the past,' said Sarakuta. 'So the human race won't be able to lie any more and they too will be able to teleport at will and build incredible buildings with just the power of their minds.'

Miranda thought that highly unlikely and, as for the human race becoming totally honest, she thought that was even more unlikely.

As they glided through the spaceship, Miranda couldn't get over how huge it was. It didn't look like any of the spaceships she'd seen in the movies. In fact, it didn't look like a spaceship at all – it was more like a floating city.

Sarakuta explained that the People of the Crystals were vegetarian and totally self-sufficient. They passed an enormous tropical park filled with strange exotic plants. She could also see large vegetable plots and even a lake!

The spaceship had a road running down the centre on which small hovercrafts were busily transporting the People of the Crystals from one end of the ship to the other. She saw shops, cafés, art galleries and even an imposing glass room which, Niger informed her, was a library although she didn't see any books, just lots of crystals on pedestals with people holding their hands over them.

'Where are the books and why are the people standing like that?' she asked.

'All the knowledge that they need is stored in the crystals, and all they have to do is put their hands over them to telepathically absorb the information.'

'This place is amazing! It's more like a small planet,' said Miranda, full of wonder.

'Yes, and it's our home until we can return to Earth,' said Niger.

'Why don't you go back to your *own* planet?' she asked.

'A very, very long time ago – when our people weren't as advanced as they are now – we made *terrible* mistakes. We had horrific wars, we were overcome with greed, we poisoned the soil with our chemicals. Money became our god and we ignored the obvious dangers to our environment. We damaged our beloved planet, Crystalia. We failed to look after it and eventually it became uninhabitable,' replied Niger, sadly. 'We don't want this to happen to Earth.'

'Why is the Earth so special to you?' asked Miranda.

'Earth is like no other planet in the cosmos. It has more species of flora and fauna than any other planet in the universe. It is indeed Heaven on Earth... if only the human race could see it,' Niger sighed.

* * *

On arriving at the meeting hall, Niger introduced Miranda to his people, who bowed in acknowledgement. He then turned to Sarakuta and said, 'I take it you have already explained to Miranda about choosing her crystal skull.'

Sarakuta nodded yes.

Niger explained to her that she wouldn't be able to physically *see* her skull – she would have to use her intuition to find it. He then placed a blindfold over her eyes. As he did this, the People of the Crystals parted, revealing solid gold pedestals with different crystal objects placed on each one. Holding Miranda's hands, he led her gently over to the first.

She stood there, mute with apprehension, her stomach churning with nerves. Everything depended on this.

Chow Yen's voice suddenly popped into her head. 'Don't think... *feel*. You did it when you crossed the river of mercury.'

How did he know I crossed the river of mercury? she thought, marvelling at Chow Yen's abilities.

As she moved from crystal to crystal, images of different shapes and sizes flashed through her mind but none of them caught her attention – until she reached the last crystal. She immediately felt the most incredible connection. As soon as she put her hands over it an extraordinary surge of energy rushed through her fingers and she felt cocooned in an overwhelming feeling of love. An image of a perfectly carved, rose quartz crystal skull formed in her mind, shimmering and beckoning. She picked it up and the instant she did so her hair lit up, sparked for a second or two and then let out a contented sigh.

Miranda removed the blindfold and there in her palms was the exact same skull she'd imagined.

The People of the Crystals all sighed in unison and stood smiling, nodding their heads. From the look on their faces, Miranda knew she'd made the right decision and she was filled with joy.

However, she also knew that the time had come to give up something of great value. Knowing that it could only be her treasured pendant, she handed Sarakuta her skull and then reached around her neck, unclasped the pendant and handed it reverently to Niger.

'Ah, Miranda, you are truly amazing – I know how much you value that pendant,' he smiled.

Miranda could feel tears springing up and turned her face away. Sarakuta nodded his head, his eyes beaming with pride and pleasure.

Niger held Miranda's hand, explaining that a ceremony must now take place in order to activate her skull to its full capacity. By selecting it, she had already started the process, but her skull still needed to be aligned with the skull that Sarakuta owned and with the one that the People of the Crystals owned. She stood, feeling the weight of the skull in her hand, wondering what kind of ceremony was going to take place. Niger and Sarakuta led her into another chamber.

As they entered the chamber Miranda saw that quite a few People of the Crystals were already there and had formed a circle around the walls. At either end of the chamber stood two large rocks. Sarakuta went to stand behind one of them and Niger went to stand behind the other. Miranda could hear a clicking sound and realised the sound was coming from the People of the Crystals.

Up to this point the rocks had seemed perfectly ordinary – until Sarakuta and Niger put their hands over them. The People of the Crystals fell silent. After a few moments the rocks began to tremble. Cracks appeared in them and suddenly the rocks shattered open, revealing two crystal skulls. One skull was bigger than the other and took her breath away – vivid colours swirled inside it, lighting up the hollow eye-sockets, making it seem almost alive! Niger solemnly picked it up and held it out in front of him. Sarakuta followed suit, picking up his own skull.

The clicking sound resumed, getting louder and louder until Miranda thought her eardrums would burst. Then, a mysterious low hum began to resonate around the hall, seeming to come from Niger's skull. Then, both her and

Sarakuta's skulls lit up and began to wail. The eerie, haunting sound sent shivers up Miranda's spine, and she felt her own crystal skull vibrate and heat up and it began to glow. She felt her arms rise up until they were level with her shoulders. The skull was becoming so hot she thought she might drop it. It was also getting heavier and heavier by the second and she was having difficulty in keeping her arms raised.

Her mind whirling, she became light-headed and she could feel her body rising higher and higher, spinning around rapidly, twisting faster and faster like a tornado. Images from Earth's history flashed through her mind. She saw cultures long forgotten and witnessed the destruction of Atlantis. The history of the human race unravelled before her and her mind was awash with gory images of war, of man's lust for power and dominance. She also witnessed moments of extraordinary love and tenderness; moments of utter selflessness. All the wars that were ever fought and all the great achievements of man were set before her, until Miranda reached her present time in history.

She stopped spinning and was gently lowered down. Sarakuta conjured up a bed with his crystal staff and he levitated Miranda onto it. She felt dizzy, sick, and terrified by what she'd just seen; she just couldn't fathom why people were so greedy and cruel, and why they never seemed to learn from past mistakes.

Sarakuta gently stroked Miranda's brow, trying to ease her horror. Niger knelt down beside her and held her hand. He apologised for her ordeal and explained why it was that she had had to witness the history of mankind.

'Miranda, the time has come for Earth to be healed. The wars, the famine, the poverty, the racial and religious intolerance and the greed *must* come to an end. It is time for the people of Earth to wake up and realise that their beloved planet cannot and will not tolerate the plundering of its resources and the continual polluting of its seas, land and air. You have already seen how the ice caps are melting and you have seen the havoc caused by floods and you have witnessed nature's destructive powers when unleashed. The time has come for change and I think the people of Earth are more than ready. Earth, ever-giving Earth, should be treated with care if Man is to continue inhabiting it. This, my child, is just a stark warning of what Earth is capable of and of what is to come. And if humans think they can conquer it, they are very much mistaken. I know this must sound incredibly daunting but it *is* your family's destiny, along with ours, to help heal Earth.'

Niger stroked Miranda's hair and continued: 'It's imperative that you find Nasty's skull. It's only then that all the skulls can be reunited and the healing of humanity can begin.'

Niger then turned and levitated both his and Sarakuta's skulls above the shattered rocks and, with a flash, the rocks were whole again, with the skulls safely hidden inside them. He carefully placed Miranda's skull in a silken bag and handed it to her.

Holding the bag close to her chest, Miranda turned to Sarakuta, her face white and anxious, saying 'Sarakuta, *how* do I find Nasty's skull? Does Nasty know where it is? Does *anybody* have any idea where it might be?'

Sarakuta looked into her eyes and could see that she was beginning to panic at the enormity of it all.

'Come,' said Sarakuta, wanting to lighten the mood. 'Red and the others will be wondering where you are.'

'Just one more question,' said Miranda. 'How does my skull work? In other words, what exactly can it *do*?'

'Your skull is *very* powerful. It can open up different dimensions, it can enable you to time-travel and it will communicate telepathically with you. Listen to your intuition and let it guide you – then you will learn more of its capabilities.'

Why is nothing ever easy? thought Miranda.

Niger stepped forward and took Miranda by the hand. 'We have great faith in you and are amazed by your courage and compassion,' he smiled tenderly. 'And as for that chariot race... What a race! All of my people were on tenterhooks and rooting for you.' As he said this, the People of the Crystals all clapped their hands.

Miranda blushed furiously; she'd never had such an accolade before. *If only Nerdy-Nigel could have witnessed this. Humph... that would shut him up.* Much to Miranda's embarrassment, she remembered that they could all read her thoughts. Cringing with shame, she thought she'd already let the People of the Crystals down by being petty and pathetic.

Sarakuta nodded his head. 'Well done for realising that such thoughts are, indeed, petty.'

It was time for them to leave and Miranda thanked them all, waved farewell and followed Sarakuta out of the hall, back to the transportation device. Once back in the Lost City, Miranda and her great, great, great, etc. grandfather hugged each other, bade farewell for the time being. This time Miranda practically danced back over the swaying crystal poles, and to her relief the door magically reappeared and opened up for her.

* * *

Miranda made her way back through the tunnels until she was finally back at the Mer-ball. By the sound of it, the ball was in full swing. She quickly changed into the bathing costume Red had handed to her previously and stepped out from behind the large rock.

Red spotted her immediately; he noted the bag she was carrying and gave her a knowing look. She could tell by his expression that he was immensely pleased with her.

She felt Orphia flutter by. 'Oh dear,' she sighed, 'did you come to a dead-end?'

'No... What d'you mean?' asked Miranda.

'Well, you've only been gone a couple of minutes.'

Miranda shook her head in confusion. 'How extraordinary!' 'I've been gone ages. Anyway, mission accomplished,' she said, beaming proudly.

She spotted Monsieur Le Grand doing the twist on a flat rock. She jumped into the water and swam over to him. Climbing out, she wagged her finger, saying: 'Monsieur Le Grand, those homeopathic pills you gave me... You know... the placebos?'

'Ah, zose,' he said, his eyebrows working overtime.

'Yes, those!'

'What's zee matter? They worked, didn't they?'

'Monsieur Le Grand, I hate being hoodwinked.'

'Well, if I'd have said that it was all in your 'ed, would you 'ave believed me?'

'Probably not,' she answered truthfully.

'Zo, I zee no problem,' he said and carried on dancing.

Miranda then made her way over to Fearless. 'That stone you gave me...'

'Och, it's amazing, is it no'?'

'Not really, considering it's just an ordinary stone that anyone could have picked up.'

'And did it no' help?'

'Yes, but...'

'Yes, but what? If I had told ye that it was just an ordinary stone, it *wouldn't* have helped. And if I had told ye that ye already possessed all the courage that ye might need, would ye have believed me?'

'Probably not,' she sighed.

'Well then, I cannae see what the problem is. Mirranda, everything that ye need is already there, deep inside ye, but ye had tae discover that fer yerself, which I'm glad tae say ye have.'

Miranda could see Red looking at her and chuckling. She swam over to him and, climbing out, she sat down next to him. Giving him a triumphant grin, she opened the bag a little and gave Red a sneaky peek of her skull.

'So, I take it that ye did everything that was expected of ye. Lassie, I canna find the words to express how pr-roud I am of ye,' he said, his eyes sparkling with tenderness. 'Of course, no' for one moment did it enter ma head that ye would fail.'

'You knew that I'd got it, didn't you! How did you know?' she asked.

'Mir-randa, surely by noow, ye'd realise that I knoow most things that are going on,' he said. 'Anyway, hoow was yer meeting with Sarakuta and the People of the Crystals?'

'Oh Red, they made me witness the history of man. It was awful; I still feel sick. It seems to me that humans never learn from past mistakes. There's so much hatred, greed and anger in the world,' she cried. "How on earth am I supposed to change all *that?*'

'Believe it or not, I think that ordinary people already know where the problems lie – but, sadly, they just don't realise that they have the ability or means to change things,' replied Red.

'Earth is so beautiful. If only people could realise this and treat the planet with love and care...,' sighed Miranda.

At that moment, Sly toppled off a ledge and did an enormous belly-flop, showering everyone in the process.

'Looks like it's time tae go,' said Red. 'Sly has obviously been drinking too much of the green liquor that the Mer-people make!'

Back on the *Wilderness* that night, Miranda lay in her hammock thinking about her skull and everything that had happened, wondering what was going to happen next.

17

Was it all just a Dream?

Miranda woke with a start to find herself in her own bed...

'Hold on a minute... I shouldn't be here! I should be on the *Wilderness*,' she cried aloud, sitting up quickly. She looked around her bedroom and noticed that her costume and goody bag were still lying on the floor where she had left them on the night of Hallowe'en.

A terrible sinking feeling began to envelop her. *What if it was all a dream?* she thought. *No, it couldn't have been... it was waay too real.* She felt for her crystal pendant but it wasn't there... then she remembered that she'd given it to Niger.

Leaping out of bed, she tore around her room looking for evidence of her adventure. *Where is my crystal skull and my magical hat? And what about the magical lunchbox from Sly?* Panic filled her heart as it dawned on her that she might never see Red and the crew again, and that perhaps it really had been just a fantastical dream after all.

She picked up her goody bag and looked inside – the hair that she'd taken from the box at Desolation Manor was still in it. She still didn't know who it belonged to but she now realised that this hair must have its own special importance... It must belong to a member of the Wyrd family but... who?

She felt as if she'd been gone for months. *Why hasn't Karmela put this away? Why is my room in the same state it was in on the night of Hallowe'en?* She crumpled to the floor and let out a sob.

Then she heard Karmela calling from downstairs, telling her that a friend had arrived. That was the last thing Miranda wanted – she wasn't ready to speak *anyone*.

'Well, if it was a dream, I'm going back to sleep and I never *ever* want to wake up again,' she mumbled, retreating to her bed and pulling the bedclothes over her head.

Karmela popped her head around the door, saying: 'I know you're tired and because of Hallowe'en you had a late night, but it's very rude to keep someone waiting.'

'Do you mean to say that it's still only the first of November?'

'Of course it is, darling. What day did you think it was?'

Miranda let out a moan. *Surely it can't have been just a dream?* she cried silently. She could still remember every detail, every adventure, the smell of Sly's cooking, Red's crinkly smile and Fearless's sense of humour. *And Mo, my bestest friend in the whole world. Will I ever see him again? How I'll miss everyone. I'll even miss silly Stavros!*

'Whatever is the matter? Did you have another nightmare?' asked Karmela in concern.

'No, it wasn't a nightmare. It was the most fantastical dream I've ever had!' she wailed.

'Oh darling, I'm sure you'll have others.'

Not like that, I won't, she thought, feeling thoroughly miserable.

'Come, come now. You'll feel better once you're up and about.' And with those words, Karmela left Miranda to get up.

Reluctantly, she got out of bed and put on her slippers and dressing gown before slowly padding downstairs. She popped her head around the sitting-room door and there – to her complete and utter amazement – sat Stavros in the middle of the sofa, with his legs crossed and his wings open and stretched out to the full! This time he was wearing a pair of rainbow-coloured goggles with tiny windscreen wipers.

'STAVROS!' she cried. 'Is it really you?'

'Flaming bandicoots… who d' ya think it is?'

She ran up to him and flung her arms around him, kissing him on the top of his head. No human had ever done that before… and he quite liked it!

'How did you manage to find your way here?' she asked.

'Well, Chow Yen got his acupuncture needles out. He said my chakras were out of balance – whatever they are – and that my inner navigation system was working back to front. Anyway, since then I haven't got lost once!'

Miranda looked around and noticed Karmela standing behind her, smiling from ear to ear.

'Mum, it *wasn't* all a dream, was it?'

'No, it wasn't...'

Miranda, realised that Karmela knew very well that it *hadn't* been a dream and tears of happiness and relief started to roll down her cheeks.

Stavros hated seeing girls cry; it brought out his soft side. He started to shift around in his seat, feeling more and more uncomfortable. In the end he just couldn't help himself and let out a loud sob, his goggles filling up with warm, salty tears.

'Well, seeing that it's started to rain, I'd better be heading off,' he bawled. 'Oh… I nearly forgot…' He got off the sofa and pulled out one of Red's giant hankies, which was tied up and knotted in the middle.

'Red thought you might need these,' he said, handing her the bundle.

Miranda opened it up and saw that the silken bag containing her crystal skull was in it. She breathed a huge sigh of relief and then noticed that the hankie also contained her magical hat and all the other gifts from the crew and last but certainly not least – her crystal pendant.

'My pendant!' she cried. 'I thought I had to give it up?'

'Yeah, well, apparently Niger and Sarakuta just needed to know that you were willing to let go of it. Red met up with Sarakuta and he gave the pendant back to him.'

Looking at her magical hat, he continued, 'And no doubt, you'll want to be able to have chats with Red...'

He yawned and stretched his wings. 'Well, I'll be off then, I've got a barbie to get to.'

He then strutted out of the front door, down the garden path and into the lane, followed by Miranda and Karmela.

'Thanks for flying all the way here to bring me my magical gifts. You've made my day!' said Miranda, giving him another kiss and patting him on his crown.

Stavros cocked his head, aiming one of his beady eyes at her and winking. 'All part of the service, matey. And dry your eyes… pirates don't cry, ya know!'

He poured the tears out of his goggles, dried them off and waited for a couple of cars to pass before proceeding to use the lane as a runway. He ran up the middle, flapping his enormous wings and took off into the bright autumnal sunlight, just missing a lamp-post by a couple of centimetres.

'See ya soon, cobber,' Stavros cried before disappearing into a passing cloud.

* * *

At that precise moment, Boudicca the goose let out a terrible babble of honks and squawks. Miranda turned around and grabbed her mother's hand.

'What's wrong with Boudicca?' she asked. 'It sounds as though Nerdy-Nigel is throwing conkers again.'

Suddenly, her hair begin to crackle and spark. Miranda knew it was a warning... but of what?! They both rushed back towards the house. As they entered, the stale smell of tobacco and the sea was overpowering.

'Nasty MacNoxious,' whispered Miranda. She felt her blood go cold.

The Weird Fate of Miranda Wyrd

Karmela silently gestured for Miranda to stay where she was, while she crept noiselessly down the hall. Slowly, she opened the sitting-room door and cautiously peered around it. The room was empty. She crept down to the kitchen and found the back door open.

'He's not here. He must have gone,' said Karmela, looking out of the kitchen window.

'But what did he want?' said Miranda. 'How did he know I'd come home?!'

'I don't know but I think I'd better double check the house to make sure he didn't take anything.' Karmela turned and went back into the sitting room with Miranda following closely behind.

Miranda was the first to spot what had gone missing. Rushing up to the glass cabinet, she turned to Karmela, shouting: 'He's taken your crystal skull!'

Karmela went white with shock and clutched the back of the sofa for support.

'We must get in touch with Red – this instant. Quick, Miranda, contact him now!' ordered Karmela, her voice quivering with fear.

Miranda had never heard her mother speak like that before and immediately put on her magical hat to contact Red.

'Are you there Red?'

'Aye, I can hear ye loud and clear. So, I see Stavros managed tae find his way…'

'Oh Red!' she interrupted. 'Nasty has stolen mum's crystal skull!'

'WHAT?' he shouted. 'Och, this is terrible news! We must get it back! And we'll just have tae bring your quest for Nasty's skull forward. I was hoping ye could have a few weeks tae recover from your last adventure, but it looks like ye'll only have a couple of days. I've a few things tae sort out and then I'll be with ye as soon as possible. Over and out.'

Miranda looked at her mother's ashen face and relayed what Red had just told her. She took her rose quartz crystal skull out of its little bag and held it up. 'Luckily he didn't get mine!'

'Yes, thank God for that! The fact he has stolen mine is terrible, but at least he doesn't know that you have found yours. The search for Nasty's skull, the one that your father has hidden, is now reaching a critical stage,' Karmela said gravely.

'So when do we start?' asked Miranda.

'Just as soon as Red gets here...' replied Karmela.

The End

A wee glossary

aboot	about
aroond	around
awfy	awfully
aye	yes
blatherskate	someone who talks too much [usually nonsense]
braiggart	braggart [show off]
cannae	can't
coudna	couldn't
didnae	didn't
dinnae	do not
disnae	does not
doun	down
fash	worry about
maself	myself
nae	no
noone	none
nowt	nothing
och	oh
oot	out
shoudna	shouldn't
tae	to
wadne	wouldn't
whit	what
yabbering	talking
ye	you
ye'd	you would/you had
ye'll	you will
yer	your
ye're	you are
ye've	you have

Lightning Source UK Ltd.
Milton Keynes UK
UKOW02f0740121015

260339UK00001B/24/P